〰️

He made a soft sound that might have been a laugh and started for his car door. She grabbed his wrist. He stopped moving but didn't turn around.

"Be my date to the wedding." She couldn't let him walk away from her like that. She hadn't planned on asking him, but seeing him again and feeling his pulse beneath her fingertips, she couldn't let him walk away.

He turned to her, leaving his wrist in her hand. "When is it?"

She ran her dry tongue across her drier lips. "Saturday."

"I'll have to trade shifts with someone but I'll be there."

Jemma nodded and let go of his wrist. He pressed his hands to her cheeks. That was dangerous. She was leaving soon, and that was good. Only bad things happened in Derring. The quicker she got to Florida, the better. She pulled away slightly and cleared her throat.

"So, uh, I have a job," she said. "In Florida."

Davis nodded. "Okay."

"I start next month. But I'm leaving soon after the wedding so I can get settled down in Jacksonville."

"That's probably for the best."

"Yeah. It probably is."

She took a deep breath and clasped her hands to keep them from touching him.

THE DAVIS YEARS

NICOLE GREEN

Genesis Press, Inc.

INDIGO LOVE STORIES

An imprint of Genesis Press, Inc.
Publishing Company

Genesis Press, Inc.
P.O. Box 101
Columbus, MS 39703

ISBN: 13 DIGIT : 978-1-58571-390-5
ISBN: 10 DIGIT : 1-58571-390-2
Manufactured in the United States of America

First Edition

Visit us at www.genesis-press.com
or call at 1-888-Indigo-1-4-0

DEDICATION

To my sister

ACKNOWLEDGMENTS

First, I would like to thank all of the people who helped me write a stronger, better book. The things you like about this book wouldn't have been possible without their help. I have to thank my line editor, Mavis, for her hard work and guidance. I must also thank the members of my critique group, the Lovestory Group, from the Internet Writers Workshop, for putting up with me and for being wonderful people all around. And I must thank my first readers, Ashley, Jen, and Pepper. Their input was invaluable.

To my Beanery writing buddies, Laurin and Phyllis, thank you. Thanks also to the Beanery staff for an inexhaustible supply of iced tea and smiles.

And, most of all, thanks to my readers. I couldn't do this writing thing without you.

CHAPTER 1

Jemma wasn't ready for the train to stop, but it did anyway. She grabbed her bags and joined the line of people in the aisle who were making their way out of the car and onto the platform. She'd come home for the first time in six years, and hopefully the last.

The humidity weighed everything down, and she felt it the moment she stepped off the train. If air could sweat, it was doing so that day. She pulled her suitcase behind her, scanning the faces of the people on the platform. She wanted to surprise Emily Rose with her return, so she'd asked Mary to pick her up from the train station. She hadn't been looking for her very long when Mary grabbed her.

Mary said, "It's so good to have you home."

She squeezed Mary's shoulders. "It's good to see you, too. It's not permanent, though," Jemma said, not wanting her to get her hopes up over something that wouldn't happen. "I'm just here for the wedding, really." She'd come home to see her best friend get married. Even accounting for the other thing she had to do, she'd be out of Derring in three weeks. Tops. If possible, she was leaving earlier than that.

Mary nodded. "I know that's what you keep telling me."

On the drive home, Mary chatted away about life in Derring for the past six years. Jemma was fine with that, as it didn't require her to say much. She was lost in thought as they passed landmarks she hadn't seen in years; they simultaneously seemed familiar and yet oddly distant.

Emily Rose and Jemma had found each other again over the internet. Whatever else had happened in the past six years, Emily Rose wouldn't get married without her.

"I knew you'd come home to us," Mary said as they pulled into her yard. Jemma stepped out of the car. Yellowed grass crunched under her brown flip-flops.

Jemma nodded, choosing not to remind her so soon that the situation was temporary. She walked to the trunk to grab her suitcase.

"No, girl, let me carry this for you. You had that long train ride and everything? You just go on in there." Mary handed her the house key and shooed her away. She wondered what it would have been like to have Mary as a mother. She often wondered that.

Carrying only her shoulder bag and her purse, she walked up to the front door of Mary's cozy house, which was more cottage than anything. The sky blue exterior paint had started to peel, but it still seemed cheerful somehow. After unlocking the door, she breathed in the familiar scent of cinnamon. Six years and nothing important about Mary's home had changed.

She walked to the room Mary had let her use for those last few weeks before she ran away. A faint smile played on her lips as she crossed the threshold. Mary had transformed the space from her quilting room into a bedroom. There was a small white lamp on a white night stand. A beige comforter covered the bed. A white dresser and matching desk were against the wall opposite the door.

"I fixed it up for you. I knew you'd be back," Mary said from behind her.

She walked farther into the room. "Oh, my goodness. Where did you find this? I don't even remember taking this picture." Jemma picked up a photo of herself, Mary, and Fred in their work uniforms. They'd all been cashiers at the Gas and Go, a small convenience store in "town", if you could call any part of Derring County a town.

She felt a brief pain inside for that sad little girl with horrible split ends and the straight, skinny body. But she wasn't that person anymore. She'd changed. She was sure of it.

Mary said, "Oh. That. You know that's the only picture I have of you? I keep a copy in my room. On the dresser."

"Does Fred still work there?" She traced the woman's dark, weathered face in the photograph with her finger. Her full name was Alfrieda, but for some reason, everyone had always called her Fred. Mary still worked at the store. She'd told Jemma that on the drive to the house.

"Yeah. She still works the day shift."

"Emily Rose come in much? Or Wendell?" She couldn't bring herself to name the one she really wanted to ask about.

"Sometimes Emily Rose does when she's home. Wendell moved away from here. He hardly ever comes back that I know of. I think he's in D.C. now," Mary said. "Well, I better try to get some sleep. I work tonight. You know you're welcome to anything I have. That includes my car. If you go anywhere, make sure you're back around eleven so I can get to work on time."

Jemma nodded, taking the car keys. She forced a smile for Mary.

"See you tomorrow."

"Okay. And thanks. For letting me stay here."

Mary disappeared down the hall, calling over her shoulder, "You know you're always welcome here."

She'd told herself that the time she spent in South Carolina was supposed to change everything. Being back in Derring, smelling the air and seeing all the places she'd grown up in, made her think maybe she'd lied to herself. Maybe time wasn't such a great healer after all.

She sat on the edge of the bed and pulled the slip of paper out of her purse with Emily Rose's number on it. She hadn't put the number in her phone yet. She stared at the black ink on the white scrap of paper, thinking about how long it had been since she'd seen Emily Rose, not counting photos online. And thinking of how long it'd been since they'd talked—really talked, not just messaging each other online.

She wanted to see Emily Rose, so dialing the number shouldn't have been so hard for her. Still, she had no idea what would happen when she dialed it. Six years was a long time, and she'd avoided the person who was supposed to be her best friend all of that time. It was wrong, she knew that now, but she'd needed to cut Derring out of her life in order to move on. Emily Rose hadn't seemed angry when they'd talked online, but things might be different face-to-face.

But wasn't that why she'd come home? To be there for Emily Rose on her wedding day? To make things right with her? With a heavy sigh, she dialed the number.

They met at the community center. Emily Rose was there doing a walk-through since that was where the reception would be and she was her own wedding planner. Jemma was halfway across the parking lot when she heard the squealing.

All she saw at first was a swirl of blonde hair against dark blue. "Jemma!" Emily Rose squeezed her close.

"Em Rose, you look great," she said, pulling back from the hug a little. And she really did. Her blue shirt dress complemented her curvy figure.

She struck a pose and laughed. "My wedding dress is a size ten. Can you believe it? I've never owned anything in a ten. Oh, my goodness. Come on, why are you still standing there? You have to meet Michael's mom. I have so much to tell you. I can't believe I'm getting married in a little over a week. I wish I had time to get you a bridesmaid dress. You should've let me know you were coming." She grabbed Jemma's hand and headed across the parking lot.

"I wanted it to be a surprise," she said, allowing her friend to pull her into the community center.

Emily Rose introduced Jemma to Ms. Fletcher, Michael's mother. She was a tall, slender, severe-looking woman with her brown hair swept into a bun and her pale lips drawn into a line. She didn't look nearly as thrilled as Emily Rose about the wedding. Then again, she didn't look like the type to get thrilled about much at all.

"Emily, dear, why don't you and your friend catch up and we can talk later about the flowers? There's a conference call I said I'd dial into if I had time," Ms. Fletcher said.

"Sure," Emily Rose said. When she was gone, something changed in Emily Rose's face. "She's really been riding me about every choice I've made. I don't think she wanted it to be here. In Derring. I think she wanted it up in Manhattan. And sometimes, I don't think she wanted me to be the bride, either."

Before Jemma could respond, the storm cloud passed over Emily Rose's face and was gone. "Well, she's right about one thing. We have tons of catching up to do. I still can't believe you're really here." They linked arms and headed out to their cars.

They went back to Emily Rose's parents' house for lunch. They were at work so Jemma didn't get a chance to say hello to them. Michael was getting in that afternoon from New York. After lunch, Emily Rose was taking her along to the airport to get him. It had been a hard-fought battle with Ms. Fletcher to get that privilege, apparently.

"You should have let me know when your graduation was. I would have totally come." Emily Rose gave her a small frown before taking a bite of her egg salad sandwich.

"It wasn't really a big deal. I was just happy to get the diploma," Jemma said with a shrug, leaving out how all she'd done was pick up the diploma from the registrar's office. She hadn't bothered with the ceremony at all. She hadn't seen the point. She knew that would have horrified Emily Rose, who loved making a big deal out of such things. She and her aunt had gone out for a quiet dinner the day she picked up her diploma and that'd been the end of it.

Jemma had been all about business for six years. She'd gotten her GED after moving in with her aunt in South Carolina while working full time. She'd continued to work until she saved up enough money for college, attending a few classes at a community college when she could fit them into her schedule. Then she'd put herself through college in three years and gotten her degree in business with a concentration in marketing. Only school and work had mattered. If she stayed focused on her goals, it was easier to stay strong and forget the past. She didn't pay attention to things like birthdays, holidays, or graduation celebrations. None of her friends in South Carolina had known when her birthday was. Having never been part of a normal family, she didn't really miss such things.

Interrupting Jemma's thoughts, Emily Rose said, "Still, these things are times for friends and family. You should have seen how many people came to see Michael get his MBA in May."

Family. Ha. Her education had never been important to Lynette. The woman had stopped paying attention to her grades somewhere around the sixth grade. "Tell me more about Michael. He's coming from New York, right?" Jemma said. "He had to stay up there a few extra days?"

"Yeah, he's been busy with interviews since a little before graduation." Emily Rose looked up from the bridal magazine she'd been flipping through. "It must be nice to have a job already, huh?"

Jemma nodded. She'd told Emily Rose about the job she'd been offered with a small PR and consulting firm in Jacksonville, Florida. She was starting as assistant director right out of college. Earlier that year, the director had decided to retire and the assistant director was taking her position. They'd liked her work as an intern so much the previous summer, they'd asked her if she wanted to take the assistant director position. That summer of working as an unpaid intern during the day and working retail at night to pay her rent had been worth it. Her new job started in about a month. Just enough time to see Emily Rose get married, take care of the other thing she needed to do, and say her goodbyes to Derring for good.

"I'm still looking for a teaching job, but I dunno. I'm not that excited to be moving to New York for good, you know?" Emily Rose said with a little frown. "I mean, I love Michael and I'd go anywhere for him, but still . . ."

"Yeah. I know," Jemma said, but she didn't. She didn't see why anybody who had the opportunity to get out of Derring wouldn't jump at it. Then again, Emily Rose's

Derring experience had been different from her own. "How's Wendell?" she asked, sipping her sweet tea. "You said you guys keep in touch."

"He's doing well. He's in law school at Howard. He's staying in D.C. this summer. He has some sort of law internship up there. He and his girlfriend are coming to the wedding."

"Oh, he's dating someone?" That was good. Wendell had never dated in high school. She was probably part of the reason why, but she didn't like to think about that. The way her friendship with Wendell had soured before she left was yet another disaster of her past. She'd been good at making a mess of things.

"Yeah, her name is Stephanie. You'll meet her at the rehearsal dinner."

Jemma wanted to ask more about him and how he'd been, but she didn't feel like she had any right to do that. He'd taken the fact that Jemma had abandoned them much harder than Emily Rose had—on the outside at least. He'd refused to even say goodbye to her.

She cleared her throat. She knew asking her next question would make things more awkward, but she had to ask it.

"And how's, um, Davis?" she asked. "Do you ever see him? Around? When you're here?" They just stared at each other for a long moment, both no doubt going back to their painful junior year of high school.

Finally, Emily Rose cleared her throat and said, "Jemma, Davis hasn't been doing so great since—well, for a long time."

"What do you mean?"

"After he lost his scholarship—"

"He lost his lacrosse scholarship?"

"Yeah. He messed up his knee really badly. He can still walk and stuff, but no more lacrosse."

"Oh."

"He dropped out of school pretty much right after that. He moved back home after staying with his brother in Pennsylvania a few months. He was taking care of his dad until a little while ago. His dad had a lot of health issues."

"But he hates his dad."

"He hates everything. He works at that restaurant near the truck stop. You know, the one near the interstate? Well, this week. He seems to get fired a lot. That place is the only one that's been willing to re-hire him. So he's been there off and on for a while."

"Why does he get fired a lot?"

"I dunno. Attitude? Not showing up for work? He seems to have both of those problems."

"Oh."

Emily Rose was quiet after that.

Jemma bit her lower lip, thinking of the last time she'd seen Davis. She'd been walking away from him. Something she'd once thought impossible. "Why did you say 'was'? You kept talking about Davis's dad in the past tense just now."

Emily Rose sat back in her chair and slid her plate back and forth between her hands a few times. "He died a few months ago. Single car accident. He wrapped his car around a tree. They say his blood alcohol level was through the roof."

"Really?" She wondered how Davis had taken that. Even though he and his dad had never really gotten along, it must have been hard. It had been for her. She'd gone through conflicting feelings of anger and loss when Lynette had died six years ago in an apartment fire. A fire Lynette herself had caused.

CHAPTER 2

Davis rolled over and squinted at his alarm clock. He groaned. Three in the afternoon. He was getting too used to sleeping the day away since his father was no longer able to wake him with his hacking cough or by shouting at him about paying some bill, being late with his rent, or drinking his dad's beer. Like Davis drank beer. Waste of time. When he drank, he got right to the point.

He thought of the months he'd spent taking care of a man who hated him and had all but tried to kill him when he was younger. Irony didn't begin to cover it.

Neither one of them had liked the other very much.

He sat up and rubbed his fingers over his eyelids. His mouth was so dry that swallowing took real effort. The phone rang and he winced at the sound. Reaching for it, he knocked an empty whiskey bottle from his night stand.

"Hello," he mumbled, blinking his eyes against the sunlight filtering through his window blinds.

"Hi," Codie said. She was amazing. It was almost painful to keep in touch with her because she'd done so much with her life and he'd done so little with his. Still, he couldn't imagine life without her.

" 'Sup?" Davis asked with a yawn.

"Davis. Please don't tell me you just woke up."

"Why?"

"Because it's nearly dinner time."

"Okay. I won't tell you then."

"So, how are things?" Codie tried to sound casual, but he knew better. She'd called almost every day since the funeral. And they'd buried his dad four months ago. It was his own fault. Stupid drunk. Davis refused to let himself feel badly about it.

"Same old, same old. How about you? How's work going?" Codie had taken a year off after graduating from U Penn's Wharton School to work for Americorps, and now she had a shiny new job on Wall Street complete with all the bells and whistles. Even with the slump in the economy, Codie hadn't been at a loss for job offers. Davis had always thought of her as a force of nature. Whenever he said something about that, she laughed him off and told him she was nothing extraordinary.

"Just loving it. I can't believe they're letting me do so much. I just graduated."

"I'm sure they're ecstatic to have your slave labor. I mean, you graduated top of your class from U Penn. Why wouldn't they drool all over you?"

"Anyway, what's going on with you? What's new? You're not getting off the hook that easily."

Davis took a deep breath. He didn't want to talk about it, but he needed to tell Codie because she'd understand. "Jemma's back in town."

"What's she doing there? How long has she been there?"

"Um, I dunno. I'd guess she's back here for Emily Rose's wedding."

"Haven't you talked to her yet?"

"Nah. She came over yesterday, but I pretended I wasn't home."

"What? Why?"

"I guess because I don't know—what to say to her."

"After the way you guys left things? The way you talk about her? Like she's the one that got away or something?"

"We never really dated."

"I know that, but you know what I mean. I would have thought you'd fling the door open and grab her."

"I'm not the guy I was then. And I wasn't a great guy then. But at least I wasn't a loser."

"I don't think you're one now. And I don't think Jemma would, either."

"Codie, I live in my dad's house and I might be homeless if my brothers decide they want to come down here and start stirring things up. I'm a server, and not a very good one, at a crappy restaurant and I just—I suck." Davis stared at the ceiling, thinking about how true his words were.

Seth, the attorney he'd hired with the life insurance money, kept trying to call him about the house, but Davis couldn't bring himself to return the calls. He was afraid Seth would tell him that his brothers' attorneys had finally gotten in touch with Seth's office. And that they wanted to sell the house. He didn't trust his brothers. They wouldn't care if he had nowhere to go. Sure, he hadn't seen or heard from them since the funeral, but they could attack without warning. They'd done it before. And with the way they had easily deserted him, leaving him alone to grow up in that house with their father, obviously they didn't give a crap about what happened to him.

And since he didn't want to deal with any of that, he hadn't called Seth back yet.

Codie's voice interrupted his thoughts and brought him back to their conversation. "You should at least talk to her. As much as you beat yourself up over what happened, don't you think you should do that at least?"

"Maybe," Davis said, trying to get Codie to drop it more than anything.

After they said their goodbyes, he rolled over onto his stomach and buried his face in his sheets. He knew Codie was right even though he didn't want her to be.

As soon as he closed his eyes, the memory hit him hard. He'd hurt Jemma so much. He could see the wounded expression on her face when he'd turned her away for what they'd both thought had been forever. At the time, that was what he'd thought he wanted. Only later, when it was too late, would he realize that telling her he didn't want a relationship with her had been the stupidest thing he'd ever done. And that was saying a lot considering he had no shortage of stupid actions stored up in his file of memories labeled "dumb stuff I shouldn't have done."

Davis walked outside barefoot to get the mail after throwing on a pair of basketball shorts. He limped slightly. There was a dull ache in his right knee that never seemed to go away. He'd been out of physical therapy for months. It was never going to get any better than it already had. He had the painkillers his doctor prescribed, but he didn't like to mess with those too much.

Of course his crappy job didn't offer health insurance, but his brother, Cole, paid for it. Davis knew it was probably out of guilt. The health insurance was the only contact they had, if you could call that contact. Whenever payment was due on the plan, Cole would send Davis a check. No note included. Just a check wrapped in a blank piece of white paper. Outside of a few hints both Cole and Davis's other brother, Ashby, had made at the funeral about selling the house possibly being a good idea, he hadn't talked to either of them in a long time.

Thinking of his brothers seemed to make his knee hurt more. There was only so much he could do about that. The pills made him completely useless when he took them so he couldn't rely on them. The alcohol helped everything, but he was afraid of turning into his father.

He stopped himself from rolling his eyes as his neighbor, Ayn, who was home from college for the summer, came up to him in a crop top and cut-off gym shorts. Her belly button ring glinted in the sun. Ayn's family had moved in next door a few years ago. She had long, black hair and green eyes and was about a foot shorter than him. Her short nose fit well into her round face. Sure, she was pretty, but also annoying. He tried to avoid her most of the time because she asked too many questions.

Ayn greeted him with a question.

"So, Davis, this black woman was knocking on your door yesterday. You were home, but you didn't answer. Is she a Jehovah's Witness?"

"Yeah," Davis said.

She followed him down to the mailbox.

"She wasn't dressed like one."

That's for sure, Davis thought, smiling at the memory of Jemma's legs. He'd watched her through the living room window. Her jean miniskirt and tank top had nearly been enough to make him run outside to her. But remembering how much of a loser he was cut that idea short.

"Who is she, Davis?" Ayn put her hands on top of the mailbox and leaned in closer.

"It's a long story." Davis backed away a little and started flipping through the envelopes. A couple of bills and the rest junk mail.

"Is there a short version?" Ayn raised her eyebrows and followed him up his driveway.

He paused at the steps leading up to his front door and turned to her. "Sure." He grinned as he reflected on Codie's words. "She's the one that got away."

"Really?" Ayn seemed to find this a perplexing thought. Her expression told Davis so.

"Oh, yeah."

"You never said anything about a one that got away before." Ayn stood next to the door, scrunching her eyebrows up in confusion, yet her eyes were bright with that eager look she always got when she thought she was getting hold of a good piece of gossip.

"Well, now you know something new about me. Imagine that."

Davis walked inside, leaving Ayn gaping after him.

CHAPTER 3

She changed her mind. Feeling like a fool for coming to the restaurant, she started toward Mary's car. She stopped when she heard her name.

He called it again, more softly this time. "Jemma."

She turned. It wasn't fair for him to still look so good to her. He'd grown his black hair out, but not much else had changed. His baby blues still had the same knee-weakening effect on her. She watched him approach her in his khaki shorts and white T-shirt. The only sound besides that of the traffic on the nearby highway was the slapping of his flip-flops against the soles of his feet as he moved across the parking lot. A warm night breeze blew, but that wasn't what made her shiver.

"I—well, it's good to see.you," he said with a smile so sad it broke her heart a little.

"Davis," she managed.

He rubbed his hand across the stubble on his cheek. "You look good. Different, though."

She nodded. She'd started wearing her hair in micro-braids during college. Becoming a runner had given some definition to her formerly straight and thin figure. She wore a beige shift dress and gold sandals. She'd even gotten a pedicure—something she didn't often do—so that her gold toenails matched her sandals. Not that she was trying to impress Davis or anything.

"You look good, too," she said, swallowing hard.

He laughed, but there was no mirth to it. She'd never heard that laugh before. "You don't have to lie."

Davis had always been slender, but now the word stringy came to mind. He hadn't shaved in at least a day or two. And there was just something about him—defeat mixed with something almost sinister—that made him not the boy on whom she'd once had a large and problematic crush.

"We should, um, I guess we should probably talk." Jemma fidgeted with Mary's car keys. Maybe coming to the restaurant had been a bad idea. She should have just accepted that he didn't want to see her when he didn't let her into his house the day before. "You busy?"

He shook his head. "I was just coming by to pick up my schedule." He paused for a moment, seeming to puzzle over something. Then he said, "What are you doing here?"

She wouldn't look at him as she admitted in an embarrassed mutter, "Looking for you."

Davis nodded. "I'll be right back."

"Okay." She watched him head toward the brick building with its green roof. It was a favorite with the locals and with the truck drivers passing through town on their way to and from the interstate. The place was kind of a dive, but the food was decent. While she waited for Davis, she tried to think of exactly what it was she wanted to say to him, but she kept coming up empty.

Davis came out of the building and walked over to his black Acura—the one she remembered very well from high school—and sat on the hood. He waved her over. She walked to him, thinking about how she'd once adored that car almost as much as she'd adored its owner. That thing was full of memories for her, both good and bad. It probably still smelled like his cologne inside. She was glad he still wore the same kind. That was one thing she was glad hadn't changed in all those years. The scent brought bittersweet memories flooding back to her.

"So what do you want to talk about?" Davis asked, scratching the back of his neck.

"The way we left things—it wasn't—it didn't feel— very . . . final." She was still struggling to find the words she wanted. After picturing this day for six years, she should have been able to do better.

Davis laughed dryly. "I dunno. Not hearing from you for six years kinda helped it feel final for me."

Jemma looked away. Sure, it'd been a crappy thing to do, but it hadn't been all her fault. He hadn't exactly made life easy for her right before she left.

He sighed and shook his head. "I'm sorry. That was an ass thing to say. I just don't know what to say or how to feel right now."

"I'm sorry, too, Davis. It was just—I needed a clean break from everything and everyone."

"Even me?"

"Especially you." She blurted the words out before she could stop herself and regretted it when his eyes filled with sadness. "I mean, I went through a lot that year. With Lynette and Smooth and well, you know the whole ugly story." She hated thinking about her so-called mother and the woman's boyfriend, and she hated talking about them more, so she left it at that. "It took a lot to get back to normal. Including cutting all ties."

"You know, everybody still blames me for you leaving. They don't say it to my face, but I know," Davis said, staring across the parking lot. He drew one knee up to his chest and rested his chin on it. He looked so sad and lonely in that moment.

She had a sudden urge to kiss him and forced herself to push it aside. "Well, you're not the entire reason. You're not even most of it. And I'm sorry they're acting like that."

He pressed his cheek to his knee, turning his gaze back to her. "That's all you have to say?"

"What else do you want me to say?"

Davis slid down from the hood and stood in front of her. He reached for her shoulders and then drew his hands back just before touching them. Putting his hands behind his neck, he looked at her with wounded eyes. "Six years, Jemma? Am I that forgettable? Six friggin' years."

She took a step back from him. "I never forgot you. I couldn't, Davis. I just—couldn't." He had no idea how hard it'd been for her to get out of bed every day for that first year. And after that, it seemed the more space and time she put between herself and everything associated with Derring, the more she felt like she'd be okay again one day.

"You know Tara and I got married? For like . . . six months. Right after I moved back from Pennsylvania. It was ridiculously stupid. She got remarried right after we divorced. And had a baby with some Navy guy or something. Lives down in Hampton now."

"Why'd you tell me that?" Her heart seemed to crash against her ribcage. She wondered why Emily Rose hadn't mentioned it. Tara was Emily Rose's sister. Then again, considering they'd never been close, maybe it shouldn't have come as such a surprise.

Davis shrugged.

"I never stopped thinking about you. And believe me, I tried."

"I never stopped thinking about you, either. And I never tried to stop."

"You got married."

"You deserted me."

"You broke me."

Davis drew in a sharp breath before saying, "I told you I was sorry before you left. I still am."

She half-heartedly brushed at his hand as he reached up to push a braid out of her face.

"How can we fix this?" he said.

She had to look away before he caught her gaze. "I'm not sure we can."

"Why'd you come to talk to me then?"

"Good question."

He made a soft sound that might have been a laugh and started for his car door. She grabbed his wrist. He stopped moving, but didn't turn around.

"Be my date to the wedding." She couldn't let him walk away from her like that. She hadn't planned on asking him, but seeing him again and feeling his pulse beneath her fingertips, she couldn't let him walk away.

He turned to her, leaving his wrist in her hand. "When is it?"

She ran her dry tongue across her drier lips. "Saturday."

"I'll have to trade shifts with someone, but I'll be there."

Jemma nodded and let go of his wrist. He pressed his hands to her cheeks. That was dangerous. She was leaving soon and that was good. Only bad things happened in Derring. The quicker she could get to Florida, the better. She pulled away slightly and cleared her throat.

"So, uh, I have a job," she said. "In Florida."

Davis nodded. "Okay."

"I start next month. But I'm leaving soon after the wedding so I can get settled in down in Jacksonville."

"That's probably for the best."

"Yeah. It probably is." She took a deep breath and clasped her hands to keep from touching him. "I still want us to be friends, Davis. I always want that."

Davis crossed his arms over his chest and tapped his fingers against his biceps. "And we will. Wedding date. Friends doing friendly things."

"Yeah."

As she turned to leave, Davis said, "I still have it."

She stopped and tried to think of what he meant. "Still have what?"

"The envelope—the letter, the CD, everything you gave me that day."

Jemma's eyes burned. In her mind, she went back to the day she'd given him the CD she'd made for him. A day she wouldn't have been able to picture just weeks prior to it. She saw herself leaving him at his front door six years ago. Leaving the only boy she'd ever wanted. And she'd come back to find him a broken man. And still the only one she'd ever really wanted. At least she'd finally come to understand that they could never work.

"Okay," she said, not trusting herself to say more.

"I listen to track ten every night."

"I gotta go, Davis. I'll see you later."

He nodded and gave her a little wave. She turned and all but ran to the car. She'd have to go back to Mary's and dig through her book until she found the track listing. She kept a scrap book of sorts with oh-so-important information like the listing of tracks to the CD she'd made for Davis before leaving home at the ripe old age of seventeen.

When she opened the book to her "The Davis Years" section, she found the track listing. She pushed the book away and closed her eyes.

"Lenny Kravitz. 'Without You'. Of course." She pressed her fingertips to her temples and squeezed her eyes shut. Why had he said that? There'd been no reason for him to tell her. Didn't he know nothing good could possibly come out of reliving such things?

She remembered the words he'd said to her that day six years ago. The last time she'd seen him before she left town. Words that had burned themselves into her heart. *I wish it could be us always.*

CHAPTER 4

Jemma and Emily Rose stood in the main hall of the community center, sipping from takeout coffee cups. They'd gotten to the center a little early and were waiting on Ms. Fletcher and Michael to show up.

The large room was almost empty. Most of the chairs and tables were stored away in a closet near the back. Jemma had almost memorized the floor plan and the different ways the tables could be laid out in the room after the previous day with Em Rose and Ms. F. Wedding planning was definitely not for her, but she was determined to be supportive and helpful for her friend. A few days couldn't make up for six years of desertion, but it was probably better than nothing.

The brown linoleum floor needed a good wax. Emily Rose kept saying it would get one, but she got that nervous heartburn-looking expression on her face whenever she said it. The same look she got every time Ms. F opened her mouth. Several large windows across the room were covered with gauzy white curtains. She could see the parking lot through them. At least they were clean, and one less thing to give Em Rose the heartburn look.

"I still can't wrap my head around the whole thing," Jemma said.

Emily Rose sipped her coffee. "What?"

"All this trouble and money for one day? And then what? Being stuck with a boring married person's life? All your friends will be married and boring. You'll be trapped."

"So not true."

"Better you than me anyway."

"Don't you want to get married one day? Meet a great guy? Fall in love? Spend the rest of your life with him?"

"Love? Yeah, I've given up on that already. It's not necessary." Jemma hadn't thought much about relationships at all over the past few years. As for marriage, she'd turned down her college sometimes-boyfriend's proposal a few weeks before graduation. She just couldn't see that kind of thing working out for her. She hadn't exactly been surrounded by examples of working marriages while growing up.

"Don't be so dramatic. I hope this isn't about Davis."

"What? Why would you bring him up?"

"I saw your face when we talked about him the other day. You still have feelings for him, don't you?"

She shrugged. "Feelings? We bonded over having crappy mothers. Not the kind of stuff lasting relationships are built on." She gestured, throwing her hands up in the air at the thought of the futility of it all. "Like it would matter if I did have any leftover feelings for him." But he was running through her mind as she spoke.

Emily Rose scrunched her lips. "He's such a loser. Forget about him."

"Done," Jemma said. But even if her head wanted to believe the words, her heart would have none of it.

"You know, there's a lot I'm curious about," Emily Rose said.

"Oh yeah?" She had an idea where this was going, and she didn't want it to go there.

"Are you okay with it? All that happened—back then. Really?"

"Yeah. I'm over it. That was a long time ago."

"What if I said I didn't believe that? I mean, when you left here, you were in pretty bad shape. And from the way you were talking when you left, I wasn't sure if I'd ever see you again."

"It's true. I've moved on. I have a great job. A great life now. I'm really sorry I left you all like I did. That was wrong. I know that now." She put a hand on Em Rose's shoulder. "I'm here now, though. I wouldn't have missed your wedding for anything in the world."

"And being back here. It's not . . . I dunno . . . weird for you?"

"Nope." She didn't want to talk about it because that would lead to thinking about it. She thought about bringing up Tara in order to change the subject. Em Rose still hadn't mentioned her at all. Then again, doing that would probably lead to talking about Davis again, and she didn't want to do that either. Instead, she picked up the flower catalog from a nearby table. "Show me these flowers you're so excited about."

Luckily, that was all it took to distract Emily Rose. They talked about flowers until Ms. F and Michael showed up.

The first word that came to Jemma's mind when she'd first seen Michael at the airport terminal a couple of days earlier was "tool", but she hadn't said it aloud, of course. He didn't seem to have very much time for anyone who wasn't on the other end of his cell phone.

Emily Rose insisted that he was very busy with his job search. She'd seemed to be apologizing for him and answering questions Jemma hadn't planned on asking.

It was Emily Rose's decision. If she wanted to marry him, then she should. And having not seen Emily Rose in six years, she had no idea of what might have changed with her. Maybe she and the tool were very compatible. There was even the possibility that he wasn't as self-absorbed as he seemed. Although she'd never seen Emily Rose look as uncomfortable as she did with the tool and his "dear old mother", as he called her.

Jemma sat in a folding chair in the main hall of the community center next to Michael and his cell phone. They'd spent the past hour or so of their lives watching Emily Rose and Ms. Fletcher fight over wedding details.

Jemma's attention to their picking at each other faded in and out. Her mind kept drifting to Davis. Emily Rose had been right. Being back in Derring was having a bigger effect on her than she wanted to admit. And he was a lot of the reason for that.

Davis Hill. He sent her heart into her throat in the time it took him to say her name. She wondered what would have happened if she hadn't walked away six years ago. If she'd been able to believe him when he'd finally confessed his love for her back then. If she hadn't just written off his confession as too little too late. Maybe she could have if he hadn't spent every moment before that being a shallow jerk. Words were easy, actions were harder, and some words were nearly impossible to prove with any kind of action.

But it wasn't worth dwelling on anymore. That was the past. And she'd moved on from the shell of a person she'd been and that person's desires. She had to because being the new Jemma was important. Old Jemma was weak and sad. New Jemma made things happen.

She was brought back to their conversation by Emily Rose's cry of disbelief. Em Rose pushed a flower catalog into Ms. F's hands. Jemma glanced at Michael. He stared at his phone as if begging it to ring. His brown hair fell around his face so that she couldn't see his expression. She then turned back to watch the latest pre-wedding battle between Emily Rose and Ms. F.

"Oh, my goodness. No. We can't have blue. That is the ugliest shade of blue I've ever seen anyway," Emily Rose said, running her hands through her blonde hair. "You really cancelled my flower order?"

"Emily, dear, we are not having those god-awful carnations you picked out, so you may as well get over that. If that is the only reason you do not want these lovely gardenias, then I'm sorry. It is not a good enough reason for me," Ms. Fletcher said. "We do not have to have them dyed, there's still time to stop them before the dyeing takes place, but you should seriously consider the gardenias. There's really no time for a change at this stage anyway."

They both turned to Michael. Jemma felt sorry for him, but very glad it was him in the hot seat and not her. He slid his phone into the holder on his belt clip and shifted in his seat.

He rubbed his jaw. "Uh, I think both are great. What do you think, Jemma?" He looked at her as if hoping to be tossed a life line.

Great. Way to punt, Michael, Jemma thought, turning to the two seething women in front of her.

"Oh yes. They're both beautiful. But it's not my day, Michael. This is a decision for you and Em Rose," she said. And apparently for Ms. F, too.

Michael gave her a look that let her know he really didn't appreciate being drawn back into the battle, and she pretended not to notice.

CHAPTER 5

Mary dropped Jemma off at the Bradens' house because she needed the car that night for work. When she got there, she found that Carolina had arrived. Carolina had rented a car, insisting Emily Rose wasn't going to take time out of her tight wedding prep schedule to pick her up.

Carolina was the antithesis of Jemma. Her personality was so big that it filled up the room and went all the way out to the sun porch. She could see why Emily Rose—or anyone for that matter—would be drawn to such a person. Jemma couldn't help but think of Carolina as her replacement. And if she was, whose fault was it but Jemma's that she'd been replaced? She'd disappeared for six years and hadn't given Emily Rose any way to get in touch with her. Still, feelings weren't always rational.

"Where's Michael?" Jemma asked after dropping her purse onto the black ottoman near a micro-fiber armchair.

Carolina laughed. "You don't think he'd stick around here for this, do you?" She had rich brown eyes and a strong Brooklyn-Puerto Rican accent. Her endless legs were clad in black tights. Carolina was a dancer and she had the long, lean body of one.

"He's at the hotel having dinner with his mother." Emily Rose tore a lavender paper lantern, swore softly, and then tossed it into a plastic bag half full of trash that was near her feet.

Jemma sat on the floor near them, realizing from the look on Emily Rose's face that she'd asked the wrong question. She tried to do damage control by changing the subject. "What are we making?"

"Centerpieces. They're supposed to look like this." Carolina held up a tea light holder shaped like a lotus flower. The glass upper part of the holder was tinted green. The base had a label around it which announced the names of the bride and groom along with the wedding date.

"Yeah, be careful with those labels 'cause the label maker just broke. We won't be able to make any more of them," Emily Rose said.

Jemma looked around and saw tea light holders in many different colors strewn across the floor. There were also several sheets of adhesive, clear labels lying around with Emily Rose and Michael's names and date printed on them in black letters. Plastic bags full of tea lights lay on the sofa against which Carolina and Emily Rose rested their backs. There were paper lanterns on the floor in colors matching the tea light holders. Jemma spotted several boxes and more plastic bags across the room from them. In the corner to her left, Jemma saw a white archway that was only partially assembled. Next to it lay piles of silk and plastic flowers.

"Yeah. The reception hall decorations. The one thing she let me have control over," Emily Rose muttered.

"Em Rose, don't even think about that bitter hag. She's trying to get to you. Don't let her." Carolina rubbed Emily Rose's shoulder. "You got your man. Nothing else matters."

The more Jemma saw Carolina with Emily Rose, the more she felt like the past six years had put up a wall between herself and Emily Rose that she didn't know how to take down. She was good at lots of things, but apparently fixing friendships wasn't one of them.

Jemma reached for a bag of tea lights just as Mrs. Braden walked into the family room.

"Jemma!" she cried. "I thought I heard you in here." She looked just as perfectly put together as she always had. She'd cut her blonde hair into a short bob and not a hair was out of place. She wore brown slacks and a sleeveless sweater. Mrs. Braden had always seemed so perfect and glamorous. She cooked, cleaned, worked all day, and actually raised her kids, unlike Lynette. And she wore a smile the whole time she did all of it.

Jemma stood and Mrs. Braden wrapped her into a hug.

She held Jemma at arm's length and looked her over. "Look at you. You're beautiful. I'm happy to see you. And proud of you. Emily Rose told me about your job in Florida."

"Thanks." Jemma smiled. Mrs. Braden had always made Jemma feel like a member of the family.

"I just wanted to say hello. I can't chat right now, I'm in the middle of making dinner for you all, but we'll eat together, okay, and after dinner I'll get right back to helping you all with this."

"Amanda, you are amazing. Nothing like our friend, Ms. F," Carolina said. Mrs. Braden had always encouraged Jemma to call her by her first name, but she never felt comfortable doing it.

Mrs. Braden wrinkled her small nose. "That woman. I can't believe she stole my Emily Rose's wedding away from us. I think she insisted we split the costs just so she could have all the control. The more you try to make her see reason, the more stubborn she gets."

"Tell me about it." Emily Rose rolled her eyes.

"I know, Em. Remember, you're to let me know if she gets too bad—well, worse than usual. But ladies, I really must get back to this roast."

Mrs. Braden headed back to the kitchen. Jemma turned back to the tea lights and glass lotus flowers.

"So, Jemma, you guys were best friends in high school?" Carolina asked, pulling her long legs to her chest.

"Yeah." Jemma knew she sounded rude, but she didn't really care. She wondered what it was about just being in Derring again that made her feel so snappy and insecure.

For a moment, all conversation shut down. Then, Carolina turned back to Emily Rose and they started talking about the honeymoon trip to Milan Michael had planned for that Christmas.

She had to remember that she'd had good reasons for what she'd done. She'd cut Derring out of her life completely because it'd been necessary. The only way to be successful was to put everything behind her that could cripple her.

Jemma had worked her fingers to the bone ever since she'd been old enough to do so. First to support her family when Lynette refused to do so, and then to save what she'd left of a life. She'd sacrificed whatever she'd needed to in order to make sure she would never be vulnerable again the way she had those six years ago. After finally creating a future for herself she could look forward to, she couldn't really regret anything she'd done to get there.

Jemma tried to think about all the times Emily Rose hadn't been there for her in high school. The problem was there weren't too many times to remember. And none of them were significant enough to warrant the way Jemma had acted—either six years or six minutes ago. She almost laughed at herself when she realized the reason she didn't like Carolina was probably because Carolina was now a better friend than she was to Emily Rose.

Later, Carolina stepped outside to answer a phone call. Jemma moved closer to Emily Rose. "I'm sorry for snapping earlier. I don't know what happened."

"It's okay," Emily Rose said, giving her an understanding smile. Jemma thought back to their conversation that morning in the community center and figured Emily Rose probably thought she knew more than there was to know. Instead of bringing up things that didn't matter—opening old and healed wounds for no reason—Jemma decided to ignore what Emily Rose thought she knew and let the subject drop.

Jemma flipped idly through the guest list as she and Emily Rose talked about the flowers Ms. F had ordered.

She gave a small frown of confusion, unable to find a name she'd expected to be there. "Hey. Tara's name isn't on here."

"Tara's—not coming." Emily Rose toyed with a paper lantern as she spoke.

"She's not coming to your wedding?" Jemma couldn't believe what she was hearing. Tara was bad, sure, but missing Emily Rose's wedding? She couldn't be that bad.

"We're not talking right now." Sadness flickered through Emily Rose's brown eyes, but she masked it so quickly that she probably thought she'd hidden it altogether. "She's been worse than usual since I went away to college. Especially since I started dating Michael."

Emily Rose had never had a good relationship with her sister, and it'd always taken such a toll on her. Apparently, it still did. She wanted a close relationship with Tara, but it seemed Tara never wanted the same with her.

"I'm sorry."

"Who cares? She's such a loser now. You should see her." Emily Rose forced a laugh, but that didn't change the fact that her voice had trembled.

"Really?" Jemma wondered what that meant, especially after Davis mentioning their short and seemingly disastrous marriage.

"You know what? I don't want to talk about her. I don't even want to think about her. Have you seen Davis yet?"

Jemma put down the guest list and fiddled with a sheet of labels. "What would make you think I'd do that?"

"The fact that I know you. Some things don't change."

There was no point in trying to avoid telling her. She was going to figure it out pretty quickly on Saturday. "He's my date. To the wedding."

Emily Rose's eyebrows rose almost high enough to meet her bangs. Jemma knew she'd have to explain. So she did.

Jemma sat up in bed that night, having given up on sleep. Being in the Bradens' house earlier, having dinner with a real family, and one she knew so well, brought back hard memories of her own family. Contrasted with the Bradens, the Jenkinses had always seemed the epitome of dysfunction.

Jemma felt her way to the kitchen, and by that time her eyes had adjusted to the dark enough for her to be able to see by the shaft of moonlight coming in the window over the kitchen sink. She grabbed a glass from the dish drying rack and filled it with water.

Lynette sure knew how to run a household—into the ground. The only thing she was really good at was making rules for Jemma. Lynette had been the epitome of "do as I say and don't you dare do as I do." Lynette had been especially hard on Jemma when it came to boys. And she'd found out from their nosy neighbor that Jemma had snuck Emily Rose and Wendell over one night while she was out clubbing. That had only happened once. Even though Jemma and Wendell had just been friends and absolutely nothing was going on, Lynette had of course assumed the worst.

Lynette's assumption had led to the first and one of the few times she'd hit Jemma. Lynette yelled and screamed all the time, but hitting was rare. At least until she met Smooth. She lost her temper more often and with increasingly violent results after she met him.

The thing that had finally landed that man behind bars was the thing he'd used to destroy her mother. He'd been convicted of drug conspiracy. They hadn't been able to get him on anything else because of issues with the evidence. But at least they got him on that.

The day after Wendell and Em Rose had come over to watch movies, Jemma worried that somehow Lynette would know. She'd dropped things all day and stammered when she talked to Lynette, but other than that, things had been normal. Still, Jemma was tense.

Then her mother followed her into the kitchen when she went to clean up the dinner dishes. Her heart sank. Lynette hardly ever followed her into the kitchen after dinner.

"Had a boy over here last night, didn't you," Lynette said so close to her ear that Jemma jumped. There was no way that was a question, although it had been phrased as one.

She gasped, putting her hand over her heart. "Mom, you startled me," Jemma said, her mind racing, searching for an answer to give Lynette.

"Thought you was slick." Lynette sneered as if Jemma hadn't said a word. She took a cigarette out of the pack and tossed the pack onto the kitchen table. Jemma hated cigarette smoke.

"I want to know why there was a boy here last night. When you was s'posed to be watching 'Monte. What kind of example is that for him?"

Hypocrite! Jemma screamed in her head. But she took a deep breath. That kind of attitude would get her nowhere good with Lynette.

"Um, all I was doing was watching TV," Jemma said.

"With a boy all up on you." Lynette blew cigarette smoke directly into Jemma's face. "Don't you lie to me. Junie saw him sneaking and creeping back and forth through the woods." Lynette's voice was calm. Too calm.

Junie. One of Lynette's friends. Of course, that woman hadn't had anything better to do than spy on Jemma. She thought they'd been careful, but apparently they hadn't been careful enough.

Lynette was harder on Jemma about boys than anything else. The one time Jemma had asked Lynette about sex, Lynette had told her that she could catch AIDS just from kissing a boy and she didn't want to know what could happen if she did more. Jemma vaguely remembered horror stories involving elements of leprosy and Ebola. Lynette had also told Jemma that she wasn't getting an HPV shot "so she could go running around, lifting her skirt up all the time." Whereas other parents might ask their children if they had a boyfriend or girlfriend, Lynette gave Jemma the evil eye and told her that "she better not be talking to none of that little trash out there."

"What you doing bringing boys in my house?" Lynette said. She had Jemma backed up against the sink.

"We were watching TV. That's it. I promise." Jemma cringed as the glowing cigarette butt came near her arm. Lynette had never touched her in anger, but Jemma knew she was really pissed. Lynette ground the butt out on the side of the sink. She was afraid to bring up the fact that Emily Rose had been there, too. Lynette would have probably considered that back talking.

"Hmph," was all Lynette said. She then backed away, calling over her shoulder, "Come with me."

Jemma reluctantly followed Lynette into living room. Lynette sat on one end of the couch and she sat on the opposite end.

"I know I don't always do right by y'all, you, your sister, your brother. But I've been all alone and it's hard." Lynette's tone changed. She was talking to Jemma for once and not talking at her or through her.

"I know, Mom."

"No, you don't, girl. These men out here ain't after love. I figured that out too late. Things went real wrong for me real fast. And you know me and your grand-mamma couldn't get along. I didn't know what else to do but get in more and more trouble, I guess. Never finished school. Never did anything. I don't want that for y'all. Never did. And Jemma, you can be something more than what I was," Lynette said. "What I am."

Jemma sat back on the couch, shocked at this rare glimpse of Lynette as a person. This person almost made her feel like she had a mother. She was caught off guard. If she hadn't been, she wouldn't have been lulled into a false sense of security.

"I'm not gonna do anything stupid. Wendell is just a friend. Really," Jemma said, thinking her mom had no idea how true that was.

"Wendell. Huh. What kind of name is that?" Her mom laughed. Jemma laughed, too, mainly because she was laughing. "Don't you ever let that happen again," her mom said, an edge coming back into her tone.

"No, ma'am," Jemma said.

"I do try to do right by you girls." Her mom sighed, dropping her head into her hands. "You and your sister. It's different for girls, you know. Always will be."

"I just wish it didn't have to be this hard. Sometimes—sometimes I feel like I have to be a mom to everyone here. Including you." Jemma didn't know what made her say that. Maybe she thought they were having a breakthrough moment. Like on the talk shows. She should have remembered that TV was a fantasy world.

"What did you say?" Lynette stood.

"I just meant—"

"Don't you ever sass me." And quick, before Jemma ever saw the hand coming, she was slapped across the mouth. Jemma's hands flew to her face. Tears filled her eyes. The fact that Lynette hit her hurt her much more than the stinging of the slap. She ran out of the room.

Lynette followed, cussing her the whole way. Jemma tried to shut her bedroom door and Lynette shoved it open.

"Mo—"

"I don't know what's gotten into you lately. Disrespecting me. Lying all the time. Think you grown, huh? Who keeps this roof over your head?"

Uncle Sam and myself, she thought. Aloud she screeched, "I'm sorry!"

"You don't know sorry yet." Lynette threw things around the room as she spoke. "And clean this room up sometime."

Jemma's hand strayed to the spot near her mouth where Lynette had hit her and she thought about something her aunt—with whom she'd lived in South Carolina—had once said during one of the few conversations she and Jemma had about Lynette.

"Lynette? Well, I think the bitterness ate that woman right on up," her aunt had said. Was that what had made Lynette so awful? Jemma didn't want to end up like that. That was another reason why she had to be over it. She wouldn't let the bitterness swallow her whole. No bitterness, no fear, none of it would be allowed to hold her back.

Jemma thought back to the night when she told Davis about Lynette hitting her. How his hands had felt over hers. The comfort in his voice. Then, the way he'd shared his own secret with her—that sometimes his dad had knocked him around when he was drunk before Davis got old enough to hit back. And after that, his dad only messed with him occasionally and only then until he was reminded that Davis was stronger, faster, and his youth had grown from a disadvantage into a weapon.

That night, she'd thought something would change between them. That there would be a bond between them that wouldn't allow Davis to pull away from her anymore. But she'd been wrong. Davis had gone right back to ignoring her whenever it wasn't just the two of them. And her heart had continued breaking for him. Best to let that memory and everything associated with it go. Too bad she wasn't as sure she could do that as she'd been a few days ago.

CHAPTER 6

Thursday morning, Jemma decided to break in her newest pair of running shoes some more. She tried to be careful with her money most of the time, especially since she was used to not having much of it—she could almost hear Lynette's voice snapping in her ear and demanding her paycheck—but new running gear was her weakness. Especially shoes. She often broke down and bought new ones whenever she ran across a pair she liked even if she hadn't run out of mileage on her current ones.

Later that day, she would meet Emily Rose at the party store in Fredericksburg to pick up some last-minute things for the reception. But she didn't have to be there until noon. So early that morning she decided to go for a run and then make Mary breakfast. She wanted it to be ready when Mary got home from her shift at the Gas and Go. Since there were no running trails nearby, she'd run a few miles down the road from Mary's house and turned back.

Jemma stared at the endless expanse of trees on either side of the road. She concentrated on the sound of her even breathing and the soles of her shoes hitting the gravel that covered the road's shoulder. Those simple rhythms always comforted her, and she needed to be soothed at the moment.

Unfortunately, thoughts of Davis crept up on her yet again. He'd been her entire world, and then he'd made her universe black. She'd given him the power to do that, that was her fault, but she'd never give it to him again. That didn't change the fact that she could still feel his pulse under her fingertips from when she'd grabbed his wrist in the parking lot. She glanced down at her fingers. She half expected them to be glowing red where they'd touched his skin.

The time they'd been almost friends in high school had started up because of Davis's idiot clique. They'd pulled a particularly horrible prank on her one day at lunch. It ended with gravy on the seat of Jemma's jeans. Out of the group, Davis had always been nicest to her. After school that day, Davis had come to the gas station during her shift to apologize for what his friends had done. They'd talked more than they ever had before. Everybody knew about Lynette, and eventually the conversation had made its way there. He knew enough even if he didn't know the whole story. He'd told her that they had more in common than she thought.

Soon after that, he started visiting the store at least once a week. Then, he gave her rides home from work some nights. She made him stop at the gate to the apartment complex so Lynette wouldn't know. Lynette was usually passed out by the time she got home, but she could never be too careful when it came to that woman. Jemma wasn't in the business of poking angry bears with sharpened sticks.

Over the weeks they spent together, he told her about his alcoholic dad and how his mother had left town when he was four. Soon after, the rides home started including detours to the parking lot of an abandoned building on the edge of town. And then talking turned into kissing. Before she knew it, she was in love, although she knew such a thing could only end badly. And it had. With him dating Tara.

Right when Smooth wrecked everything, Davis told her they could never be together. And she was supposed to forget that later when he allegedly changed his mind and said he loved her? She'd been a fool, but not a big enough one to buy that story. He'd probably done it out of pity for her after her mom and brother died. Not that it mattered anymore. Whatever she and Davis had done, whatever quasi-friendship they'd shared, that was the past. She'd moved on to South Carolina where she'd had school and work and an okay sort of life.

She was supposed to be renewed. Successful. She needed to start acting like it again. It was as if she'd forgotten how as soon as she'd gotten back to Derring. Enough of that.

But there was another problem with being back in Derring. That problem was the other reason she'd come home.

She slowed to a walk as she entered Mary's driveway.

Jemma had bought her train ticket to Jacksonville at the same time she bought one to Derring. She'd scheduled her departure date for the day after her interview with the parole board. She wanted to be out of town before Smooth's interview with the parole examiner.

The parole board had notified her of his upcoming hearing because she'd signed up to receive notice of changes in his parole status. Any concerned citizen could do it, and she'd felt she qualified since she was the daughter of his dead girlfriend. She'd seen and heard a lot of things back then and felt like she definitely had something to say that the board needed to hear. In fact, she'd been called to testify against him at his trial based on things she'd seen and some of the things he'd said to her. She hadn't seen him since the day of his sentencing hearing.

She remembered the day she'd gone to the mail room near her dorm and found the other letter in her mailbox. Every time she thought of that day, she went cold all over again, but it was especially bad now that she was back in Derring, so close to that apartment and the graves she hadn't visited since the funeral.

Smooth had sent the letter to her aunt's house and her aunt had forwarded it to her at school. He knew that she'd gone to South Carolina to live with Lynette's sister after Lynette and Demonte died. The letter had been short and to the point. He'd told her he assumed she'd been notified about his parole hearing, and asked her to come visit him at the prison before her interview with the parole board if she was going to set one up. Or to come visit even if she didn't set one up. Of course she was going to do an interview with the parole board. What she didn't know was whether she ever wanted to come face-to-face again with the man who'd taken her family away.

Out of all the mistakes Lynette had dated, Smooth had been the worst. He'd taken sub-par Lynette down even lower by introducing her to crack. Jemma had wanted out, but she had to stay for her little brother. If not for him, she would have emancipated herself and left. None of that had mattered in the end. An apartment fire took Demonte away from her. He was only four. Just a scared four-year-old boy and she hadn't been there to help him—to save him.

Jemma had shouldered all the responsibility while Lynette drank, went out with her friends, and spent way too much time with her boyfriends. This had been especially true after Jemma's sister, Patrice, had run away from home. Lynnette took every cent Jemma earned. She claimed the money belonged to her until Jemma turned eighteen. At least Lynette left her enough most of the time to do groceries and take care of the most important bills so they'd had light and heat. But all that changed in the time it took an unconscious Lynette to drop a lit cigarette from her fingers into a pool of spilled bourbon on the carpet.

She didn't know if she was going to see Smooth or not. Part of her wanted to go and show him that he hadn't destroyed her after all he'd done to her family. The other part of her was sick at the thought of him.

She had some time to think about it, though. Her interview was almost two weeks away. She had a full day of wedding prep ahead of her, she had to find something to like about Carolina, and she had a bachelorette party to attend that night.

After coming in from her run, Jemma showered, put her hair up, and pulled on slacks and a bright blue T-shirt. Then, she started cooking. By the time Mary got home from work, Jemma had the table loaded down with scrambled eggs, sausage, pancakes, freshly squeezed orange juice, and grapefruit halves. There was bread stacked by the toaster just in case Mary wanted toast instead of the pancakes.

When Mary saw what waited for her in the kitchen, she clapped her hands. "Oh. Jemma. You didn't have to go to all of this trouble."

"Just a small way of showing my appreciation of you letting me stay here while I'm in town."

Mary crushed Jemma to her chest. "I wouldn't have you stay anywhere else. You don't know how happy I am to have you here again, do you?"

Jemma smiled. "Let's dig in before it gets cold."

Once they had food on their plates, they started talking about the store and how things had changed since Jemma had worked there.

Mary wiped her mouth on a napkin and then set it aside. "Jemma, there's one thing I always wanted to ask you, but I never wanted to get in your business. When you went with that boy, when I covered for you with Lynette and told her you were at the store those times, was he part of why you left? I knew where you were going, but I didn't want to meddle and I certainly never went to Lynette, but I hate the thought of anyone hurting you. But if I thought he hurt you . . ."

Jemma pushed her plate away. "You know what, Mary, looking back on it, I think we hurt each other. All I know is we were never any good for each other. I don't know if I could ever be good for anyone. But us two? We could only cause disasters to happen."

"Why do you say that?"

Jemma twisted her right-hand diamond ring around her finger. She'd bought it on the day she'd turned down a marriage proposal from her on-again, off-again college boyfriend. It'd seemed appropriate at the time. "I never really told you what it was like living with Lynette. I don't like to talk about it." The only person she'd ever talked about it with was Davis.

"All I know is it must have been a burden for you. A terrible, terrible burden." Mary reached across the table for her hand. She gave it.

"It still is."

"You shouldn't let it be. You owe it to yourself to let go."

Tears spilled over Jemma's cheeks. She could only bear to see it in bits and pieces, so that was how she told Mary about what it was like living with Lynette for the first seventeen years of her life. Starting small was better than not starting at all.

"Oh, you poor baby. You never had anybody to love you, did you?" Mary came around the table to stand behind Jemma's chair.

"I had Emily Rose and Wendell."

"You had good friends, yes. But that can't take the place of a mother's warmth, a mother's comfort—you were robbed of that, Jemma." Tears stood in Mary's eyes as she spoke. "I never had a daughter, Jemma. I never had anybody to give those things to."

"I never had a mom." Jemma turned around in her chair and looked up at Mary. "You can have a daughter now. If you want me."

"Of course I want you, Jemma." Mary pulled Jemma up out of her chair and hugged her close.

CHAPTER 7

It was one thing to know better and another one altogether to do better. Thursday night, Davis leaned against his car, toying with a pack of cigarettes although he'd quit for what must have been the fortieth time that morning. It was too hot to quit smoking. Derring was in the middle of a heat wave, and if he was going to be that uncomfortable, he at least ought to be able to have a smoke when he wanted it.

His shift had ended a few minutes earlier. He didn't want to go home and he didn't want to stay at the restaurant—they might put him back to work if he hung around. He didn't know where he wanted to go or what he wanted to do.

Seth had called again. Left a message that it was urgent for Davis to get back to him. Davis didn't want to hear anything Seth had to say. He probably wanted to tell Davis to pack his bags—that his brothers had found a way to sell the house out from under him.

Davis tapped his fingers against the cellophane, thinking about Jemma and how dumb he'd been and how stupid it was to let himself think about something starting between them. Jemma would be gone soon. To Florida. And that was a good thing. He'd screwed up enough lives. He'd almost screwed up hers. They'd go to the wedding together and that would be it. So why was he allowing himself to get wrapped up in some fantasy of them having everything that had been missing in high school?

He'd been a real idiot back then. He'd denied his real feelings for her for a ton of stupid reasons. Because of his absent mother and the father he wished had been absent. Because of his stupid friends. Guys he didn't even talk to anymore—none of them had been real friends. But none of the reasons really mattered. None of them should have kept him away from her.

Anyway, Jemma needed out of Derring and it would be stupid and selfish of him to try to keep her there. He couldn't think of asking her to give him another chance. Even if she was the one his heart ached for. Ironically, she'd taught him the meaning of true love by breaking his heart.

He smiled thinly, thinking of how happy she'd been in high school in those few moments they'd shared, even with all she had going on at home. That'd been before he'd been among the number of people who'd broken her. Those nights in his car when it was only them, they'd shared something that their lives outside of it hadn't been able to touch.

Davis tensed at the sound of a voice behind him. "Hi." He knew he had to deal with her eventually, and maybe that was subconsciously a part of the reason he hadn't left the parking lot yet.

"Hey there," he said as Rosa stepped in front of him. She was another server at the restaurant. They'd been flirting for the past few weeks, and it had gotten a lot heavier right before Jemma came into town. They'd gotten to the point where something needed to be said or else it would look like he was playing games. He didn't want to be that guy. He'd only been that guy once, and nothing good had come out of that.

"We haven't talked much lately," she said, giving him a sexy, full-lipped pout.

"I know." Davis slapped a mosquito away from his neck. Night had cooled the summer air off a little, but it was still wet and muggy out and the critters loved that sort of weather. Especially the flying, biting ones.

"Did I do something wrong?" she asked, moving closer, giving him a perfect view down her blouse. She didn't have the first three buttons fastened.

He backed up, shaking his head. Should he tell her the truth? But what was the truth? He was in love with a woman who was leaving for Florida in a few weeks? That sounded like a lame and made-up stupid way to blow her off. He didn't want her to think of him as a jerk even though he probably was. "No. Nothing you did."

"Then what is it?"

He leaned back against his car, pressing his palms into the hood. What could he say? He had a rash? He'd met someone? That last one was kind of sort of true. "I should go."

She frowned. "What? That's all you have to say?"

"Trust me, Rosa. You'd be thanking me if you knew my whole story." And how screwed up he really was.

"People told me you were an ass and to stay away from you, but I said no. I'd give you a chance. Guess I should have listened, huh?" she said in a sharp voice, her Mexican accent becoming more pronounced than usual.

He shrugged. "Probably." No, he really wasn't that great of a guy, so what could he say for himself?

"Fine. I'll see you around." She turned and walked off without giving him a chance to respond. He let his head thud against the roof of his car.

At the end of the night, Jemma helped a very drunk, very happy Emily Rose into the Bradens' house and up to bed.

They'd gone to a club in Richmond for the bachelorette party and Jemma had volunteered to be DD. They'd already dropped Carolina off at her hotel and Meg, Emily Rose's bridesmaid, off at home. Emily Rose was Jemma's last stop before heading back to Mary's.

Meg and Emily Rose had gotten close during their senior year at Derring High. Jemma hadn't met her until that night. Meg had been out of town at the beach with her boyfriend until that day. She'd come back in time for the bachelorette party and the rehearsal dinner.

Emily Rose wanted her three closest girlfriends to get along. Jemma wanted to try for Emily Rose, but everything felt forced. She felt further away from Emily Rose than ever around Carolina and Meg. The friendship the three of them shared seemed so easy and natural. Especially when it came to that Carolina.

Jemma realized that although she'd had a decent time that night, something still felt off. She and Emily Rose hadn't had a real conversation since she'd gotten to Derring. Even in the few times they'd been alone, they mostly talked about Michael and their new lives. They rarely discussed anything deeper. They definitely didn't talk about the past six years.

Jemma supposed it was best to move on. Still, something felt unfinished and not quite settled in every conversation they had. Standing right next to her best friend, she felt further away from her than she ever had in any of the six intervening years.

"Did I ever tell you you're my best friend? Ever? I love you, girl." Emily Rose giggled as she collapsed on top of the bed.

"I know," Jemma said, removing Emily Rose's sandals.

"You've always been here when it matters." Her head lolled back against her pillows. She closed her eyes and smiled.

"Yeah."

"I don't need these." Emily Rose shoved away the pain killers Jemma handed her.

"You will in a few hours," Jemma said. Especially when Ms. F called her at six in the morning to get her going for a final day of wedding prep.

"See? You take care of me and everything. You're the best. My sister," Emily Rose said. She lay precariously close to the edge of her bed. Jemma moved her closer to the wall so she wouldn't be in such danger of falling off the bed.

She patted Emily Rose's arm. "Yeah."

Emily Rose wrapped her hand around Jemma's arm and looked up at her. "I hope we'll always be close."

Jemma pushed back the urge to say what she wanted to—that they needed to talk and their friendship felt almost dead to her. "Me, too."

"Thanks for coming home for me. I know how you feel about this place."

"I'll always be here for you when it matters. Remember? You just said it yourself."

"I know." She closed her eyes and Jemma walked out of the room, blinking back tears.

Late Friday morning, Davis ran some errands before the start of his shift at the restaurant. He was supposed to be there by noon, and it looked like he was actually going to be on time. Maybe that would shut his supervisor up for once.

On the way out of the post office with a fistful of mail, Davis was cornered by his lawyer. He froze in the doorway of the post office, staring up at Seth. Seth's black hair was cut close and his naturally tan face was darker than usual. Davis knew he liked to drive out to the lake whenever he could spare a few hours. Seth wore a light colored suit with a green and white striped shirt underneath and no tie. Seth made it known that in his opinion ties were only good for two things—court and church.

Seth put a hand on Davis's shoulder and smiled broadly. "Well, look who I've run into. I'm glad I didn't send my assistant to do the morning mail drop-off and pick-up. Figured I could use the exercise," Seth said, patting his stomach briefly, which extended slightly over his belt buckle. "You'll have this problem one day, too, skin and bones. Once that metabolism wears off. Man, I miss those days."

"Hi, Seth," Davis said, not really in the mood for small talk. Especially with Seth. He glanced down at his watch. "I really gotta go. I'm gonna be late for work."

"Oh, not so fast. This will only take a minute, son. Here, let me walk you to your car." Seth swung an arm around Davis's shoulders and walked in the direction of the parking lot. "You've been ignoring my calls, Davis. And I sent you three letters. There's one of them there." Seth nodded to the envelope on the top of the pile of mail that Davis clutched.

He looked down at the envelope with Seth's business address and a red "urgent" stamp on it. "Yeah, I guess I've been busy lately."

"Sure," Seth said, but he didn't look convinced. "Well, son, let me get right to the point. Your brothers are coming to town, or so their lawyers say. They say if they can't get in touch with you, they're coming to see you."

Davis sank against the Acura and looked up at Seth, who'd stopped just in front of him. Seth crossed his arms over his chest. He looked down at Davis with firm brown eyes, his lips set in a line.

"What, why?" Davis ran a hand through his hair and then pushed himself onto the hood in a sitting position.

"They don't want to say too much until they can talk to you. No lawyers involved. All I know is what you probably already guessed. It's about the house and whatever else remains of your father's estate."

Davis snorted. That the few trinkets and dollars left behind were being called an estate was funny to him. "When are they coming?"

"Apparently, they're both planning time away from work and making other arrangements as we speak. They say they hope to be in one day next week. They'll call you. And it won't do any good not to answer, son. They kind of know where you live," Seth said with a wink. He put a hand on Davis's shoulder. "But seriously, Davis, it's going to be fine. You know they can't do anything to you. If they threaten to, give me a call."

"Cole didn't say anything about bringing his family, did he?" Davis asked.

"No."

Davis hadn't expected him to. There was no way Cole wanted his kids knowing Uncle Davis. When Davis had left Cole's house in Pennsylvania after the accident, Cole and his wife had just had their first kid. That one probably didn't even remember Davis. He'd only been a few months old when Cole had kicked Davis out.

"I need to get back to the office, and I should let you get to work as well," Seth said.

"Yeah." Davis nodded and hopped off of the car, making sure to land on the leg connected to the good knee. "Thanks, Seth. Sorry about, you know, the run-around stuff."

"Don't worry about it. I billed you for all of it, so it's no skin off my back." Seth chuckled—his idea of a joke. "Remember, call me if you need anything."

"Yep." Davis got into his car and slumped against the driver's seat, staring down at the pile of envelopes in his lap. He flipped through them idly, trying to decide if he should be proactive and call his brothers, or do what he wanted to and change his number.

CHAPTER 8

Friday afternoon Jemma met Carolina, Emily Rose, Michael, and Meg for lunch at the restaurant where Davis worked. It was probably going to be a little awkward to see him after the first and only time they'd talked since she'd come back to town, but it wasn't like they had a lot of restaurants to choose from in Derring.

The restaurant's worn brick façade was visible from the turning lane where she sat waiting for a green light. Two of the large windows facing the road had signs in them advertising $9.99 lunch specials. Once she reached the parking lot, Jemma spotted Emily Rose's car and Carolina's rental. She got out of Mary's car, straightened the skirt of her paisley sundress, and told herself that she wasn't going to make a big deal out of it if she saw him. They were just two people who'd shared something small in another life. That was it.

She entered into the cool, dark interior of the restaurant and was hit simultaneously by a blast of cold air and the smell of onions and stale cigarette smoke. Couldn't have a restaurant that was popular with truckers that was non-smoking. Sliding her sandals over the worn brown tile, she took her time going from the entryway to the cashier's station at the front of the restaurant.

After their run-in in the parking lot, she'd had lots of feelings about Davis that she wanted to be able to control, but she hadn't been able to. It wasn't possible for those feelings to lead to anything good. The logical part of her knew that. In fact, she was starting to regret asking him to be her date to the wedding. Still, there was the feeling of his skin under hers again. And Lenny Kravitz. It was dangerous to want the things she wanted. She knew that. That didn't make her want them any less.

Low watt bulbs lit the place. They cast a dim glow over the green booths and dull wooden tables. The low lighting didn't really hide the worn and greasy look of the dining room.

A petite blonde with obvious bleach damage to her hair stood behind the cash register. She smiled and welcomed Jemma to the restaurant.

"I think my friends are already seated. Tall, brown-haired guy with three women?" Jemma said.

She nodded, pointing to the back of the non-trucker section. "Right back there, hon." Jemma walked to a table near the back where Michael, Emily Rose, Carolina, and Meg sat. She took the only empty seat, which happened to be next to Carolina, said hello to everyone, and picked up her menu.

Carolina said, "So everything's set for dinner tonight, Em Rose?"

Emily Rose nodded, her blonde hair bouncing with every vigorous movement of her head. "Yes. We have to go over to the community center after this. Oh, and we'll need to make a little stop by the church before that. But everything is pretty much good to go." She placed her hand over Michael's.

Michael looked greener than he had all week. He smiled weakly back at her and nodded. Jemma had a bad feeling about Michael. Granted, she hadn't known him long, but he had a shifty look about him. Maybe it was because he was under a lot of pressure from his mom. Ms. Fletcher was admittedly intense, but Jemma wasn't sure that was it. Or maybe it was the stress of his job search. Still, there seemed to be more going on between them than Emily Rose was willing to admit.

After that, Michael turned the conversation away from wedding talk and to himself and the fabulous job he was sure he had in the bag.

Carolina leaned toward Jemma. "Michael can be a little full of himself sometimes, huh?" she murmured.

Jemma was surprised to find herself agreeing with Carolina for once. "Yeah." Maybe Carolina wasn't so bad after all.

"He's not always like that. Don't worry. I wouldn't let Em Rose marry a total jerk."

Jemma smiled. "She's lucky to have a friend like you." She fought the urge to get defensive. It wasn't like Carolina had implied that Jemma was a bad friend. Jemma's guilt was causing her to jump to that conclusion. The rational left side of her brain knew that.

Carolina laughed. "It's a hard job, but what can I say? I'm a superstar."

Jemma agreed, going along with the joke.

"You guys ready to order?" Davis broke in. Jemma looked up. Her heart pounded as she watched him standing there, tapping his pencil against his order pad. He wore a white collared shirt with grease stains at the cuffs and black pants. Even in his shabby uniform, he was sexy. His upbeat manner was clearly forced, but only someone who knew him well could tell. He'd always been pretty good at masking his real feelings.

She shifted in her seat and hid her trembling hands beneath the table. He was right behind her chair, so close they were almost touching.

"Yeah. You can take my order," Carolina said, beckoning to Davis with her index finger and a sexy grin. Jemma tensed. Davis stepped closer to Carolina.

Jemma watched Carolina flirt with Davis as she asked questions about the menu. He grinned back and answered her, but it seemed he was just trying to be nice. Jemma hoped it was his concern about his tip that made him not look completely disinterested in her.

Davis took the others' orders and came around to her last. When he stood by her chair, she grinned up at him. "So, you coming to the rehearsal dinner with me tonight?" she asked.

"I guess." Davis narrowed his blue eyes at her in a look of confusion. "This is the first I'm hearing of this, though."

"Oh, I guess I forgot to mention it to you." Jemma put her hand on his arm.

"Yeah, I'll go," Davis said. He looked at her hand and then into her eyes. She supposed her sudden friendliness was kind of unexpected.

"Good."

Davis smiled warily as if he wasn't sure if he was being tricked or not. "So . . . what are you, um, what do you want to order?"

"Surprise me."

Davis seemed thrown off for a moment by her change in behavior from the last time they'd talked, but it warmed him up to her. One side of his mouth curved in a lopsided smile.

"I can do that," he said. The words sent a thrill through Jemma. Her ears burned as if he'd said something intimate and inappropriate to her in front of a table full of people. His stare reinforced her feeling that he had.

"I'm glad." She rested her chin on her hand after putting her elbow on the table.

"Me, too." He continued to hold her eyes with his as he said this.

Jemma wasn't sure what they were talking about, but she was pretty sure it was no longer food.

An attractive Latina much shorter than Davis tapped him on the shoulder and told him that he was wanted in the kitchen. That was what it took to break the spell that had fallen over them. There seemed to be a tension between Davis and the woman, but she was gone before Jemma could be sure if she'd imagined it or not.

"I have to go put this in the kitchen. Give it to the cook." He cleared his throat, eyes darting after the petite woman. "I'll be back to check on y'all." He strolled toward the kitchen.

Jemma turned back to the table as Davis walked away. She noticed for the first time that all conversation had stopped. She cleared her throat and took a sip of her water. She felt their eyes on her, but pretended like she didn't.

"So, you know him?" Carolina asked.

Jemma almost laughed. Did she? "Yeah."

Carolina's mouth dropped open and her eyes filled with realization. "Wait, is that wedding date Davis? The Davis? Davis Davis?"

"Yeah. We're uh—good friends. He's my date to the wedding, that's right."

"Oh, sorry girl, I didn't know. Shoot, you go. He is fine," Carolina said.

"It's cool," Jemma lied with a shrug. "Like I said, we're just friends."

"Sure you are." Carolina's wink was followed by her braying laugh. "I wish I had a *friend* like Davis, then."

"I'm leaving in a couple of weeks, give or take. We wouldn't have time to be anything else to each other."

"It don't take weeks, honey. It only takes one night," Carolina said.

"Trust me. There's nothing going on between us." Jemma wondered who she was trying to convince—herself or Carolina.

Later, Davis and the Latina server came back to the table with the first of their entrees. Her name was Rosa according to her gold plated nametag. Davis couldn't stop stealing glances at Jemma, and neither of them could stop grinning. Rosa slammed down Jemma's plate and left the table, mumbling something about checking on the rest of the food.

"You know," Carolina said to Davis, "we were just talking about you."

Davis stood still, his hand in mid-air after putting Carolina's Cobb salad in front of her. He raised an eyebrow. "Oh really?"

Jemma could feel her ears burning and readied herself to do damage control in case Carolina said something outrageous—something she'd be completely capable of from what Jemma had seen.

"Yeah," Carolina said. "It's nice to be able to see old friends, huh?"

Davis looked at Jemma. He gave her what seemed to be a wistful look. "Yeah. It is."

Jemma gave him a weak half-smile, turned her attention back to the table, and asked Emily Rose some mundane question about the wedding decorations—anything to get away from that look in his eyes. Next, conversation turned to the latest political scandal and Jemma was distracted for the moment by a debate with Michael over campaign finance reform. But when Davis was nearby, she was never distracted for long.

In fact, as her mind wandered to him yet again, he came up to the table with a water pitcher. She made sure their fingers brushed against each other as she handed him her water glass. She'd been thinking about him ever since he'd walked up to take their order. They couldn't have forever, but did that mean they couldn't have anything at all?

It was so hard not to give in to the idea of having the most amazing few days of her life. Maybe they could spend time together until she had to leave for Florida. But she was afraid that if she gave into that desire to be near him even for a little while, she'd never leave. And if she never left, she might never really move on. And if she didn't do that, her biggest fear might come true—she might turn into Lynette.

Florida symbolized a new life for her. A second chance. Everything she'd worked so hard for wouldn't be fully in place until she was there.

No, it was a bad idea. It was hard to think straight, though, with her eyes glued to his sky blue ones—the color of the sky on a cloudless day with no chance of rain.

Halfway to the community center, Jemma made a U-turn at the next light and headed back to the restaurant. She realized that was where she wanted to be, and it was stupid not to be there. What was she afraid of? Why not spend as much time with Davis as she could? If she never saw him again, did she want to always regret throwing away the chance to be with him at all? After all, nothing lasted forever. At least they'd both know when the end of this was coming. If Davis wanted her, she was going to let herself have him.

No matter what happened with Smooth, how tangled up and messy her emotions were, or anything else, she had to hold him again. Be held by him.

She threw back her head, laughing at herself. She didn't care who saw or thought she'd lost her mind and shouldn't have been on the road. She'd been about to give up what she might always look back on as the best, most spontaneous days of her life.

No overthinking it. No over-analyzing. No labeling it as wrong or right. She'd have plenty of time for that once she was in Florida. Carolina was right. She didn't have to worry about relationships or complications or anything. Just Davis.

She hurried from the parking lot back inside the restaurant. Davis looked up from the counter where he'd been talking to the bleached blonde at the cash register. He smiled and Jemma smiled back, giving him a little wave. Her palms were sweaty and her heart beat so fast she thought it would start aching. Davis said something to the blonde, she nodded, and he walked over to her.

He leaned in close enough for her to smell the clean scent of his cologne over the grease. "What's wrong? Why'd you come back?"

She fought the urge to grab and kiss him right there in the front of the restaurant. "For you. I came back for you," Jemma said, wondering how he would take those words and wondering how she wanted him to take them.

He stared down at her, his light blue eyes unreadable.

"I—three weeks, Davis. Three weeks of you and me and not thinking about relationships or pain or anything serious. Three weeks."

"Uh, c'mon," Davis said, taking her hand. He pulled her to the back of the restaurant and into the break room.

He pulled out a chair for her at the square table, its black vinyl top cracked. She sat. He pulled a chair up next to her. After sitting in it, he hunched over and stared at his hands.

"Davis?" Jemma shifted toward him.

He looked up at her and swallowed hard. "I'm not the fun, wild type anymore. I'm not going to give you some great adventure. I can't."

Jemma traced her finger along his jaw line. He let her for a moment and then pulled away. She leaned in closer. "I'm not looking for an adventure."

Davis bit his lower lip and shook his head. "What are you looking for then?"

"Time. I just want time. That's all." She dropped her hands onto her lap. "With you."

"You don't even know how much I've wanted you here. All this time. And now . . ."

Jemma clasped her hands in her lap and looked down at the pastel paisley swirls on her dress. Her throat ached when she remembered those lonely days back when all she'd ever wanted was for him to say things like that.

He put his hand over hers, which she had resting against her thigh. "And now I don't know what to say. To that. To what you want."

She pulled her lower lip into her mouth, sucking on it a moment, before she continued. "I want to hold you and not feel like I'm falling apart. I want to be with you and not talk about forever or what we're doing or not doing. Just you and none of the stuff that's too hard to talk about." Jemma put her arms around him and he sagged against her. She held him tighter and felt him shudder a little against her. "Davis?"

"You can't avoid the stuff that's hard to talk about. Even if you don't talk about it."

"We can try. We at least deserve a chance at a real goodbye. What we had—it deserves more than how it ended, even if what we had wasn't much."

He pulled back and cupped her chin with his hand. "It was always a lot to us."

Jemma moved his hands to the sides of her face. "Please tell me I can have you this one last time." She tried her hardest not to tremble although she felt a mixture of anxiety, desire, and pure adrenaline.

He pressed his face against her hands. "My brothers are coming here. And I don't know how to feel about that."

"You know the great thing about living in the moment? You don't have to know how to feel about it. We can talk about it if you want. If you're not ready, that's fine, too. Right now, just let me hold you."

He nodded against her shoulder. She ran her fingers through his raven black hair and let them rest at the base of his neck.

"My dad wrapped his car around a tree, driving drunk. Single car accident. At least he only killed himself. I think my brothers want to take the house from me."

Jemma kissed his cheek and held him tighter.

"I took care of the evil old bastard until he died. You know what our relationship was like. Now they want to take the only thing he ever gave me worth anything."

Jemma thought about what Davis had told her all those years before. How his brothers had left him there with their dad. First Cole had run away to college, then Ashby. Jemma rubbed her cheek against his.

"You could be right. Maybe we should just live in this moment."

She pressed her face into his neck, not moving, not speaking. She concentrated on the rhythm of their breathing.

"You really do mean more than anything to me." Davis murmured the words into her hair.

She pulled back from him. "Hey. You know what? I hope your shift is over soon. Because we're going to be late if we don't get out of here and get changed." It was already close to four. They'd had a late lunch.

He smiled wryly and nodded. He reached over and kissed her cheek. That brief touch of his lips set her on fire the way no other kisses ever had. The way they always had. She remembered what she used to say about them: *his kisses are like home.*

She plastered a smile on her face and stood on shaky legs. He rose from his chair and stretched his arms over his head.

"Meet you at Emily Rose's parents' house? Seven-thirty?"

He rolled down the sleeves of his shirt, nodding. "I'll be there. Am I supposed to wear a suit to this thing?"

"Nah. Just not jeans. Khakis or slacks and a nice shirt or something."

"Jemma."

She paused at the door to the break room, her hand still on the knob.

"I'm glad you came back for me."

Jemma bit her lower lip. "Me, too." Florida. Escape. She had the train ticket at Mary's house. On the white dresser. Propped up against the mirror. One-way. Nothing was more important than that.

Jemma ran the thin, gold chain she wore around her neck back and forth through her thumb and index finger. "I'll see you at seven-thirty."

"I'll be there." Davis's voice was soft. She didn't dare turn to see the expression on his face that went with it.

Jemma meandered back to the car in a daze, her head filled with thoughts of Davis. She'd either made a huge mistake or the best decision she ever had. Either way, she wanted the next few hours to fly by so she could see him again.

"So that's the reason, huh?" Rosa said.

Davis jumped, startled out of his thoughts about Jemma. She'd come outside to find him on his cigarette break. "Huh?"

"The reason you were so weird when I asked you what was happening between us that night. The reason you act all strange with me now. Jemma, that's her name, right? She's the reason." Rosa's jaw tightened.

He stubbed out his cigarette and watched the big rigs lumber across the parking lot that was behind the building that housed the restaurant and travel store. "Don't, Rosa. Just let it go."

"I just want to hear you say it," she said, her voice wavering. "I walked in on you two. In the break room. I cracked the door, saw you there, and ran out when I saw . . . what I saw." Her words were barely audible over the rumble of the diesel engines. Trucks were moving in and out of the parking lot.

Crap. Why did he have to make them cry? He didn't know what to do when they cried. Maybe if he wasn't such a bad person, it wouldn't have happened so much. "I'm sorry. I know it sounds like something people just say in these situations, but you really can do so much better than me."

"I know," she said with a watery smile. She gave his shoulder a playful punch. They laughed. "I'm sorry. For crying. I feel so stupid."

"Please don't apologize for that. You're making me feel worse."

"Who is she? I've never seen her around before."

He grabbed a couple of napkins from his pocket. He couldn't remember why he'd stuffed them in there earlier, but they were clean. "Someone I knew in high school. We have a history." He handed the napkins to Rosa.

She took them. "Thanks."

"No problem."

"She's pretty."

He smiled. "Yeah."

CHAPTER 9

The Bradens held the rehearsal dinner in their back-yard. Emily Rose's mother seemed more excited than Emily Rose was. Mrs. Braden loved hosting things. There'd always seemed to be a large party in the Bradens' backyard during the summers back when she was in high school.

Jemma stood back, observing Mrs. Braden's handi-work and the guests. Dinner would start at eight and everyone was still mingling. Jemma had no desire to mingle. In a place like Derring, they'd want to know about her parents and her family and investigate her whole life story because they'd be convinced they had some connection to her. She didn't even like to think about Lynette, let alone talk about her. What would she tell them? That her mom was a dead crack addict? Worse than that, what if they knew of Lynette? Derring was big enough so that not everyone knew everyone else's busi-ness, but small enough that its residents thought they should know everything about everybody.

Mrs. Braden had done a great job with the yard, as usual. She should've had one of those home-decorating shows on cable. Paper lanterns of pastel pink, blue, and cream hung over the tables, casting a soft multi-colored glow onto white lace table cloths. The candles in the chrysanthemum-laden centerpieces cast a matching glow up to the lanterns through their glass, rose-tinted globes. She inhaled the scent of the magnolias and looked up at the large white flowers on the tree next to her.

Groups of people, mostly friends of the Bradens' Jemma didn't know, stood around, talking and laughing amongst themselves. A few had already taken seats. The few Fletchers present and their friends stuck together in a small group near the house. A very perturbed-looking Michael split his time between the Fletcher group and Emily Rose and her family.

Emily Rose made her way over and hugged Jemma hello. She looked the part in black pants and a sleeveless peach top, though it was a bit warm for silk. They talked for a few minutes and then off she went with Michael in tow.

Emily Rose, a lover of the spotlight, was in heaven. That weekend was what she'd always wanted in more ways than one. Jemma wished she could find more enthusiasm. Em being happy made her happy, but she knew she wasn't showing it. From Smooth's letter to whatever was happening with Davis, it took a lot of energy to keep her mind from wandering into dangerous territory. And when she noticed the smile on Em Rose's face become a bit strained, and then Michael and Em Rose disappeared, she worried even more.

Jemma's attention was caught by the sound of a laugh she hadn't heard in six years—a sound she remembered perfectly. She looked across the yard and saw Wendell, his arm linked with that of a slender, attractive, brown-skinned woman. Not knowing if she should run up and give him a hug or wait and see if he would come to her, she watched as he and his date hugged Emily Rose. Emily Rose pointed Jemma out and said something to Wendell. Carolina stepped in front of her before she could see Wendell's reaction.

"How you doin', girl?" Carolina asked. She wore a tight navy blue skirt and an ivory blouse.

"Great." Jemma forced a smile. "You, uh, having a great time?" She moved her eyes between Carolina and Wendell, who'd started toward her. He was intercepted by Mrs. Braden.

"Yeah," Carolina said. Unfortunately, she followed Jemma's eyes. "Ooh, Wendell. I hear you two have a history." Carolina brayed a laugh.

Jemma's jaw tightened. It wasn't like that, but she didn't owe Carolina an explanation and she didn't feel like giving one.

"You have all these sexy guys falling all over you. What is your secret?" Carolina gestured to indicate that Jemma should share, as if there really was one.

Jemma tried to laugh off the comment. She glanced at Carolina's newly manicured fingernails. "Your nails look great." She winced, counting how many times she'd said that word. She glanced up. Wendell was now only a few feet away.

Carolina beamed and held out her hand, wiggling her fingers with their peach-colored nails. "Thanks. They match the dress. Oh, you haven't seen our dresses yet, have you? You will die when you see them tomorrow, okay? Em Rose has taste. But of course you know that. You've known her longer than I have," Carolina said.

She nodded and smiled in all the right places.

Jemma had almost stopped paying attention to Carolina's ramblings when she said, "Wendell!" She hugged him and Stephanie.

Jemma almost threw her arms around Wendell's neck, but caught herself at the last minute and held her hand out for an awkward handshake. "Hi, Wendell. How've you been?" It felt odd to be so formal with someone who'd been one of her closest friends, but she was in foreign territory. A handshake felt like the least inappropriate gesture to make, and nothing she could think of seemed like a great idea.

"Jemma." Wendell adjusted his black-framed glasses on his nose. The frames looked more expensive and stylish than the ones he'd worn in high school. He gave his head a small shake as if he was trying to pull himself together and put his hand on his date's back. "This is my girlfriend, Stephanie. Stephanie, this is my . . . friend, Jemma."

Stephanie gave Jemma a cool smile and extended her hand. "Funny. Wendell's never mentioned you."

Jemma shook her hand and smiled back. "Yeah. We haven't talked in a while. We used to be friends."

"I figured that much." Stephanie moved closer to Wendell.

They all stood staring at each other for a moment. Stephanie kept giving Jemma sharp little once-overs. Not that Jemma could blame her. She'd probably be feeling the same way if she were in Stephanie's situation. Stephanie didn't have anything to worry about, but she obviously didn't know that.

Carolina took Stephanie's arm. "I haven't seen you since Emily Rose's birthday party. Come catch me up."

"Right now?" She spoke to Carolina, but kept her eyes on Jemma.

"Yeah, why not?" Carolina said.

Wendell seemed to snap out of the trance next. "Yeah, baby. I'll be over in a minute. Save us seats?" He kissed her cheek.

She kissed his lips and put a hand on one of his polo shirt covered biceps—he'd developed real biceps at some point over the past six years—and said, "Don't be long." She gave Jemma a final glance and then sauntered away with Carolina.

Wendell said, "That was interesting."

Jemma gave him a tentative smile. "Yeah, I guess it's difficult to know what to say. We didn't end on such good terms, huh?"

Wendell laughed. "Yeah, I guess storming out of the house when you were trying to say goodbye to Emily Rose and me wasn't really the best move. But Em Rose helped me a lot after that. We talked about it once I calmed down enough. She told me—you know, what you said. To tell me goodbye and that you loved me. I held on to those words for years and tried to make them make everything hurt less." Wendell picked a leaf from the magnolia tree and fiddled with it. "I want you to know I'm not angry anymore."

"Wendell—"

"Hear me out, Jemma. I understand now. Seventeen was a while ago. You weren't in love me the way I was with you. That's nobody's fault. I have Stephanie now. I'm happy and I want you to be happy, too. I also want us to be friends. Really be friends again." His brown eyes seemed sincere when they landed on hers.

She smiled, relief making her feel feather-light. "I want that, too."

"Good. Can you do me one favor?"

"What is it?"

"Please don't disappear on me for six years again."

She laughed. "I think I can manage that."

"All right." Wendell hugged her.

"That's enough of that. Stephanie's eyes could cut diamonds right now."

He forced a laugh and hid a look from her that she had a feeling she wouldn't have wanted to see anyway. "Aw, she'll be fine."

"I'm sure. She made a great catch. I'd be protective of you, too."

They laughed. Wendell's laughter was cut short and Jemma followed his gaze to find the reason for it.

Once she turned, she couldn't stop the corners of her lips from lifting. Davis wore a light blue shirt with khakis. He walked up and wrapped his arms around her. She felt the heat of his touch through the thin fabric of her sundress.

"You look amazing tonight," he murmured to her, kissing her cheek. She wanted to melt in his arms.

"Thanks," she managed to say.

He pulled back a little and slipped his arm around her waist.

"Hi, Davis," Wendell said.

"Oh, hey Wendell. How's it going?" Davis asked.

"Pretty good. Uh, I'm going to grab my seat with Stephanie. I'll talk to you two later," Wendell said, talking and moving like a man making a getaway. They said goodbye to him. She felt too overwhelmed by Davis standing so close to concentrate on the things that needed to be done and said when it came to Wendell. The way he'd gone away was unsettling. His words and actions hadn't matched during their brief conversation. She could feel the nagging under the surface, but she tucked it away. She was good at promising herself "tomorrow" and "later".

Jemma sank into Davis's side, thinking about how right being next to him felt. She was tempted to imagine that it could always be that way. Just being by Davis's side no matter what. Forgetting all the scars Lynette and Bill had given them.

She listened to him chat and be social and charming and all the things she'd always adored about him. She was happy simply to be held close to him throughout the evening, barely aware of what was going on around her anymore.

Emily Rose came up to them right before everyone sat down to eat and whispered to Jemma, "Is it weird? Having Wendell here? I'm sorry, but I had to invite him. You understand, right?"

Jemma nodded. "He's your friend. You should invite your friends to these things." She gave Emily Rose a one-armed hug. "Of course you want Wendell here for this. He's one of your closest friends."

She smiled and gave Jemma a look that increased her feelings of guilt tenfold. "And you're the other one." She rolled her eyes and waved to Mrs. Braden, mouthing that she'd be there in a minute. "Mom needs me. We'll talk some more after dinner, okay?"

Jemma nodded and watched Emily Rose hurry off.

"They really went all out for this thing, huh?" Davis whispered to her.

She grinned. "You could say that." She loved the intimacy of Davis's whisper. He could have been telling her the weather for the next day and it would have thrilled her.

Mrs. Braden stood and tapped a fork against her glass. "If I could have everyone's attention, there are a few toasts in order tonight."

Someone cackled from the far corner of the yard. "Toasts, huh? Does anybody mind if I go first?" Everyone turned at the sound of the newcomer's voice. Emily Rose's uninvited sister, Tara, stood by the fence that led into the backyard, tottering on high-heeled sandals and holding a large bottle of malt liquor. Her long blonde hair lay in limp tangles against her bare shoulders.

Surprised murmurs went up around the guest tables, especially from the Fletcher section.

Mrs. Braden flushed and she nearly dropped her glass. Mr. Braden caught it right before it fell from her hand. "Tara. What are you doing here?"

"Surprised to see me, Mother? I'm sure you are, too, my stuck-up sissy."

"Tara—"

"What? Every since she started seeing Mister Perfect, I've become the hidden, horrible family secret." Tara tottered a few steps closer and Jemma could see smudges on the straps of her white halter. Her long legs were now skinny and badly sunburned. Mascara buried lashes which framed red-rimmed eyes. Nothing like high school cheerleader Barbie Tara.

"Tara, you know that's not what happened. We're not the ones who threw you away. We barely see you since you moved to Hampton." Mrs. Braden's hands balled into fists. Mr. Braden attempted to calm her down, but she wasn't having it.

"Right. She wants to pretend I never existed." Tara glared at Emily Rose.

"Like you pretended I didn't exist all the way through high school?" Emily Rose glared back.

Tara's eyes fell on Davis. She laughed. "Even my ex-hubby's been invited. But no invite for sis. Not to the stupid dinner. Not to the wedding. Nothing. How you been, Davis?"

"Hi, Tara," Davis said. Jemma moved closer to him almost without thinking about it. He tightened his hold on her and she relaxed a little against his side.

"You're here with . . . is that Jemma? What is she doing here? Where did you come from?"

"Tara, I don't think this is the appropriate time and place for you to—"

"Oh, shut up, dear mother." Tara sneered when she said the word *dear*. "I don't care what you think anymore. You're done ruining my life with your opinions."

Emily Rose jumped up from the table. "You're not going to ruin this for me. You've ruined everything my whole life and you are not going to ruin my wedding." She stomped over to Tara. "Leave!"

"This is my parents' house, Miss Piggy. I don't have to leave, and I'm not going anywhere."

Jemma winced at the nickname the always thin Tara had given the once heavier Emily Rose longer ago than Jemma could remember.

"If you want to stay here, I can't stop you. But you get in the house because you're not invited and you won't ruin this."

Tara put one hand on her hip, the other still holding the malt liquor bottle. "So I ruin everything, huh?"

"You're a washed up, selfish bitch. An old, faded-out cheerleader who's only good at one thing and it ain't raising a kid."

Tara slammed her fist into Emily Rose's face and then stormed into the house. Mrs. Braden, Carolina, and Meg ran to Emily Rose's side.

"If this bruises, I'll kill her. The wedding is tomorrow," Emily Rose screamed. She continued screaming as they helped her into the house.

Guests stood up and started milling around the tables, seeming uncertain about whether they should stay or go. Mr. Braden went to the Fletchers' table and started talking with Mr. and Ms. Fletcher. Emily Rose's father kept running a fist across his forehead and patting his pockets as if looking for his handkerchief, which he was always misplacing.

Davis touched Jemma's arm. She turned to look at him.

"I'll wait out by my car for you," he said.

She nodded. "I'll be there in a sec."

Jemma watched Davis walk toward the front yard before she stood, intending to follow Emily Rose inside. Then she changed her mind mere feet away from the house. Emily Rose seemed to have enough support. She probably wouldn't need Jemma. Besides, she didn't have much of a desire to go into a house which contained Tara.

As Jemma walked past the kitchen door, Carolina came out of it and they almost ran into each other.

"Where are you going?" Carolina asked.

"Home," Jemma said.

"What, right now?" Carolina raised her eyebrows and scrunched her lips into the facial expression equivalent of a question mark. "Emily Rose wants to know where you are. I told her I'd come out here and check."

"Tell her I'll see her tomorrow." Jemma started to walk away.

"Oh. Really?"

"What does that mean? Why'd you say it like that?"

"Just seems kind of strange and selfish that you'd leave your best friend like this. Really, Jemma, you haven't seemed like much of a best friend. I know I haven't known you long, but—"

"You really haven't."

"Look, I don't know why you would, like you said we barely know each other, but you seem to have a problem with me. Now whatever that problem is and why ever you have it, I would think you'd let Emily Rose come first. She always says such good things about you. You disappear for six years, miss all kinds of stuff in her life, shut her out of yours, you finally show up again, and you act like you don't want to be here."

"Well, with you and Meg around, who needs me? You two are always crowding me out." She should have stopped there, but she couldn't. "Maybe I'm afraid I've already lost her. She was one of the most important people in my life and now . . . everything seems wrong between us. Maybe I'm coming off as a bitch, but I don't know how to handle that. Any of it." Jemma wanted to take it back as soon as she finished telling Carolina all of that, but she knew she couldn't. Carolina had poked and prodded until she'd forced the truth out of Jemma.

Carolina looked down, her black hair falling around her brown face. For the first time since Jemma met her, Carolina didn't seem to know what to say. She finally looked up again, flipping her hair over her shoulders. "I guess I wasn't thinking about it that way."

Jemma shrugged, sniffling, and dug into her purse looking for tissues. Carolina nudged her arm and Jemma realized she was holding a tissue out to her. Jemma murmured her thanks and took it.

"You know, Emily Rose never would say all that much about why you left."

Jemma nodded, grateful to Emily Rose for that. "Let's go in there."

"Okay." Carolina held open the kitchen door for Jemma. She walked through to the living room and up the stairs to Emily Rose's room.

Jemma stayed long enough to make sure Emily Rose was as okay as she could be and to say goodnight. Then she left Emily Rose in the capable hands of her bridal party after telling both Emily Rose and Carolina to let her know if she was needed. She hated that Carolina had caught her in a vulnerable moment. She never liked feeling out of control of things. However, she felt a little better when she went outside and found Davis waiting for her by his car as promised.

He held his hands out to her as she moved closer. "You okay?"

She nodded, taking his hands.

"Even with what happened out there, I'm glad I was here with you."

She smiled, pulling him close. "Me, too." Her mind went back to prom and the perfect couple. Prom queen Tara and lacrosse jock Davis. High school royalty. And then there was Jemma.

Davis's face came close to hers, bringing her back to the present. "For now can we pretend you're not leaving and that this mess of a rehearsal dinner didn't just happen?" Davis whispered against her lips.

She nodded, resting her hands on his shoulders.

He started to speak again.

She placed her fingers over his lips. "No talking."

Davis nodded, moving her fingers aside and placing his lips over hers.

His fingers found hers and he brought their hands to rest on his hips. She sighed, pressing her lips closer to his. Squeezing his fingers, she moved herself closer to him until there was no space between them. He turned their bodies so that she was pressed between him and the car. She wanted to stay right there forever. From her ankles to her knees and upward, her body craved Davis Hill.

"I like kissing you," he whispered when their lips finally parted. "I missed it. A lot."

She grinned into his shoulder. "I like that you like kissing me."

"Good." He stroked her hair.

When she was able to think again, something occurred to her. "That had to be weird for you. Seeing Tara like that."

His fingers stopped moving through her braids.

"Just out of the blue like that. And it's probably been a while since you saw her last?"

He nodded, staring down the street into dusk and streetlights.

She brushed her fingertips along the backs of his hands. "If you want to talk about her or anything, I—"

"No. I don't," Davis said, kissing the tip of her nose. "For now, it's only us, remember? Your rule. Only us."

CHAPTER 10

Always a wedding guest and never a bride. That was how she wanted it. Jemma had no plans to become anyone's bride. Definitely not soon and maybe not ever. She wasn't sure people like her were meant to be wives. People who weren't able to put a lot of faith into the word "love."

Saturday morning, she sat sideways on the bathroom sink so that she could face the mirror and concentrate on applying eye shadow. She didn't wear it often—usually she went with only eye liner and mascara for eye makeup—so the task was a challenging one. Yet it still gave her too much time to think about Davis and being pressed between his car and his body.

He was coming to pick her up soon to go to the wedding. She needed to finish getting ready. At least she didn't have to worry about her hair. Her braids hung free over her back. Still, she needed to get done with the makeup so she could throw on her dress. She'd decided on a strappy pale-mint-colored sundress with eyelets. She paired it with white sandals and a matching jade earring and necklace set.

Not a moment sooner than she'd slipped on her sandals and checked the mirror to make sure everything worked together, she heard a knock at the front door.

When she answered it, Davis's eyes moved appreciatively over her. She returned the appraisal. He wore a light-colored sports coat with matching slacks and a white shirt unbuttoned at the throat. They draped a little on his lanky form, but he still made them look good. He pulled a bouquet from behind his back and he had to speak first because the simple gesture tied her tongue.

He ran a hand through his hair, briefly lifting it off his forehead, and gave her an awkward yet adorable smile. "Uh, dahlias. Because you don't like roses—especially red ones—and because if I remember right, dahlias are your favorite."

A shaky grin stretched across her face. "I only said that to you once and it was years ago. I didn't think you were listening."

He put the flowers into her trembling hands. "I bet you'd be surprised at what I've heard when you think I'm not listening."

"I guess these need some water." She stepped back so he could come inside. After closing the door behind him, she stepped back a little. She wanted to at least try to resist temptation.

He kissed her cheek. "You're gorgeous."

The flowers almost slipped through her fingers. "Ready for our first date?" Jemma asked with a nervous laugh.

Davis looked at her with a mixture of regret and desire in his eyes. "This is how it should have been at prom. Not me with Tara trying not to watch you across the room. And you looking so sad and—it wasn't right."

"That's in the past now." Jemma looked down at his loafers.

"I wanted . . . things should have been different. I wish they had been." He caressed her chin. "Different."

"You were so beautiful that night," he whispered, tilting her chin up so that she was forced to look at him. The pad of his thumb was smooth and warm against her skin.

She tried to laugh off his words so they wouldn't drown her. "When you say I'm beautiful now, I can understand it better. Then? I was a joke."

"You've always been beautiful to me. Just because I was being a jerk back then doesn't mean I couldn't see it." His eyes searched her face as if looking for answers her words couldn't provide.

Davis reached out and slid his hands up her arms. He leaned in close, grazing his lips against her throat, murmuring into her skin about how it should have been her at prom. That it should have always been her. Heat blazed under every inch of her skin his lips touched.

She backed away a little. "I'll put these away. We have to get going." She pulled him into the living room by his jacket sleeve, careful to put as much distance between them as possible. That plan didn't work so well. He closed the distance between them and put his hands on the back of her arms.

She breathed in the familiar scent of his cologne. By itself, it wasn't anything special—available at any department store in the country. What made the scent special was the fact that it was on his skin. It brought back so many good memories. Funny how selective her memory could be. At that moment, with her back pressed to his chest, her mind was definitely working against her. She could only associate good things with the clean scent on his skin. Things she missed so much, her heart ached when she thought about them.

"Davis . . ." She trailed off as he led her to the couch. He sat and pulled her onto his lap. She tossed the flowers on the coffee table and then pressed her body to his.

He wrapped his arms around her. "I'm so sorry for the jerk I've been. I am."

"Don't," she whispered over his lips. She was too distracted by need for him to finish her thought, but thankfully he didn't take her single word to mean he should stop kissing her. Because that wasn't what she'd meant by it. At that moment, she didn't know what she'd meant by it. He trailed a series of lazy kisses down her throat and across the rise of her breasts, his lips pressing across the boundary between dress and flesh.

She caressed his cheeks as he continued to give her those gentle kisses.

She pushed his blazer away from his shoulders and he shrugged out of it. She traced her hands over the area between his shoulder blades, massaging it through his shirt.

He pressed his hand into her thigh and she kissed him again, wrapping herself up in the taste, the feel of the kisses she'd missed so much.

"Always wanted you," he whispered before running his lips over the side of her neck. She threw her head back.

She locked her fingers behind his head. "Show me how much."

Davis hesitated for a moment and then she felt his hand on her inner thigh. "You make it so hard for me to be good."

Her teeth nipped at his earlobe. "Maybe you shouldn't try so hard." She moved down to his neck. "Please don't try so hard."

And then she heard her phone vibrating on the coffee table. She stared over her shoulder at it for a moment, knowing she needed to answer it, but not wanting to move.

"You better get that, I guess," Davis said, but he seemed reluctant to let her move far enough to grab the phone. She gave him another longing kiss and then reached for her buzzing phone. Emily Rose's number was displayed on the screen. "Hey, I know. I'm about to leave right now."

"Jemma, she's really freaking out," Carolina said, throwing Jemma off for a moment since she'd called from Emily Rose's phone.

"What's going on?" Jemma turned her attention away from Davis and his kisses.

"The bruise—her face—she's threatening not to get married today," Carolina said. Jemma could hear Emily Rose shrieking in the background. "No one here can calm her down. She won't listen to any of us."

"We're on the way," Jemma said.

"Emily Rose?" Davis got to his feet while helping her to hers.

93

Jemma nodded. "We, uh . . . need to get going."

"That is very unfortunate," Davis said as he handed her purse to her.

Jemma agreed while thinking of the touches and kisses he'd given her a few moments earlier. But she knew Emily Rose needed her, and despite all else, there was nowhere else in the world she would be but at the church.

Emily Rose was practically in hysterics. She flew around the small room, screeching about Tara and concealer and bad omens and cold feet. Apparently, Michael had made the bad move of telling Emily Rose it was okay if she wanted to postpone the wedding until her face healed. She blew that out of proportion, saying that Michael didn't want to marry her. Plastic shopping bags, clothes, and garment bags were all over the place, as were other things like giant makeup cases. As in more than one.

Carolina chased Emily Rose around the room with a makeup pad and a bottle of foundation. Meg sat in the corner on a bench between two racks of choir robes, calling soothing words out to her and begging her to calm down. Emily Rose yelled at both of them that they weren't helping while swiping at tears. That was the overwhelming and slightly chaotic scene Jemma walked into.

"How late do you want this wedding to be? Your makeup isn't started yet. Would you please sit your butt down?" Carolina slammed the bottle of foundation down on a nearby table and picked up a tube of concealer.

"You've ruined the little bit of progress I made. Now I'm going to have to start all over."

Carolina and Meg looked beautiful, if angry and worried. Carolina had been right about the dresses. They wore strapless, silky peach dresses with tight bodices and flowing skirts and matching peach pumps. Meg's black hair was swept up into a French roll and accented with sprigs of baby's breath. Her bangs, which were cut to lay straight across her forehead normally, must have been bobby-pinned back into the rest of her hair. Carolina's hair fell over her shoulders and back in glossy hairspray-secured curls. She had baby's breath and Ms. Fletcher's gardenias woven into a thin, almost invisible band that she wore like a headband.

Emily Rose glared at Carolina, the angry bruise on her right cheek making the expression more menacing than it normally would have been. With her wheat blonde hair piled on top of her head and gentle tendrils of curls falling into her face, she would have looked angelic if not for that expression and the accompanying bruise. She wore a gray zip-up hoodie emblazoned with her alma mater's name and white cotton shorts along with purple flip-flops. Jemma spied a tiara sitting on the table behind her.

Emily Rose snatched the tube of concealer from Carolina and waved it in the air. "Concealer. What good is concealer going to do? There might not be any wedding. My face is monstrous and Michael may as well have said he didn't want to marry me. He's been acting weird all week. He just wants a way out of this." She slammed the tube onto the table next to the tiara. Jemma walked further into the room. Nobody had noticed her arrival yet. That wasn't surprising with all the commotion going on in there.

Carolina put her hands on Emily Rose's shoulders. "Calm down, honey. Michael loves you, okay? You know that man wouldn't be here if he didn't want to be. He was only trying to help, even if he's really bad at it."

Emily Rose burst out laughing before she could regain her scowl. "That's not funny. Stop trying to make me laugh when my life is falling apart."

Carolina shrugged, smoothing concealer across Emily Rose's cheek. "It got you to stop moving long enough for me to apply this stuff. Goal accomplished."

"I have the most awful mother-in-law ever breathing down my neck, a giant bruise on my face thanks to my trashy sister, who finally left this morning, and these ugly flowers thanks to that same fire-breathing mother-in-law," Emily Rose muttered as Carolina worked away with the foundation. She'd put down the concealer for the moment.

"Tara's gone?" Jemma asked.

"Yeah. She's ruined my life again. Made sure that everything continues to go to crap for me. Mission accomplished, so what does she need to stick around for?" Emily Rose said.

Carolina stood back, admiring her handiwork. "You know, you really can't see it now unless you're like—this close." Carolina leaned in so that her nose was very near Emily Rose's. They laughed.

"Yeah, I guess you done good," Emily Rose said with an exaggerated drawl, holding up the mirror that Carolina handed her.

Carolina and Meg talked her down enough to get her through the rest of her makeup and started on the six thousand steps that went into successfully getting her into her dress. While they worked, Jemma tried to keep Emily Rose thinking happy thoughts by telling her how great everything looked. But once the corset and the underskirt were in place, Emily Rose backed away, shaking her head.

"Em Rose," Carolina said, eyeing the dress still under its plastic cover and then looking down at her watch.

"I can't do it. I can't. I'm sure Michael will be ecstatic to find out he's free." Emily Rose wrung her hands.

"You've been planning this for over a year. And you and Michael can't get enough of each other," Meg said, putting a hand on her shoulder. Emily Rose pushed it off and started pacing the room.

"Tara ruined it, like she ruins everything. I can't get married with a swollen face, makeup or not. Nothing's the way it's supposed to be, and it's all falling apart. They're probably all out there talking about me and what a joke this day is. I know his mother is." Emily Rose threw a water bottle across the room, followed by a plastic bag containing something that sounded breakable once it hit the opposite wall.

"Emily Rose, calm down. Sit down for a minute," Meg said.

"No, there's nothing that can fix this, especially not sitting down." Emily Rose's scarlet face was hidden behind her shaking hands. Jemma went over to her. Past high school and college, Tara still had the ability to make Emily Rose crazy. Only one person could fix this. Unfortunately, that was the way it'd always been.

Emily Rose sunk down on the floor, sobbing. Jemma sank down with her and held her. She knew what she had to do. Finally, she felt like there was something that she could.

"What if we postpone the wedding? For a few hours," Jemma said.

Three faces turned to Jemma, their expressions asking if she'd lost it.

"I'll go to Hampton. Talk to Tara. And try to make her understand what she's done. You guys . . . I dunno— stall. Somehow. Tell people to leave and come back? It'll be an evening ceremony and we'll party into the night."

"What if the preacher can't come back?"

"Then we'll think of something. Shouldn't we at least try?"

"I don't want to see her," Emily Rose said, but she didn't sound convincing in the least.

Carolina helped Jemma to her feet, put an arm around her shoulders, and pulled her away from Emily Rose. Speaking in a low voice, she said, "So, you want to go to Hampton, get Tara, and come back. Which will take at least three hours. In the meantime, you want us to do something with all these people?"

Jemma looked Carolina straight in the eye and nodded. "Sure. Unless you have a better idea."

"What makes you think she's not going to come here and act a fool again?"

"Tara does this kind of thing because she knows how much her opinion matters to Emily Rose, no matter how Emily Rose tries to pretend that isn't the case. She does it just to get to her. I think that maybe if I can talk to her one-on-one, I can get through to her. I owe it to Emily Rose to at least try."

Carolina stared at her for a moment before laughing and shaking her head. "This is the craziest thing I've ever been a part of, and that's saying a lot. But why not? Nothing else seems to be working."

"Okay. I'm going to get Davis. You guys talk her down and patch things up the best you can. If you need me, call me."

Carolina nodded, although she still looked pretty shaky about the plan. Jemma told them everything was going to be fine and then she went to find Davis in the sanctuary. Maybe she couldn't face her problems with Smooth, and she might not have been able to decide how she really felt about Davis. Still, she could try to do something for the friend she'd neglected for so long out of her own selfishness.

Jemma spotted Davis in the fourth row, talking to some of Michael's friends. She smiled and, for a moment, all the bad melted away. His smile. Large hands on the back of the pew in front of him. His laugh. The small rash of acne scars on his cheeks didn't take away from his pretty face.

She put her hand on his back. He looked up at her and despite the stress of the moment, she felt lighter. "I need to talk to you. Over there." Jemma pointed to the doors at the back of the church.

He nodded, told the guys he'd been sitting with that he'd see them later, and then followed her to the back doors.

"So what's up?" He put a hand on her waist. "You look worried. Is Emily Rose okay?"

Jemma shook her head. "Not really. I kind of . . . need you to take me to see Tara."

Davis's light blue eyes widened. "Huh?"

Jemma explained the crisis and her theory that if she could get Tara to apologize, Emily Rose might calm down and get back to normal.

"So will you do it?" She grabbed one of his hands between hers.

"Yeah. If you think it'll help, sure. Anything for you, Jemma. Always."

She smiled and threw her arms around his neck. "Thank you."

She followed Davis to his car, wondering what things would be like once the wedding was finally over—if it ever began. Bad things awaited her on the other side of that wedding. Her interview with the parole board representative, for one. Whether she decided to go see Smooth or not, there was still the interview. After that, she had to face saying goodbye to Davis forever. She didn't want to think about how hard saying that goodbye would be, so instead she thought about what she would say to Tara.

CHAPTER 11

The drive to Hampton was a mostly silent one. Jemma was trying to prepare herself for the tornado that was Tara, and Davis seemed busy with his own thoughts. She kept glancing at his profile, but he looked straight ahead most of the time. She caught his eye a couple of times, but he just smiled at her and turned his attention back to the road when she did.

She wanted to know what was going on with him, but she was preoccupied with her own worries. Including whether or not Tara would let her through the door. She did have Davis with her, so maybe if Tara didn't open the door for her, she would open it for Jemma plus Davis.

She didn't have a plan for when she saw Tara. She just knew she had to get to Hampton. Tara had created the problem, and she could and would solve it. As much as Emily Rose hated to admit it, she still looked to Tara for approval. Not having Tara at her wedding, and on top of that having Tara show up to try and sabotage it, had likely hurt Emily Rose more than she'd ever say. And there was a good chance there really wouldn't be a wedding if Tara didn't fix the damage she'd done.

Tara had always been the perfect sister when the two of them were growing up. She was thinner, more popular, and Emily Rose thought their parents liked Tara better.

Emily Rose had tried to deny she looked up to Tara, but everything Tara did mattered to her. All she'd ever wanted was Tara's love and respect. Tara was never generous with either of those when it came to Emily Rose.

Jemma looked up as Davis slowed, turning off the main road into an apartment complex. The three-story buildings with white vinyl siding looked like skinny tract houses glued together. He pulled into a visitor's spot and gestured to his left. "Over there. Apartment twenty-four."

She reached up and kissed his cheek. "You coming in?" She let her fingers linger on his opposite cheek.

He shook his head. He didn't move away from her touch, but wouldn't look at her. "I don't have anything to say to her. If you really need me, come get me. I wouldn't abandon you to her."

Jemma kissed his cheek again. "Thanks for doing this." She got out of the car and leaned back in. "You okay?"

He nodded, still not looking at her. She closed the door and headed for apartment twenty-four.

Tara came to the front door with her hair in a messy ponytail and a screaming toddler on her hip. The toddler had a bright red face and bright yellow hair and was grabbing and smacking at Tara's face.

Tara grabbed his hand and snapped at Jemma at the same time. "What do you want?"

"To talk to you."

"Well I don't wanna talk to you."

"Same here, but this is for Emily Rose."

"That Davis's car out there?" Tara craned her neck out of the doorway, looking toward where Davis was parked.

"Yeah."

"That mean he's out there?"

"Yeah."

After a pause in which she stared at the car with something close to sadness in her eyes, Tara walked toward the living room, calling over her shoulder, "Come in."

Jemma walked into the cramped apartment, stumbling over a brightly colored plastic toy fire engine as she entered the living room. To the right was a small kitchen. Doors led off of either side of the back wall of the living room into what Jemma assumed were two bedrooms. She inhaled a blend of overcooked pasta and trash that needed to be taken out days ago.

"Is your husband here?" Jemma asked, remembering mention of this alleged man by both Emily Rose and Davis.

"Out to sea," Tara said flatly. "What are you doing here?"

"I told you. I'm here for Emily Rose," she said.

"What about her?" Tara set the toddler on the floor and he went to work throwing toys and generally destroying the living room. It seemed the only word he'd learned so far was "no". That was the only one he cared to use, at any rate.

Jemma took a deep breath and began. "She's threatening not to get married. And this day and her fiancé mean more to her than anything else in the world. What you did yesterday was really out of line. Even you should know that. And I think it would help a lot if you apologized and maybe talked to her a little. Without being a bitch."

"You come into my house, cussing at me, and ask me to do something for that worthless, stuck-up cow? Thinks she's better than everybody 'cause she went to college and she lives in New York. She only came back here to have her stupid wedding so she could show off. Good. I hope she doesn't get married. Michael owes me one if they don't. On top of all that, you're dating my ex-husband. Why should I listen to anything you have to say?"

For some reason, Jemma didn't want to correct Tara about she and Davis dating. Maybe it was wishful thinking. "Tara, you mean a lot to her even if she doesn't want to admit it. And I think you care about her, too. You're sisters."

"You're wrong. I have no family. They all forgot me a long time ago. You know they haven't asked to see Branson for over a year?" Tara pointed to the tow-headed terror throwing CD jewel cases across the living room and laughing with glee.

Maybe they feared for their lives, Jemma thought. Aloud, she said, "I'm sure there's a lot to the story I don't know, but I think it hurts them as much as it hurts you. I think you need to talk to your parents, but right now Emily Rose needs you. She'd never admit it, but she does."

"I really don't care what you think," Tara said, wiping mascara-caked crud from the corner of her eye. "They think I'm a druggie and a whore."

"Have they really called you those things?"

"No, but I know it's true. So I have a girlfriend and a few guy friends I hang out with when Thom's out to sea. I get lonely. He's out there a lot. People have nothing better to do than talk. And I like to have a little fun, and I don't always like to drink. Alcohol has so many calories. I don't see the harm in taking a few pills sometimes."

Jemma was at a loss for words. She couldn't believe she was actually starting to feel sorry for Tara.

Still staring at Branson, Tara continued. "I don't touch the hard stuff anymore. That's how I lost the first baby and how I lost Davis. I wouldn't do that stuff anymore."

Jemma couldn't hide her surprise.

Tara smirked. "What? Davis hasn't told you why we divorced?"

"I guess I never asked," Jemma said, too stunned to think of anything more to say.

She laughed bitterly and turned her attention to the toddler. "Branson! Get out of that before you kill yourself." She ran over to her son, who was tottering on the entertainment stand.

Tara put Branson on her hip and turned to Jemma. "So are we done here?"

She stood and studied the scene before her, trying to come up with something else to say that might convince Tara to listen. Nothing came to her.

"'Cause I have a son to try to control, and there's nothing you can say to me that won't be a waste of both of our times."

"You shouldn't try to ruin Emily Rose's life just because you screwed up your own." She hadn't meant to come off like that and put Tara on the defensive because she knew that wouldn't get her anywhere. She didn't know where all of the emotion was coming from all of sudden, but she was feeling really angry and hurt. Suddenly, she was taking the situation very personally. As if not succeeding meant both she and Tara had failed Em Rose.

"What the hell do you know? I don't have to listen to a word you say. I don't care about any of them, and I'd punch her again before I apologize. Fuck my family and fuck you. Get out, get out, get out. Out of my house!" Tara shouted. And then Jemma realized Branson added a new word to his vocabulary as he shouted it and clapped his hands with glee. "Oh, shit, don't say fuck, Branson. For fuck's sake."

"You're horrible, Tara. Emily Rose really should cut you out of her life. I hope she's able to."

"Get out!" Tara screamed at her all the way to the door.

Jemma looked back over her shoulder to tell Tara something else about how evil she was and saw tears in her eyes. Jemma closed her mouth, stunned. When Tara slammed the door in her face, Jemma didn't try to get her to open it again.

She crossed the parking lot, stumbling in the direction of Davis's car, feeling disoriented. Thinking about the things Tara had said.

"Tara was going to have your baby? She lost it?" Jemma sank into the passenger seat.

"She lost it doing crank." Davis didn't act surprised that she knew.

"That must've been hard," Jemma said. "That's why you guys broke up?"

Davis leaned back against his seat, but kept his head turned toward her. "That. And the cheating. And the lying. It seems like it was always something with her."

"Did you love her?"

"I . . . good question." Davis spread his hands over the steering wheel and looked at them instead of her. "Should we get back?"

"I guess. Yeah."

"You get what you wanted from her?"

"No, I really don't think so."

"Not surprised," Davis murmured as he pulled the car out of a visitor's spot.

Neither was Jemma, but that didn't make her frustration any less.

"This wedding has to happen, Davis," Jemma said. Of course she wanted Emily Rose to be happy, but something even stronger than that was driving her now. She felt guilty for giving Emily Rose so little over the past six years. She had to be able to give her this one important thing. There had to be a way. Besides, if it couldn't happen for Emily Rose, what chance did anybody have? Jemma was tired of sad endings. There were enough of those going around already.

"You know, you never asked me to try," Davis said matter-of-factly.

Jemma looked up at him. "Huh? Try what?"

He laughed, turning out of the parking lot. "To talk to Emily Rose. I mean, I was married to the terror that is Tara. I probably know her best outside of her family. Em Rose and I got to be pretty cool back when we were in-laws whenever she was home from New York. Even if we haven't talked much since. Maybe I could say something to her to bring her out of this."

"Thank you." A huge weight lifted off Jemma's chest. She leaned over and slipped one of her arms between his back and the driver's seat. She wrapped the other around his waist and locked her fingers together. "This has to happen for her. I want her to be happy." She rested her head on his shoulder.

"I know."

"I'm sorry Tara hurt you."

Davis didn't say anything, but he put his free arm around her.

Once they returned to the church, Davis went to find the Bradens and update them. Jemma went back to the dressing room.

Emily Rose barely looked up at her. "You went to see her? Waste of time, right?"

Jemma shook her head. "Emily Rose, she's not what's important today."

Emily Rose was quiet for a long time after that. Finally, she said, "Tara ruined it all. Ruined everything. And she didn't even apologize. She never will. She doesn't care. She's probably so happy right now. She couldn't stand it that maybe I could do one thing—*one thing*—

better than her. She failed at marriage so she had to make sure I never made it to the altar. I hate her."

"Don't say that."

"Why not? It's true. It's okay 'cause she hates me, too. What other explanation is there for this?"

Jemma could think of a few, all having to do with Michael and none appropriate to mention at the moment.

"I don't know," Jemma finally said. "I wish I had a better answer than that, but I just don't."

"Well, I can hate my sister if I want to."

But Jemma didn't see hate anywhere in Emily Rose's expression. All she saw was pain.

Emily Rose said, "I've been betrayed. Betrayed by everyone who's ever pretended to love me."

"I've never betrayed you. Your parents never have. Carolina doesn't seem like the betraying type. Or Meg."

"Well, you guys never pretended to love me. You always have."

Jemma smiled and threw her arms around Emily Rose. "I want you to talk to somebody else before you make any final decisions about calling this wedding off."

"Huh?"

"Just one more person. Please? This is an important day and I really want you to make the decision that's going to make you happiest."

Emily Rose shrugged and turned to look out of the window behind her.

When Jemma came out of the room, Meg and Carolina attacked her. Just then, Davis walked around the corner.

"Emily Rose is melting down. She almost destroyed her dress. She found a pair of scissors . . . oh, it wasn't pretty. Most of the guests are coming back in an hour. Or at least they said they would. Some have started their own cocktail party at the open bar at the community center. I think Ms. Fletcher wants to cut off our heads, and Michael has been drinking. Please tell me you can fix this." Carolina said all of this in one breath. Jemma was amazed and impressed.

"Well, there's good news and bad news," Jemma said, squeezing Davis's hand after he offered it.

Carolina crossed her arms over her chest and raised an eyebrow. "I have just spent the last three hours with Bridezilla from hell. The good news better outweigh the bad."

"The bad news is Tara is not going to apologize. The good news is Davis is going to try to talk to Emily Rose."

"Davis?" Carolina gave Davis a skeptical look. Meg seemed to understand a little better.

"Yeah, that might work," Meg said. She turned to Carolina. "Did Emily Rose ever tell you about Davis being her sister's ex-husband?"

"She told me her sister had an ex-husband . . ." Realization seemed to slowly dawn on Carolina. "Davis—you—Tara? Wow. All the things I never knew about Emily Rose. Didn't know her sister was a crazy drunk who'd punch her in the face the day before her wedding. Didn't know about you and Tara. Hmm. You think you know a person."

Carolina's last words particularly stuck with Jemma.

"We all have things we don't like talking about, I guess," Jemma said. She put a hand low on Davis's back and looked up at him. "You ready?"

"Yep," Davis said. He kissed her forehead. "Wish me luck."

She hugged him close. "All of it in the world." She looked up and found him smiling down at her. It was one thing to know she still cared for him. Falling in love with him all over again was another thing altogether. And it was something she was in danger of doing. Especially if he kept looking at her like she was the center of the universe.

She tore her gaze away from his and gave him a gentle push in the direction of Emily Rose's makeshift dressing room. Ignoring the curious eyes of Carolina and Meg, she watched Davis disappear into the room.

CHAPTER 12

When Davis entered the room, Emily Rose's head jerked up from where it had been resting against her knees. She wore shorts and a hoodie and sat on a low bench that ran against the far wall beneath the windows. She hugged her knees to her chest. Davis sat down on the bench a few inches from her feet.

"They sent you?" Emily Rose's voice was a little rough, and that wasn't the only sign she'd been crying. Her face was red and puffy and she had a box of tissues on the windowsill next to her. She clutched a crumpled one in her fist. "I wasn't expecting them to make you take a turn at trying to get me out of here. Oh, and you're wasting your time, by the way."

"Maybe." Davis shrugged, leaning back against the wall, still looking at her.

"So you guys went to see Tara. A big waste of time, right? I could have told you that."

Davis smiled, but didn't respond to her comments. Instead, he said, "You remember what you said to me right after Tara and I got married? We were standing on the steps out in front of town hall."

Emily Rose laughed and her face grew redder. "Yeah. Sorry about that."

"You shouldn't be. You were right. But say it. Out loud. What you said to me."

"I said she had better be worth all the lying you had to do to yourself to marry her, but I didn't think she was worth much, really, either way myself."

"Yeah. You did," Davis said, still smiling.

Emily Rose removed her feet from the bench and moved closer to Davis. "And? Your point is?"

"No, she didn't apologize. And yes, she's a bitch. But she doesn't hate you, Emily Rose. She's not out to destroy your life. Not the way she sees it, anyway. She has . . . a lot of issues she needs to work through. We both know that. And unfortunately, she won't take any help with them. But you know what else?"

"What?"

"She had better be worth all the lying you'll have to do to yourself to walk out of here today without marrying Michael. But I don't think she's worth much, really, either way myself."

Emily Rose laughed and punched his shoulder lightly. "Hey, Davis Hill, you're not allowed to use my words against me like that."

"I think you're a great person. And you're also very important to Jemma. And she's the most important person in the world to me no matter what's happened or what will. For those reasons, I want you to be able to let go. Let go of Tara until she deserves to be a part of your life. If she ever does," Davis said quietly, patting the back of her hand, which lay on the bench.

"She doesn't have any hold over me."

"Then why aren't you married right now? Why aren't you at your reception instead of sitting on a bench in this hot little room?" Davis asked.

"Michael doesn't want to marry me." She bit her lip and opened her palm. She looked down at the huge diamond ring she'd twisted backward on her finger.

"You know, I was talking to Michael earlier while we were all waiting to see what the hold-up was. And he was really excited. Nervous, but excited. Chad said he was shocked when Michael became a one-woman man. And that he knew when that happened, you were special. Michael agreed."

"But all this week, he's been acting so weird."

They both looked up at the sound of Michael's voice. "Because I've been stressed. And I've been an idiot."

"Michael." Emily Rose stood. "How long have you been in that doorway?"

"Once I realized Jemma and Davis were back, I poked my head in the door, but you guys were having such an intense conversation, you didn't notice. So I stood here, eavesdropping for a while." Michael came into the room. He was still wearing his tux, but no bowtie. "I've been worried about finding a job. You would think these things would be easy for an NYU MBA, but not so much. Mom's been really crazy—"

"I know she doesn't like me. She must be thrilled about all this."

"Em, this day isn't about her or your sister. And that's why I left like an idiot earlier and went out to that bar. I was so frustrated that I couldn't make you see that. But Chad talked some sense into me—he's good for that— and I'm back now. To say that no matter who, what, when, or where, I'm here for you. And whenever you want to get married, whether it's today, tomorrow, or next decade, I know where you can find a groom. If you'll have me."

"How do I know you're not lying to me?" She chewed her bottom lip, looking uncertain, but like she wanted to go to him at the same time.

"Have I ever?" he said. "Besides, I'm still here, right? Through everything that's happened today, look where I'm standing right now. The only place I want to be."

She took a tentative step forward. "The only place?"

"The one and only." He held out his arms. "I love you, Em Rose. That's how it's always gonna be."

"I love you, too." She ran to Michael, hugging him. Then she sprinted out of the room, holding his hand and shrieking that the wedding was back on.

She stuck her head back into the room, beaming. "Thanks, Davis." And then she was gone again.

Jemma walked slowly into the room while Michael, Emily Rose, Carolina, and Meg talked in the hallway about guests, the preacher, and the reception.

"What in the world did you say, Davis Hill?" Jemma asked, reaching for his hands.

"All things magical," Davis said, putting his hands in hers.

"Apparently." She kissed his lower lip, letting her lips linger over his.

Davis put his arms around her waist and stared into her eyes. He'd never tell her what he was thinking because he didn't want to scare her off. If he did that, he wouldn't get the few amazing days he wanted to have with her. Still, he didn't know how he was going to handle her leaving. From where he was standing at that moment, he couldn't think of a way to possibly be okay with letting her go. Again.

With a little teamwork, everything came together. Jemma and Davis helped Meg get all of the guests back and find the preacher while Carolina helped Emily Rose finish getting ready. Michael and Chad spent almost the entire time arguing with Ms. Fletcher, but when that was done, the three of them managed to salvage most things for the reception at the community center. There was not going to be an ice sculpture, though, and the chocolate fountain had overheated and stopped working, so that was a no-go as well.

Emily Rose was gorgeous in her flowing, backless halter ivory dress and tiara surrounded by baby's breath and gardenias. Her makeup really was fantastic. Carolina was good—she'd wanted to be a makeup artist at one point, and, judging by her work, she probably would have made it. Still, Emily Rose wasn't disappointed that they hadn't been able to get the photographer to come back. She was paranoid about her face.

Jemma and Davis sat next to each other at the ceremony, holding hands and whispering to each other. Wedding guests who didn't know them kept commenting on what a gorgeous couple they were. Jemma tried not to get used to hearing that, but it was hard. She liked hearing it. Worse than that, she liked believing it.

Everyone seemed relieved to make it to the reception. They were skipping dinner—the caterers had given up on them already. The Bradens and a couple of their friends had made a nice spread out of the finger foods the caterers had left behind and added a few dishes of their own. Everyone seemed more interested in the open bar, though.

The bride and groom were announced and Emily Rose floated in on Michael's arm. Everyone stood to watch the first dance and Jemma pressed her hands to Davis's shoulder and stood on tiptoe to reach his ear so she could whisper to him. "You know, this might not have happened without you."

Davis put his arm around her waist and whispered to her. "Yeah?"

"You're kind of like a hero."

"Kind of?"

"Kind of."

"I'll take it." Davis grinned and nuzzled her nose with his, Eskimo-kiss style.

"This day really was something like magic," Jemma said, placing her hands low on Davis's waist.

"You're something like magic," Davis said, pulling her closer, placing his forehead to her cheek. She closed her eyes and her heart jumped a little when she felt his lips against her eyelids. They slid into the next song after the first dance was finished.

Jemma pressed her face to his shirt and breathed in the sharp, clean scents of his cologne and laundry detergent. She was aware of every move his body made against hers, but she was most aware of his fingers. At first intertwined with hers, fingers playing gently against fingers. Then, she felt his fingertips moving up and down her spine through the thin fabric of her mint green dress. Next, they moved through her hair, exploring several individual braids. They seemed to be drinking in memories independent of the rest of him. On her shoulders, sending pleasant chills all over her body and through to the center of her. Then, back to her fingers.

"What's that line from Romeo and Juliet? Let lips do what hands do?" Jemma murmured the words huskily into Davis's ear.

"Oh, you just wait." Davis pulled her closer and they laughed.

"You mean so much to me." Jemma was barely aware she'd said the words out loud until Davis stopped moving. The expression on his face made her regret what she'd said. She tried to laugh off her comment. "I don't know where that came from. I'm hungry. You want to go get some food?"

Davis didn't say anything, but he took her hand and headed in the direction of the food tables.

"I know this has to be—" Jemma started before Davis shoved a large strawberry into her mouth.

"All this has to be is perfect," Davis said, licking strawberry juice from his fingers. The sight of tongue against thumb sent thrills of desire through Jemma.

"Perfect? That's all?" Jemma quirked an eyebrow and smiled as she chewed and swallowed the last of the strawberry.

"Yep. That's all." Davis handed her a plate. "Now. What do you want to eat?"

Jemma smiled, seeing Davis in HD. Living in stereo. He'd never been like this before. If her heart had been in danger then, how in the world would she keep it safe this time? But she wasn't going to worry about that for the moment. At least she would have this one, perfect memory no matter what else happened. And what was life about if not chances to stockpile good memories to get you through the bad times?

That night, Jemma danced hard and laughed harder. Especially when Davis attempted to teach her the Electric Slide. She felt like the only person in the world who didn't know the dance when she looked around the crowded dance floor.

She also realized that night that Carolina wasn't so bad and it was only Jemma's own jealousy that had kept her thinking otherwise. It did her no good to be jealous over anyone else's relationship with Emily Rose. She had to repair her own relationship with her best friend. And she was working on that.

For Emily Rose, that night was about the spotlight and about Michael. And for Jemma, that night was about being happy for Emily Rose; and also for Davis.

Talking to Davis. Laughing with Davis. Catching up on inane stories about life from the past six years. Rediscovering. Bringing the sun back into her cloudy world. It was all about the new and wonderful. Every moment of it. Until Wendell and Stephanie came to their table.

CHAPTER 13

Jemma and Davis sat at a table near the back of the room, their chairs drawn close together, people watching and commenting on what they saw. She rested her head on his shoulder and her arms were locked around his waist. She was missing him already. She needed to get those distracting thoughts about love and forever out of her head.

Wendell and Stephanie walked up with a camera and that just didn't seem like a very good idea. Stephanie, who'd been snapping pictures all evening, asked the three of them to squeeze in for a picture, which was something of a surprise.

After the picture was taken, Wendell said, "Can we sit here?"

Jemma said, "Sure."

Stephanie grabbed Wendell's arm and smiled across the table at them. She seemed to have recovered from the night before. "So you're just in town for the wedding?"

Jemma nodded, not letting her eyes go anywhere near Davis. "I leave next week."

"Where do you live now?"

"Florida," she said, liking the sound of it.

"Oh. That's nice. Six years. Long time to be away from home. I could never go that long without seeing my people back home." That glint of a challenge was back in Stephanie's eye. The Stephanie she'd met at the rehearsal dinner was back.

Jemma smiled. She started tearing the napkin she'd been toying with to shreds. "I guess it's kind of been a while. How did you two meet? You and Wendell."

Stephanie lay her head on Wendell's shoulder and patted his arm. She either hadn't noticed how tense Wendell had gotten or she was ignoring it. "Wendell came down to Hampton, where I was going to school, one weekend with some of his frat brothers. It was homecoming weekend. Anyway, we met at a party, couldn't get enough of each other. We talked for hours. He asked me out before he went home. He came back down to Hampton a few times. I went up to D.C. a weekend or two. It was love at first sight. For me, anyway." She leaned her head into his and he gave her a weak smile and mumbled something in an agreeing tone. "After graduation, I moved up to D.C. for grad school and Wendell started law school. We moved in together this summer. After I graduated from American."

"Oh? What were you studying?"

"I just received my Master of Social Work degree."

"Congratulations," Jemma said.

"Thank you," Stephanie said, head still pressed to Wendell's. She looked around the room before settling her eyes back on Jemma. "Hopefully, it won't be too long before we have one of these ourselves." She patted Wendell's arm.

He choked on his punch.

Stephanie patted his back. "You okay, baby?"

He nodded, rasping, "Yes. Yeah, I'm fine."

Davis squeezed her knee and murmured, "I think you guys probably really need to talk, huh?"

Jemma just leaned her head to the side and peered into her cup, avoiding two sets of eyes, one brown and behind glasses across the table, one light blue and too close.

A Maxwell song came on, and so did Davis's easy charm. "I love this song. Stephanie? Would you dance with me?"

"You want to dance with me?" Stephanie latched on tighter to Wendell as if Davis might try to pull her away from him.

"Yeah. Isn't this a great song? Could I steal you away from Wendell for just a little while and take you out there to the dance floor?"

"Um, okay." She looked unsure about it, but she made a show of kissing Wendell and telling him she'd be right back and then walked off with Davis.

"I told her everything last night. After the dinner," Wendell said once Davis and Stephanie were on the dance floor. "She's normally not like this. I never thought she was the jealous type. I guess she's just nervous, although I told her there was no reason to be."

"I can see where she's coming from. It's fine," Jemma said, tucking her feet under her in the chair. Even though her back was to the dance floor, she had the feeling they were under Stephanie's skeptical gaze every second.

"You're still in love with him."

It wasn't a question, and that was fine because Jemma didn't have an answer. The best she could do was if she was, she didn't want to be.

He said, "Did you ever wonder what it would've been like? You and me?"

"Wendell, there's no point in talking like that. You have someone who's good for you, better than I ever could've been. And anyway—there's just no point." Someone who would probably make a great wife and mother. Two things Jemma wasn't sure she would ever be capable of being.

Wendell leaned forward in his chair. "I can't help it. I've moved on, sure. But I don't think I'll ever completely leave the idea of us behind. I can't stop thinking about what could have been. I was too in love with you to let it go completely," Wendell said. "I don't know if I'll ever be able to." He started to reach across the table and then stopped himself, dragging his hands back and dropping them onto his lap.

"You were such a good friend to me and I'm sorry I hurt you. You have no idea how much I am. I wish a lot of things could've been different, but there's no way to know what would've happened if they had been. What if I'd had a real mother? What if there'd been no Davis? What if what if what if? Why torture ourselves like that?" She wrapped her arms around herself. "Things are the way they are. The only thing I know for sure is I have no regrets about us not dating with the way things were. Because with the way things were, I think I would have only hurt you even more than I did."

He hunched over the table. "But I could have been so good for you." His face crumpled and she wanted Stephanie and Davis to come back. If he said much more, something else inside of her would break and so much in there was already broken. "I'm gonna have a good job when I graduate. I could have given you a real family. We could have been everything you always wanted." His eyes flitted across the dance floor and hardened a little. "Well, almost everything."

Jemma sat back in her chair and stared at him, arms still crossed over her chest. "I have a good life now. I found what I left here to find. And you have a good one, too. You have Stephanie. And your future career. We need to just leave it at that, okay?"

"I guess I have to, huh?" Wendell said. "I just wanted you to know I still think about it is all. I had to make sure you know that. Regardless of . . . just in case . . . whatever."

Jemma was trying to tell herself he didn't mean what she thought he meant while she stared down at the table-cloth. She was still hoping he wouldn't do something crazy like offer to leave Stephanie for her or tell her he was still in love with her and Stephanie could never compare when the others came back to the table. She was relieved when Stephanie told him they should go congratulate the bride and groom since they hadn't done that yet.

Davis sat next to her and took her hand. If he noticed it was clammy, he didn't say anything.

"They're gonna do the bouquet and stuff in a few minutes," Davis said. He rubbed his thumb over the back of her hand.

Jemma nodded. "I'm going to go say my goodbyes to everyone then so we can slip out right after."

"Hey. You okay?" Davis gave her a small frown.

Jemma forced a smile. "I'm just tired. Really tired." She kissed his cheek and stood.

While Davis waited for Jemma, Emily Rose and the others—including Stephanie—danced one last dance together and took a million more pictures at Emily Rose's insistence. Then Wendell came up to him. They nodded greetings to each other and then Wendell took a place against the wall next to him.

"What did you say to her? While I was dancing with your girlfriend?" Davis said.

He crossed his arms over his chest. "The truth."

"About?"

Wendell turned and narrowed his eyes at Davis. "Do you really care about her? You really love her?" After a pause during which he must have figured Davis wasn't going to answer him, he said, "You know she barely survived what you did to her before."

Davis swallowed hard. He knew. He didn't like to talk about it, but he knew. "Jemma means more to me than anyone ever has." He'd never been so honest about his feelings out loud to anyone besides Codie, but it didn't matter anymore who knew. He was still losing her again. He'd never deserved to be a part of her life and he didn't think there was anything he could ever do to change that.

Wendell snorted. "That's saying a lot considering how you treat the people in your life."

"Why's it such a big deal to you? She's going to be in Florida in a few weeks. She came to me. No one's playing any games here with anyone else." He almost said no one was going to get hurt, but that might not have been true. At least if someone did, it would be him. He wouldn't let it be Jemma.

"Why is it such—did you really just ask me that?" Wendell's blasting laugh was full of disbelief and outrage.

"Yeah. I just asked you that." Davis could play the asshole game, too. Heck, he'd invented it.

"I love her. I always have. I won't let anything bad happen to her."

"What about Stephanie?"

"What about her? She's my girlfriend, yes. She's going to be my girlfriend in the future, yes. Maybe even my wife. But that doesn't mean that I'll ever get over what I felt for Jemma or that I'll stop being her friend. And I will certainly never stop caring for her." Wendell stared him down. "I just want to make sure we're clear about that."

"You think you know me so well, Wendell." Davis shook his head, grinning in disbelief. "You don't know a thing about me at all."

"I know you're worthless."

"It doesn't take much to figure that out."

"If you hurt her, I will hunt you down."

"I'm not afraid of you, but I'd never hurt her." Davis watched Jemma squeeze in between Emily Rose and Carolina for a picture. "Again."

Before she left, Jemma found everyone and said her goodbyes. She told Emily Rose, Carolina, and Meg she'd see them the next day. There was going to be a big brunch for everyone before Carolina and Michael headed back to New York on Monday.

Carolina had a dance audition in a few days and Michael had to get back on the job search. He had interviews lined up during the upcoming week. Emily Rose was driving back to New York at the end of the week. They weren't honeymooning until they both had jobs. They'd planned a trip to Milan at Christmastime because they hoped they would both have jobs by then.

Jemma stood at the edge of the group of women waiting to catch the bouquet. She didn't want to risk getting close enough to catch it. After watching Michael throw the garter, she found Davis and they left.

Davis stopped at Mary's so that Jemma could throw some things in an overnight bag and then they went to his house. He started to get out of the car until he noticed that she wasn't moving. He sat back in his seat and closed the door.

"Hey. What's wrong?" He leaned over the console and toward her.

"Would you mind if I just wanted you to hold me tonight? The mood . . . kinda gone," Jemma said while staring out of the windshield at the creamy half moon.

"What kind of crazy question is that? Would I mind. All I want is to be near you, Jemma. To be as close to you as I can for as long as I can."

He unbuckled her seatbelt. She felt as if he'd released her from all of the dark thoughts weighing her down with his words and that simple gesture.

They walked hand-in-hand to his front door, him carrying her bag. She looked around the foyer, remembering the first time she'd come to that house. She swallowed hard, thinking of that disastrous afternoon before prom. After locking the front door, he led her to his room. The only other time she'd been in that room, things had been completely different between them. It'd been that same afternoon before prom. Standing right there next to his desk, Davis had told her there was no way they could ever work as a couple. And it was still true. But for completely different reasons.

"You change here. I'll be back in a minute," Davis said before kissing her neck.

"No. Hold me for a minute first. Real tight. Like you're afraid to ever let me go," Jemma said.

Davis did as she asked. He had no idea how she wished it could have been different. Wished that they'd never hurt each other. That others hadn't hurt them so badly that they didn't know how to do anything other than damage their own chances at happiness. That there was another way she could fix it all besides going away to

Florida. And most of all, she wished that she never had to let go of Davis.

"I'm sorry I ever said all those hurtful things to you back then." Davis was apparently visiting the same memories that she was.

"What did we say? What have we been saying all along? Nothing exists past or future during our time together, right?"

"I wish I could—I dunno. I want to do something really big and wonderful for you. To show you how much—I mean you made me so happy today. I want every day to be today."

"The biggest and most wonderful thing you could do for me right now would be to show me the bathroom. 'Cause I really have to go," Jemma said. She was afraid if she didn't break the seriousness of the moment, her feelings would suffocate her. He laughed and then told her where to find it and she headed off in that direction. Her head ached with the pressure of unshed tears.

Davis shifted his body away from Jemma's slightly, afraid that if he didn't, she would know how much he wanted her despite how cool he'd tried to play the situation earlier. She lay on her side and he was curled up behind her. He let her pretend she was asleep because he wasn't sure what he'd say to her if they acknowledged she was awake.

Man, he could use a cigarette, but he'd decided to quit yet again that morning, knowing Jemma wouldn't like the idea of him smoking. A drink would have been good also, but he wasn't sure that'd be a good idea, either. Besides, he didn't really want to leave his bed as long as Jemma was in it. Being so close to her warm, soft body after dreaming about it for six long years was a sweet kind of torture.

He moved his hand from her shoulder and smoothed it over her braids, then let the backs of his fingers rest against her cheek. He thought he heard her breathing quicken, but there was no other sign of movement from her. She still wanted to feign sleep. Fine with him.

He wondered exactly what Wendell had said to her, but she hadn't wanted to talk about it. Wendell might have been smarter and more successful than him, but the guy was still a jerk. He hated the idea of anyone making her feel badly. He wanted to protect her from anything and anyone who would hurt her, including himself. She had such a good heart no matter what all had happened. He'd been one of the people to break that good heart all those years ago. And Wendell rehashing the past she obviously didn't want to relive angered him. And then the idiot had the nerve to assume he knew what Davis wanted.

When she'd come back to him in the restaurant Friday, there'd been only one answer he could give her. His heart hadn't let him give any other when it came to spending as much time with her as he possibly could. Still, he was seeing a problem with their so-called arrangement already. He'd never gotten over her. Holding her so close again, burying his face in her hair, remembering the feel and taste of her lips under his made the thought of having to let her go again almost unbearable. Still, couldn't ask her to stay for him. Knowing all she'd been through, including the stuff he'd put her through, doing that would be stupid and selfish. He had to remember that. She would have probably said no anyway.

She'd asked him earlier about his marriage to Tara. He was over that. It hadn't taken long because clearly marrying Tara had been a mistake. Most importantly, he'd never really loved her. He'd done it because it'd been easy. She'd been there. They'd dated in high school. She was attractive. Or at least she had been at the time. But Jemma? Thinking about losing her all over again was painful. But it was just another pain he had to endure because the alternative—having her be so close but not being able to see, touch, and feel her—was not an option.

He pressed his face into her neck and draped his arm over her waist. He felt her fingers weave through his. He squeezed them.

CHAPTER 14

Sunday morning, Davis dropped Jemma off at one of Derring's few hotels on his way to work. The post-wedding brunch was being held at the hotel's restaurant.

"I'll pick you up from Mary's when I get off work?" he said, scratching his jaw.

"Yep." She leaned over and kissed his cheek, wanting to apologize for the previous night. However, it felt strange to mention the previous night at all. So much had happened, and she was still trying to digest it all.

He started to say something and then closed his mouth.

"What?"

He pressed a hand to her hair, letting it drop to her ear, which he caressed between his thumb and forefinger. "I can't wait 'til this evening. That's all."

She felt like that wasn't all, but who was she to push? After all, she'd been the one faking sleep last night because she didn't want to talk about anything that'd happened. They were both closed books. What a pair they made.

"Me, neither." She took his hand from her ear and kissed his fingers before letting go. "Okay. I have to go and you do, too." That didn't mean she wanted to.

Hopping out of the car, she hurried into the hotel to avoid the light rain that misted from the gray sky.

She looked forward to downing a couple of cups of coffee. She still had her headache from the night before. Thinking over what Wendell had said made her sick with guilt every time she did it, but she couldn't stop.

Then there was Smooth. She wanted to go see him, to let him know that he hadn't ruined her life, and that she hoped he rotted in there for what he'd done. But could she look into his face again? In her mind, at least, he was a murderer even if there was no way to convict him for the actions of her mother. If she went to the prison, what would she say to him? She definitely hadn't figured out that part yet.

She was startled out of her intense thoughts by a tap on her shoulder. She turned around to see Wendell.

"Hi." She tensed while trying to gauge his mood. She couldn't deal with any more dysfunction at the moment.

"I'm sorry about last night. I kind of freaked out on you, huh?" he said with a smile.

His words gave her a sense of relief. "It's okay."

"Stephanie and I had a fight about it last night and I realized how stupid I was being." He studied the carpet for a moment before giving her an earnest look. "I want my friend back and I'm going to act like it," he said. She caught a hint of sadness in his eyes, but she could tell he wanted to hide it from her and she was going to respect that.

"Okay, friend."

"It really is good to see you again."

"And I really do promise not to disappear anymore." They laughed. "Seriously, I'll keep in touch this time. In fact . . ." She dug one of the business cards she'd had printed up after getting the job offer out of her purse. Handing it to him, she said, "Here."

He read the card and gave an approving nod. "Assistant director. You really are doing well for yourself, huh?"

"Told you."

He slipped the card into his pocket. "Tell me more."

She told him about college, Florida, and her new job. He then told her more about Stephanie, law school, and his life in D.C. They talked until the others showed up.

Emily Rose ran up, throwing an arm around each of them. "Hey, you two. I'm so hungry. Let's go get some brunch. Where's Steph, Wendell?" Jemma could hear the rest of the group behind them.

Wendell put his arm around Emily Rose's shoulders. "We're staying here. She's up in the room, married lady. I left her up there getting ready. She'll probably be down, oh, sometime before tomorrow."

They laughed.

Michael slid up next to Jemma. She let Wendell and Emily Rose walk into the restaurant ahead of her. Michael looked at her, his brown eyes serious. "You know, we haven't talked much. I want to thank you for yesterday. And to let you know Em Rose is in good hands. I love her more than anything in the world."

They stopped walking. Carolina and Meg gave them curious glances, but continued around them to the restaurant.

"After yesterday, who could doubt that?" Jemma said.

Michael chuckled. "I just wanted to say that. Because . . . you haven't seemed so sure about me since we met."

So Michael had picked up on that. Between his comments and Carolina's, Jemma was realizing she wasn't as good at hiding her feelings as she'd thought she'd been.

"I've had a lot on my mind," Jemma said. She sighed and then added, "Maybe I wasn't. At first. Sure about you, I mean. I was too quick to judge. You're a better guy than I gave you credit for. Besides, Emily Rose loves you and that's all that matters."

A slow grin spread over his face. "Emily Rose isn't like any girl I've ever met. My grandmother says she's sunshine and thunderstorms all rolled into one. As strange as that might sound, it makes total sense to me. I like it. Gram's from the South, too. I think that's one of the biggest reasons she and Em Rose have bonded so well."

Jemma nodded. "Em Rose is special."

Michael held the door to the restaurant open for Jemma. "Yeah, she is. I don't know what I'd do without her." The enraptured look on Michael's face at that moment both warmed and pained Jemma's heart.

She wanted what Michael and Emily Rose had. And she had no idea how to go about getting it.

"She gets me in a way no one else ever has, Jemma. I don't have to try to be perfect for her." Michael made all kinds of wild hand gestures as if trying to make sure Jemma understood exactly how he felt. "She knows me so well. It's so good to be loved by someone who knows how to live with the flaws. Who knows not to expect the world from you and how to be grateful for what you can give. And who knows that, like the people who give it, love is not perfect."

Emily Rose skipped over to them and threw her arms around Michael, kissing his cheek. "What are you two talking about back here?"

"Southern girls," Michael said, squeezing her to him and kissing the top of her head.

A thought struck Jemma and she said, "Yeah. What is it you used to always say about Southern girls? Something about sweet tea and charm?"

Emily Rose did her best impression of Julia Roberts's Shelby accent in *Steel Magnolias*. That was her favorite movie and she'd long ago named herself an honorary Steel Magnolia. "Sweet tea, charm, and giggles. We have it all."

They laughed. Carolina and Meg looked at each other and then turned their puzzled looks on Jemma and Emily Rose. Emily Rose turned to them to explain the inside joke. Jemma took a seat at the table next to her and across from Wendell. When Stephanie came down, she sat next to Wendell.

"Hi, Jemma," she said with a sweet smile. Apparently, having it out with Wendell the night before had helped.

"Hi," Jemma said, surprised by her mood change and grateful for it. Things were well on their way to normal when it came to Wendell, at least.

All through brunch, Jemma thought about Michael's words. Especially what he'd said about love not being perfect. Davis had disappointed her, hurt her, yes. But what about second chances? Maybe there was a chance he wouldn't do it again.

But did she want to take that chance? Even if he didn't hurt her again, and that was a big "if" Davis was a reminder of a past she didn't care to dwell on. Could she be with him and stay in Derring, without being haunted by that past? Probably not.

No, it wasn't only about second chances. It was about finding a way to move on as well. She decided in that moment that she did want to see Smooth. Then, after meeting with the parole board, she would leave. There was nothing else to stay in Derring for any longer.

She looked at Wendell and Stephanie. Then at Michael and Em Rose. Both couples had something she and Davis lacked. Or she and Davis shared something the two couples lacked, depending on how a person looked at the situation.

Jemma was distracted with similar thoughts throughout the brunch. Emily Rose and the others had to call her name several times any time they wanted her attention. She barely touched her omelet and only picked at her fruit.

Eventually, Emily Rose turned to her and said in a low voice, "Do you even want to be here?"

"Of course I do," Jemma said.

"I get the feeling—now don't get me wrong, I'm forever grateful for what you did for me yesterday—but, sometimes I get the feeling you don't really want to be around me."

"No, Emily Rose." She put her hands over her friend's. "No, it's not that."

"Then what? Jemma, you're not—it's like we're strangers now."

Jemma's heart sank. Emily Rose hit on one of the things that had been bothering Jemma since she'd arrived home.

Em Rose narrowed her brown eyes and leaned in closer. "Carolina keeps hinting that I really need to talk to you. Did you say something to her about me? What's going on with you?"

She twisted her lips to the side for a moment before answering. "She's right. We do need to have a long conversation about some things. Really talk. But not around everybody like this. Why don't you come to Mary's tomorrow afternoon?"

"What's wrong with today?"

"Well, it's your last day with Michael for a whole week. He goes back to New York early tomorrow morning. And you won't see him again until you go back at the end of the week. I don't want to take any of your time with him."

Emily Rose still looked unsure, but she nodded. "Okay. But only if you promise to tell me what is really going on with you tomorrow."

"I promise. We'll talk about what's happening between us," Jemma said, choosing her words carefully.

Emily Rose turned back to Michael, interrupting a story he was telling about Emily Rose giving a homeless man a drunken serenade in Central Park. She shouted at him that he was telling the story wrong. Jemma had to do a better job of paying attention. She didn't want the spotlight on her again.

Later that morning, when they were leaving the hotel, Jemma grabbed Carolina's arm. "Can I talk to you for a second? Before you go?"

Carolina gave her a confused look but nodded and walked with Jemma to the parking lot.

"Emily Rose told me what you said about her and me needing to talk," Jemma said.

"My big mouth always gets me in trouble. I'm sorry if I was butting in where I don't belong, but Em Rose means a lot to me and she's so sweet. This thing is getting to her, whatever it is going on between you two."

Jemma nodded. "I know. You're a good friend to her, I can tell that. And it's good you said something. We do need to talk."

"Good," Carolina said. The two of them stood there for a moment, looking around the parking lot.

Finally, Jemma said, "We didn't get off to the greatest start, huh?"

Carolina grinned. "Didn't seem like it."

"Sorry about that. I just wish we had more time to get to know each other. I start coming to my senses right before you leave."

Carolina shrugged. "What about now? You need a ride anywhere? I don't see that car you've been driving around."

"Actually, I do."

"Let's go." Carolina nodded in the direction of her rental.

"So what's this audition for?" Jemma asked as they walked to the car.

"Comeback tour for a has-been pop star."

"Oh, yeah?"

"Yeah, actually he used to be a pretty big deal. It's a closed audition. I'm lucky to have it, I guess."

"You don't sound very excited about it."

They got in the car. Carolina made a noncommittal noise and pulled out of her parking space. "It's just—it might be my last audition."

"Why?"

"Because . . . it's probably time I got realistic about some things. I've been thinking about going the practical route and becoming an agent for a while. I'm not going to make very much money off a few dancing jobs here and there. Not enough to support myself."

"Isn't dancing what you went to school for?"

"Yeah, but I minored in economics and I know this guy who works for a dance company. As a business manager. He knows people. I've been thinking about the agenting thing for a while now."

"But dancing means a lot to you, doesn't it?"

"Yeah, but I'll be working with dancers and I'll still dance, just not professionally. And nobody gets everything they want, right?"

That was certainly true. "I guess not."

"And I figure that sometimes, you have to decide which dreams are worth fighting for and which dreams are just too unrealistic to hold on to. And then you have to make some hard decisions. Sometimes painful, but necessary, decisions."

Jemma nodded and her thoughts immediately went to Davis.

CHAPTER 15

Sunday evening, Davis picked Jemma up from Mary's as soon as he got off work. They went to his house so that he could shower and change. He kept telling her he had a surprise for her, but he wouldn't give her any hints. He'd only say that he wanted to do something special for her.

She tried to guess after he came into the living room with his black hair still wet and slicked back from his forehead.

"Is it food?" Jemma asked.

He sat down next to her and kissed her cheek. "No."

"Is it in this house right now?"

"Uh-uh." He kissed her throat.

"Are you taking me to get it?"

"I guess you could say that." Davis kissed her shoulder over the strap of her tank top.

"We have to leave?" She pulled him closer and kissed his lower lip.

He grinned, pulling her onto his lap. "I went by the Bradens' after I dropped you off for the brunch thing and before I went to work. To get this." He pulled a brass key out of his pocket and showed it to her.

She didn't get it. "A house key? Why?"

"I asked if we could borrow their lake house for the night. Up near Louisa."

"Really?"

"Yeah. Thought it'd be fun. What do you think?"

"When do we leave?"

"How about . . . right now?"

Jemma grabbed the bag she'd packed to stay at Davis's that night and he told her he'd packed a duffel bag and put it in the trunk earlier. He took her bag and they headed out of the door. She enjoyed the feel of the heat of the early evening sun on her skin as they walked to the car. She was glad the sun had finally come out after the morning had been so gloomy.

Davis drove with one hand on the steering wheel and the other in one of Jemma's.

He brought her fingers to his lips and kissed them before placing their hands on his lap. "How's Mary?"

"Good, but the poor woman. She's still in denial. She doesn't think I'm really leaving." She looked straight ahead while answering him.

"Oh."

"But I am. My train leaves in less than three weeks. The movers have already picked up my stuff from South Carolina. They're paying for my moving expenses. The job is, I mean. Did I tell you that?" It was like he'd asked her for hard proof she was leaving or something. Why did she think he needed to know all of that?

"Yeah," Davis said. He didn't want to talk about her job or anything that had to do with her upcoming move to Jacksonville.

"I never lied to you about it."

He pulled his hand away from hers and dropped it onto the bottom of the steering wheel. "Yeah."

"It's for the best, Davis."

"Man, this song is awful." He fiddled with the knob on the car's radio. "You bring any CDs?"

"I think I have a few in my bag," Jemma said. She gave him a look, but didn't try to change the subject back. Instead, she reached behind her and grabbed her purse off of the backseat.

"Good. Hopefully they don't suck."

"What? I have great taste in music."

"Says the world's number one Vixen Vengeance fan."

"Hey, shut up about Vixen Vengeance or you won't like the consequences."

"Consequences?"

"It's going to be a long and lonely night sleeping by yourself up at the lake house," Jemma said, handing him the CD.

"Point taken. Lips sealed." Davis slid it into the player.

"They better be until tonight."

"That's a promise."

"'Cause I don't make threats," Jemma said, completing their old inside joke. It made him happier than even made sense that she remembered it. "I can't believe you remember that. You're full of surprises, huh?"

"I try to be," he said.

"Yeah, yeah, yeah. Full of something, anyway."

"Oh, Jemma, the impossible, c'mere," he said, hugging her close.

She smiled, settling into the crook of his arm. If only he could keep her there. If only they never had to go back.

Jemma fell asleep, pressed to his side. He brushed a few stray braids out of her face and grinned down at her. He told himself not to get used to having her there, but he knew that wouldn't stop him from doing so. Or from missing her when she left for Florida.

It wouldn't be news to say he loved her. But it was amazing that he could fall in love with her all over again when he hadn't thought it was possible to be more crazed over her than he already was.

"I love you and I don't know how I'm going to be able to let you go," Davis whispered. "But I have to. I know it's what you need."

He thought back to those midnight moments in high school. There was nothing he wanted more than to go back in time and shake some sense into that idiot version of himself. He had no idea how many times he'd had that thought. He'd had it even before his accident. And after his accident, the thought plagued him, haunted him until he wanted to reach into his brain and physically rip it out. He knew dwelling on the past wouldn't do any good, but knowing wasn't doing.

"I want you to stay with me, but more than that, I want you to be happy. I know you can never be happy in Derring. Especially with me," Davis whispered. Then, he laughed at himself. "I never woulda seen this day coming six years ago. But who would have?"

He smiled, going back to his favorite memory.

She hadn't known he was watching. He'd been at the Bradens' house to pick Tara up for a date. Emily Rose's door was cracked and he'd peeked into the crack out of curiosity. A flash of orange had caught his eye. She danced around to The Cure's "Just Like Heaven" in an orange tank top, laughing at her own tone-deaf singing. He'd watched, barely noticing that his lips had curved up with a slight smile.

At that moment, she hadn't seemed like the heavily burdened, always-sad girl who was way older than him in emotional years although he was a year older than her in physical years. It really was just like heaven, being able to watch her dance around that room and sing loudly and out-of-key. That was the moment that he realized he was in love with her. And in that moment, he was too mesmerized to be scared. The fear would come later and screw everything up.

But in that moment, he could only see and feel love. Her warm brown eyes. The slight flush beneath the perfect brown of her cheeks. A long-fingered, slender hand reaching up to brush her hair out of her face. The swaying of her hips and arms.

He wanted to kiss the lips that sung those out-of-tune notes. When he heard Tara coming from her room, he'd almost been angry. He'd had to remind himself that Tara wasn't interrupting anything. That Tara was the one he was there for. She was the one he wanted. After all, Davis

Hill couldn't be seen with the biggest loser at Derring High. So he'd kissed Tara and continued to ruin his life by making the wrong choices.

Now, he heard the words that haunted him in his dreams. Words that had made it sink in that he was too late even though he'd finally realized he loved her too much to want to hide it from anybody anymore and didn't want to try. He'd finally convinced her to come over to his house after school one day near the end of the year and talk. It'd happened a little while before she'd left town. The words that were stamped across his battered heart were never too far from his mind's ear:

"I wish there was something I could do to keep you," he'd said.

"There was," Jemma said, staring at him from across the kitchen table. "Back when I needed you most."

"That's not fair."

"None of this is. You think I wanted things to be this way? You made this necessary. All I wanted was you, Davis. All I wanted was you."

And then. Even worse. The memory of what had followed.

"So there's nothing I can say? Nothing I can do to make this right?"

"I wish there was."

"What if I swore on my life to never hurt you again? To come home from Pennsylvania or Charlottesville every weekend possible? To always love—"

"Stop."

"You're taking the life out of me right now. You can at least listen to the words that torture me every minute."

"No. Because you weren't there when I fell apart. My friends had to suffer through that. And I won't make them suffer again. That's why it's best if I go."

"You wouldn't stay? Not even for me?"

"Why would I? You're not good for me—you're not enough for me."

Davis's face froze. Then, he slumped forward against the table, burying his head in his hands. "You can really just give up?"

"You gave up a long time ago. We have to live with that now."

And then she was gone.

Davis sighed, the memory having drained him emotionally, as it did every time he gave over to it.

Whenever he visited those memories, he always wanted to hold her close. Now, with her lying next to him in the car, he could. He tightened his arm around her. She stirred in her sleep and slung an arm low around his waist without ever waking. He kept absolutely still for a moment, afraid of doing anything to ruin the moment.

How would he ever be able to let her go again? He took every moment he could spare from looking at the road to look down at her head, curled into his side. He shook his head. There wasn't enough time left with her—there never would be. Biting his lip, he forced himself to concentrate on the road. He wouldn't fall apart and ruin the few moments he had left with her.

They reached the lake house a little before sunset. The house was close to the lake. A dock led from the backyard and into the water. They stood near the dock and watched the orange-red glow of the sun's dying rays skimming across the surface of the lake. A couple of canoes bobbed in the water near the dock.

"This is gorgeous," Jemma breathed, letting Davis take her hand.

Davis stepped in front of her, pushed her hair back, and left his hands framing her face. "This is the kind of moment I've been dreaming about, Jemma. For six years. And now that I have it . . . I can't stand the thought of anything taking it away."

Jemma wouldn't meet his eyes. She didn't know what to say to that. It wasn't fair for him to say that. He knew what this was supposed to be. A simple time of not thinking. No past. No future. But how could she get mad at him when she knew she'd asked the impossible when she asked for that? She exhaled and her breath whistled through her teeth as she searched her brain for a response, carefully ignoring her heart. "That little grocery store back up the road is going to close soon. We should get going if we're going to get some things for dinner."

"Yeah. I'll—uh, bring in the bags before we go," Davis said, looking away from her. He'd been acting like that ever since they'd arrived. Strange.

She nodded. "Thanks."

"Yeah," he muttered, heading for the car.

She followed him with her eyes for a moment and then headed for the front door.

She looked around the house while she waited for Davis to bring in the bags. The downstairs consisted of a living room, a kitchen, and a dining room. It was simple, but airy and spacious. And full of memories of summers and weekends with the Bradens.

She wandered upstairs to check out the bedrooms. There were three. She went into the master bedroom and looked around. The room was warm and dark. The color scheme was burgundy and cream. She smiled, hugging herself and inhaling the faint scent of lavender potpourri. Mrs. Braden was a potpourri fanatic and had probably left some after her last trip to the lake house.

Moving over to the bed, she traced her fingers over the intricate patterns on the wine and gold-colored duvet. Jemma imagined candles throwing shadows onto the dark walls while she and Davis lay in tangles on that bed. She heard Davis walk into the room, but she didn't turn around. He walked up behind her and wrapped his arms around her waist. She sank back against his chest. He rested his chin on top of her head.

"This feels almost too perfect," she murmured.

"This is the nicest thing I've ever felt. And I don't want to stop feeling it," Davis said, weaving his fingers through hers. "I'm tired of things being ruined for us."

She started to pull away, but Davis didn't let go of her. She sank back against him. "You know what I said about food earlier? I'm starving. We better get going."

"Okay. You know, I was thinking we could make chicken fried steak and mashed potatoes. Maybe have some greens with it." His lips grazed the back of her neck and a delicious shiver ran down her spine.

"You know what I like." She turned in his arms and ran her hands down his arms, stopping at his elbows.

He bent his head, bringing his lips close to her ear. "What I don't know, I'm dying to learn."

She reminded herself that love—even when it existed, which was rare in her experience—couldn't be trusted. Love was blind, all right. Too blind. And it blindly led people into making bad decisions. It had certainly led Lynette into more than one, the biggest one being Smooth.

Jemma kissed him because it felt so good and because she was afraid of talking at that moment. She forgot to want anything else. His mouth on hers was the only thing she had left in the world. When he tried to pull back, she kissed him harder.

CHAPTER 16

Brady's Country Store was only a few miles down the road from the lake house. Jemma had been there before with the Bradens when Jemma had come with them to the lake house, which hadn't been all that often with Lynette breathing down her neck. Those were some of the best memories Jemma had. Visiting them made her both look forward to and dread her talk with Emily Rose the next day. She wanted things fixed between them, but was afraid it wouldn't happen.

From the outside, Brady's looked like an old country house. It was a wooden structure painted dark red with a matching peaked roof. In the front were several picture windows. One was missing its screen. The white wooden door was swung open and the screen door had an "open" sign on it as well as one advertising Brady's hours.

Jemma and Davis walked into the cool, dimly lit store. Several ceiling fans rotated slowly, circulating air throughout the building. There were more fans on the floor near the front of the store. Coolness that could only come from air conditioning still hung in the air as if someone had recently turned off the A/C in anticipation of the sweet, cool evening air they were experiencing.

They walked down the aisles, holding hands. Davis carried a red plastic shopping basket. He let her hand go only to put things in the basket.

"Gross," Jemma said as he threw a jar of olives into the basket.

Davis grinned and threw in another jar.

She took both jars out and put them back on the shelf. He set the basket on the floor and tickled her until she was laughing so hard that the few people in the store with them turned and stared over the short rows of shelving.

"Jerk." She was laughing as she said it and playfully punched him in the chest.

He stumbled backwards, pretending her punch had more force than it did. "You better not forget about me when you go to the far and distant sunny lands," Davis said. He then began singing "Don't You (Forget About Me)" by Simple Minds.

Jemma laughed. "Of course I won't. You never forget your first—well, whatever you were to me."

He raised his eyebrows. "I wasn't your first love?"

Jemma turned her attention to the shelves in front of them, picking up jars and putting them back without reading the labels. She didn't like the direction in which the conversation was going. "I don't think it counts if only one person's in love."

"What? I do love you. I did then, too."

She stepped away from the hand he put on her shoulder. Her heart beat a little faster at his telling her he loved her. She wouldn't acknowledge it, though. She'd expected he'd say something like that. She'd been preparing herself for it. She refused to talk about love in the present tense. She tried to keep her tone light when she said, "Right. You told me you loved me after everything was wrecked. Once it was too late."

"Okay. So things were a little rocky between us. And maybe a little sketchy, too. I'll give you that. I still believe we had love."

"Since when does making out in your car in an abandoned parking lot and keeping any interaction between us a huge secret because you were embarrassed about me qualify as love?"

"Yeah. I screwed up, but I was never embarrassed to be with you." Davis picked up the basket and looked into it, avoiding her gaze.

"Liar."

"Okay, but I got over it in a big way and I wanted to tell everyone I loved you—"

"Once it was too late."

"Yeah. Unfortunate." He looked up at her. "For both of us."

He put the basket down again and took her hands in his. She tried to pull away, but he held on and kissed her fingers one by one.

She bit her lip and forced herself not to say the things she wanted to say. Saying them could have ruined everything. There hadn't been a time that mattered when she hadn't loved Davis Hill. But it'd always been a hard love. He'd hurt her so much both intentionally and unintentionally. Sure, he said it was real and true now, but what was ever really true? Especially when it came to love.

Losing her whole family in a matter of weeks and having Lynette as a mother hadn't done much for her faith in love or it being able to overcome all. Even if he did really love her. Maybe the kind of love that Michael had talked about, and what he and Emily Rose had, could only happen for people who didn't share a painful past.

"What is it?" He teased her earlobe with his lips, then nearly melted her with kisses.

"Thinking about how much I want you."

"Well, I'm right here." Davis nuzzled his face against her neck.

She put her hand behind his neck and pulled his lips to hers. He kissed her slowly, thoughtfully. As if trying to memorize every place his tongue touched. When he finally pulled back, she was still reaching for his lips.

"What else do we need? Let's hurry so we can get back to the house." She grabbed the list from him and hurried to the next aisle.

Davis put an arm around her waist and brought a spoon to her mouth at the same time. "This better?"

She tasted the gravy that she'd told him earlier needed more pepper. "Perfect."

He kissed her neck before moving back across the kitchen to the stove. She followed him with her eyes, wanting more than gravy.

"When did you learn to cook?"

"Long time ago," Davis called over his shoulder. "Living with my dad. It was either that or we were gonna both starve to death."

"This man is full of secrets," Jemma said, coating the steak in the flour mixture she'd made, getting it ready to fry.

He turned toward her and they locked eyes. It was funny how memories came back. The stuff her mind pulled out of what happened in the past. At that moment, all she could remember was the night Davis had first kissed her all those years before. And how perfect that kiss had been. All she'd wanted that night was for Davis to be her husband one day.

No use dwelling on the past. She'd been a stupid, naïve girl back then. Traitorous memories. She turned back to her work, concentrating on fixing their steaks so she wouldn't be able to think of anything else.

After dinner, Jemma washed dishes while Davis dried.

"That was really good," she said.

"We make a good team." Davis took a plate from her and moved closer, pressing his hip to hers. In fact, he was so close that she barely had enough room to move the sponge over the dishes, but she wasn't complaining.

"Oh?" Jemma handed him a bowl.

"Yeah." Davis moved behind her, slipping his hands into the water and covering hers. "Don't you think so?"

"Um." It was hard to think at all with him so close. His lips brushed the tender skin behind her ear. He pressed in closer and she reached up for another kiss, barely realizing she was doing it.

"So?" He trailed his wet, soapy fingers up her arms.

"Huh? I mean, well, we should finish washing the dishes—I mean, that gravy's going to be really hard to get out of the pan later," Jemma said, needing some space. She wasn't sure she was ready for what would happen if he didn't back away. The more she thought about it, the more she was afraid that if she let him go too far, let him get too close, she would cross that line she'd been toeing for over a week. If she crossed it, she wasn't sure she could get back to the safe side.

She had to leave Derring. She could never be free of all her personal demons if she didn't. She couldn't trust the love, believe that it could be enough even if they both really did feel it, when it had never been enough before. Love hadn't saved her brother. Smooth had supposedly loved Lynette, but he'd still destroyed her. Lynette and love—putting those two words next to each other didn't seem right.

"Okay," he said with a sigh, moving over and picking up the dish towel again. She had to want him to move closer to the dish rack. She stopped herself from pulling him back to her.

They sat down to watch a movie once the dishes were done. The little bit of tension from earlier had passed. The movie was something basketball related and Jemma quickly lost interest. Davis kept catching her falling asleep and teasing her about it.

Jemma yawned. "I think I'll make some coffee." She stood and Davis pulled her onto his lap. "What?"

"I know a better way to wake you up," Davis said, his eyes twinkling. "Let's go for a walk."

Jemma raised her eyebrows. "You know it's midnight, right?"

"Yeah. Best time for a walk." He said it as if everyone knew this was true.

A smirk of disbelief spread over her features, but she let him take her hand. They padded out of the living room on bare feet and went through the kitchen and out the back door. He led her down the steps. Her toes curled around the cool, moist sand as they walked out onto the beach.

"Hmm. That feels nice," she said and smiled. "The sand." She stared up at the moon, so bright that night. She caught his eye from the corner of hers. "Yes?"

"You're so beautiful in the moonlight. Then again, you're beautiful everywhere," Davis said, encircling her waist with his arm and drawing her closer. They walked down to the lake's edge.

"You brought me all the way out here in the middle of the night to tell me how beautiful I am in the moonlight?" she asked with a grin, resting her head against his shoulder. She admired the moon's reflection on the shimmering stillness of the lake's surface.

"No. I can tell you how beautiful you are anywhere. I could tell you all day, every day."

"Oh. That's nice." She was starting to get carried away again, but she couldn't stop it this time. The scariest part was she didn't want to.

"I should thank you."

She looked up at him, confused. "For what?"

"For coming back to me. Even if just for a little while. Saving me. Again," he murmured into her hair. "I wasn't—I wasn't doing so well before you came back."

He didn't seem to be anything like what Emily Rose had led her to believe she'd find. He didn't seem nearly as broken as she'd expected him to be.

"You've done so much for me. And you mean the world to me. You keep saving me. I feel so whole—so happy here next to you. I can't believe I'm holding you in my arms again. You're such a large part of my life. Even when you're not physically in it. We don't have much time, and I don't know how to tell you everything that's in my heart."

Jemma felt as if her own heart would disintegrate. "Then don't."

"Don't?" His brow puckered in confusion.

"Remember? That's part of the deal we made," Jemma said. "Enjoy this night with me." She walked backward into the lake, reaching out for his hands.

"What are you doing?" His voice was wary, but he gave her his hands.

"Enjoying this moment with you," she said, walking further backward. She didn't stop until the water was waist high. The water she'd disturbed by walking in pushed against her waist in small, pleasant waves. She leaned her head to the side, enjoying the contrast of Davis's dark hair with his pale skin. Her eyes lingered on the angular line of his jaw. In moonlight and shadows, his face was perfection. The face of all her favorite dreams. But that was all he was meant to be now. Dreams and memories. They would have never lasted as a couple. Trying wouldn't have been good for either of them.

Davis said, "Why are we standing here with all of our clothes on?"

"'Cause I can't do this on land." She splashed water into his face.

"Oh. It's on now," he said, splashing her back. She reached down to scoop up an armful of water to fling at him and he grabbed her arms. She laughed, struggling against his grasp until they both lost their balance and went crashing into the lake. Once they surfaced, dripping clothes adhering to their skin, he pulled her close, and kissed her hard and sweet with a passion that would have sent her right back into the lake if he hadn't been holding her so tightly.

"It's not so bad being in here now, is it?" she said between kisses.

"It's not anything but perfect when we're together like this."

She smiled against his lips.

"I still can't believe we did that," Davis said. "That water was freezing." He wrapped a towel around her and rubbed her shoulders. "I'm glad we did, though."

Jemma nodded. Her dress lay on the bathroom floor and she wore only her wet underwear and the towel Davis had just wrapped around her.

"You okay?" he asked.

"Yeah," she said. Needing to feel him close, she sank back against him. "Just a little chilly."

She felt his breathing, gentle and quick, against her neck. She put a hand over his, which lay against her shoulder. She was just going to have to deal with the pain of leaving. She wanted to enjoy every minute she had left with him in the fullest way possible. She needed to listen to what she kept telling him. All that mattered was living in the moment. Enjoying what time they had left to say a real goodbye to each other—something they'd never gotten the chance to do.

She turned around in his arms and locked her hands behind his neck, letting them rest against the nape. And then she drank him in with her eyes. She let them move over the shadowy planes of his face—crooked nose, cheeks, and finally eyes—those eyes a perfect, clear blue. The sky on a cloudless autumn day when everything seemed so perfect it was almost believable that all was going to be okay. That kind of blue.

He traced his fingertips along her cheeks, over her ears, down to her shoulders. Up again, under her chin. He moved them across her collarbone and then up and down her arms from shoulders to elbows. The whole time, they watched each other. They kept their eyes locked as if trying to tell each other all the things they'd forbidden each other to say out loud.

She slid her arms down to his waist. He stroked her hair away from her face. Everything seemed so perfect in that moment. If only there was a way to trick herself into believing it could always be that way. Too bad she knew better.

Davis pulled Jemma's towel open and held the ends of it in his hands. She wore only a soaked black lace bra and panties. Her nipples strained against the transparent material of the bra. She started to move closer. He shook his head, not yet done drinking her in with his eyes.

"What?" she whispered.

"I'm just admiring." His eyes traveled over the rise of her breasts, down to her flat stomach, over her navel, and to the scrap of lacy fabric between her perfect legs.

"Admiring?"

"Yes. Admiring." He dropped the towel and moved closer.

"Oh."

His hands slipped over her hips as he hugged her to him. She moaned, pressing her hands into his lower back.

He tried to absorb every inch of her. He only had days left with her, and he had to be able to remember everything perfectly. From the way her neck curved into the slope of her shoulders to how his name sounded coming from her mouth. To how good it felt to run his fingers over her silky skin.

He knew she was right and that was why it was good she was going to Florida. But that didn't mean he wanted her to go. He wished he were more selfish. Selfish enough to beg her not to go. To ask her to marry him although he had no right to ruin her life by making himself a permanent part of it.

"Davis?" she asked in a soft murmur as his lips found their way up one arm.

"Hmm?" He hummed into the flesh of the opposite arm, working his way down to her fingertips.

"I'm glad you brought me here."

He nodded, his lips pressed to the flesh between her breasts. He let her bra slide from his fingers to the floor. Holding her eyes with his, he spread his fingers over her shoulder before tracing them down to her navel. His lips touched the places his fingers had been. He kneeled in front of her, his hands pressed to her thighs. He took the top of the black scrap of fabric between his teeth and pulled it slowly over her thighs and then released it from his teeth, letting it fall to the floor.

He kissed her inner thighs, inhaling her sweet scent, his hands on the backs of them. He felt her fingers in his hair and his kisses became deeper. While he pressed his lips into the skin of her hip, one of his hands found its way from the back of her thigh to the wet warmth between her legs.

He pulled away and she moaned in disappointment. He stood and took her hands, pulling her over to the bed. Lying on top of her, he said, "I want you to be happy." He'd almost said he wanted to make her happy, but he wasn't sure he was capable of doing that. He represented things from a past she wanted to forget. A past anyone would want to forget.

"I am," she said before kissing him.

"Good." His kisses moved lower and lower until he once again found himself between her gorgeous legs. He drowned out his thoughts with the scent and taste of her.

CHAPTER 17

Monday morning, Davis limped into the kitchen to find Jemma making breakfast. He kissed her cheek before grabbing a mug and going over to pour himself a cup of coffee.

Jemma said, "I've had such a good time here. You sure you can't call in sick?"

"Only if I want to get fired again today." Davis went to the fridge to look for cream.

"Are you okay?"

He looked up from the fridge. "What? Yeah. I'm fine. Why?" No cream. Maybe there was some non-dairy creamer in one of the cabinets.

"Well, it's just that you're limping. And the Vicodin . . ."

"I'm okay. I don't even take the Vicodin. Have you seen me take the Vicodin?" He slammed a cabinet shut. He put a hand over his eyes and winced. He felt bad for snapping at her, but he didn't like to talk about his knee. That, combined with the previous night making him so much more aware of what he was about to lose, led to him being on edge. He also hadn't been able to sleep well, thinking of those things.

"Sorry. You looked like you might be hurting is all." She flipped the eggs that sizzled in a black skillet.

She had no idea how he hurt. "It's okay." He dumped some of the powdered creamer he'd found into his coffee. Then he went to find a spoon.

"I hate to think of you in pain."

He stirred sugar into his coffee.

"Davis?" She put a hesitant hand on his back. He tensed, but didn't move away from her. "I'm sorry. About you and Tara and your . . . what happened between you two. I wanted to say that the other day. And I didn't."

He nodded. "Thanks, but that was a long time ago. Tara was another part of me. A part I didn't like very much. She's not important anymore."

"It has to hurt, though. If you ever want to talk about it—"

He shrugged away from her hand. "Ever? Don't you mean if I want to talk about it sometime in the next two weeks or so before you take off for Florida?"

"I'm sorry, Davis. I am. But you have to know it's better for both of us this way," Jemma said.

"What I know is that it hurts. I love you, Jemma. I've always wanted what we shared this past weekend. Last night. I'm only letting go because it's what you want and what you deserve. I know it's my fault—a lot of the reason you hate being in Derring."

"I don't want to talk about this. It's all in the past and the past can't be changed."

He turned his coffee cup in circles on the counter, looking at it instead of her. "Regardless, I wish I could take it all back."

She was rougher with the plates she pulled from the cabinet than she needed to be. "Like I said, we can't change the past. Only move forward. That's what I'm trying to do."

"I wish I could have been all that you needed. I wish I could be now."

Jemma turned off the stove burners and put her hands on her hips. She stayed facing the stove. "I'm sorry if I hurt you. Maybe this was a bad idea. If you want me to leave you alone for the rest of the time I'm here—"

"Shh. No. Never. I want the time we have left. I know you're going to Florida at the end of it. That may be a little hard for me to deal with, but I understand you need that. I wanted you to know how I really feel. That's all. I thought about it all night, and it might not be fair to you to say anything, but I'm done with the days when I don't tell you what's really in my heart."

"I don't want to hurt you. I don't." He could hear the tears in her voice even if he couldn't see her face.

"Don't worry about me. Go. You deserve a real chance at a happy life."

She turned to him. "I'll never forget you. Even if I can't—I mean, you're important to me." He moved closer and she placed his hand over her chest.

He wanted forever, but he settled for pulling her close.

"I want you to know that no one has ever taken your place, Jemma. Definitely not Tara. Not anybody. And no one ever will."

"Hey, don't you—"

"Forget about me."

"That's a promise."

"'Cause I don't make threats."

Their old joke again. This time, it made her a little sad.

He pressed his lips to hers. For a moment, there was no sound except for their uneven breathing and the racing of their hearts in their own ears. She pressed her thumb against his chin, parting his lips. She held his lower lip between her teeth for a moment before pushing her tongue against his. Their slow kiss deepened as they pulled each other closer, trying to shut out the world.

He lifted her onto the counter and pressed his body into hers. Maybe if he never stopped kissing her, they'd never have to leave.

Monday afternoon Jemma sat in the living room at Mary's house, reading over some files for work. She'd offered to get up to speed on some files and do other client research so she would be up-to-date coming through the door. Her new boss had happily sent her the needed info. Her having the files wasn't a problem because she already had a confidentiality form and all the other appropriate paperwork on file from her summer internship with the firm. She planned to make herself indispensable to them as quickly as possible. The job was a very important step in her career.

Besides, working was good for her. It was easier to avoid the things it was hard to think about when she had something to preoccupy her mind with like reading client files and brainstorming new marketing strategies.

She was so involved in her work, she didn't realize it was time for Emily Rose to come over until she heard a knock at the door.

Once she and Emily Rose were sitting in the living room, Jemma took a deep breath and decided to begin with the beginning. She said, "Smooth's up for parole." And then she told Emily Rose all about the letter and her upcoming interview with the parole board.

"That's what you're doing here," Emily Rose said in a dangerous monotone.

"What?"

"You don't care about me anymore. Maybe you never did. You came back to Derring because of him—his parole hearing. Why am I always such a fool for you, Jemma?"

"No, that's not why I came back."

"It makes perfect sense. You hated helping with the wedding. It's like you couldn't stand to be around me. I was just something to pass the time, huh? Maybe make yourself feel good that you showed up for at least one important thing in my life since high school."

"Emily Rose, it's not like that at all." Jemma reached for her, but she pushed Jemma's hands away.

"You don't care. You're not the Jemma I knew. You've changed, and I don't like this person you are now. At all." Emily Rose walked across the room.

"So you want me to be broken and pitiful like I was back then?"

"I never felt that way about you. And no, I just want you to be Jemma again. I want you to care. I want you to laugh and joke with me and—I want it to be like before. Not the awful parts—I'm not a bitch like you are now. The parts with the sleepovers and the days of us hanging out doing nothing all day. I want you to be something other than this selfish, uncaring thing you've become. Is that what going away made you? This is what you call a better life?"

"Emily—"

Emily Rose made long, angry strides back and forth across the room. "I hate the way you are now. You're a liar and you're so cold. I can't believe what I'm hearing, what I see before me—I can't believe it. You're no better than Tara, you know that? And you know why? All you care about is yourself. You used to be such a good friend, but not anymore."

"No. It's not like that. I thought about you all the time. All of you. It really did hurt to leave you all behind, but I couldn't come back. It's hard to explain, but I just couldn't." Jemma felt like she'd been punched in her heart. Em Rose was right, but there had to be some way to make her see. Some way to get their friendship back the way it should've been.

"Don't I mean anything to you? Does Wendell? Your friends are nothing? Everything we had is nothing? Obviously our friendship is nothing. Was. You're not a friend to me anymore. I don't know what you are." She came to a stop in front of Jemma.

"I was wrong, okay? I'm scared to death, Emily Rose. I'm confused. I don't know how to be or how to act around anyone anymore."

Jemma thought Emily Rose's face fell, but she couldn't see all that clearly through the stream of tears pouring from her eyes. The truth, which made her seem stupid, petty, and small, had tumbled out before she really meant for it to.

"What are you talking about?" Emily Rose spoke in a softer voice.

Jemma threw up her hands and shook her head. She pressed her hand to the side of her head after passing it across her eyes to knock some of the tears away.

"I don't know what I'm talking about. It was stupid, okay? To run away. To leave you. Not to let you guys know where I was. I thought I needed to do that in order to move on. I thought starting fresh would make me happy. But really, the thought of what I did to the few people in the world who ever cared about me? It made me miserable. It's eating me up more now that I'm back." Her breath hitched and then she continued. "You don't think it was hard for me? But what was I supposed to do? How could I stay?"

Emily Rose on the opposite end of the couch. "How could you abandon us? You wouldn't send us an address or call us—you knew where we were even if we didn't have a clue about you other than you might or might not have been somewhere in the state of South Carolina. You said when you left you weren't even sure if you were going to go live with your aunt. That you were going to visit her and you'd take it from there."

"My memories of you were all mixed up with Lynette and Demonte and all kinds of painful things. I was so hurt—so lost. Sometimes, I think I still am."

"I thought you cared about us, Jemma. About me."

"I do."

"And you can honestly tell me Smooth's not the only reason you came back." Emily Rose moved a little closer to her.

"He's not."

"Then how could you leave me? Why aren't we close anymore? I want us to have 'us' back. Why can't we have that?"

"I want that, too." Jemma slid closer to Emily Rose on the couch and they shared a box of tissues Emily Rose had grabbed from an end table.

"Remember how I always said I wished you were my sister instead of Tara?" Emily Rose put her head on Jemma's shoulder.

Jemma nodded, lying her head against Emily Rose's.

"I still do."

"I am your sister."

"Don't leave me like that anymore then, okay? Even after I'm in New York and you're in Florida. Don't disappear on me ever again. You're—you're just not allowed."

Jemma laughed a hard, relieved laugh. Things would be better now that all of what had gone wrong with their relationship was out in the open. She could feel it.

"Okay." Jemma blotted at the corners of her eyes with a tissue. "Never again." She threw her arms around Emily Rose.

Jemma and Emily Rose spent the next few hours catching up. Jemma got the full Michael story, including all of the stories she'd felt left out on earlier that Emily Rose, Carolina, and Meg had shared. Jemma felt like a part of Emily Rose's life again by the time they left for Emily Rose's house. Wendell was going by there before he left for D.C. and Jemma wanted to be able to say goodbye to him.

Jemma was sitting on the porch with Emily Rose and Mrs. Braden when Wendell's car pulled up in front of the house. He drove a black Honda Accord and it looked relatively new. He and Stephanie got out and walked toward the house. Jemma was glad to see that they actually looked like a happy couple for the first time since she'd seen them together at the rehearsal dinner.

Stephanie hugged all three women. Jemma was a little shocked, but in a good way, when Stephanie's arms went around her. She smiled and said, "The way I acted before . . ."

"Don't worry about it." Jemma patted her arm.

"Don't get mad, but Wendell told me everything. Not just about you and him, but everything. And if I'd known, I wouldn't have . . ."

"No, really. It's okay," Jemma said, both because she didn't want to talk about it and because she really did understand Stephanie's position. "I'm just glad he found you."

She smiled, tucking her hair behind small, shell-like ears. "Me, too."

Wendell stepped up. Jemma prepared herself for another handshake just at the moment when Wendell wrapped her in a bear hug. "Come to D.C. and visit us sometime, Ms. Assistant Director."

She squeezed him before letting go. "Of course I will."

He leaned over and whispered, "I'm going to ask her to marry me. I just have to get the ring first."

"I'm glad," she whispered back. "I'll be looking for my invitation in the mail."

"For what it's worth, I think he really does love you. And you know that's not something I'd say lightly."

Jemma stood there, stunned speechless as the others waved and shouted final goodbyes to each other. She watched Wendell and Stephanie go back to the car, hand-in-hand. Watching them drive away, she was still unable to speak.

"What did he say to you?" Emily Rose said, waving a hand in front of Jemma's face.

"Um." Jemma finally managed to make a sound. "Um, something I'm sure I heard right." She started with the part that made sense. "He's going to ask her to marry him."

"He told me that already." Emily Rose narrowed her brown eyes in that Nancy Drew way of hers. "That's not all he said, is it?"

Jemma shook her head, trying to decide if she should repeat what she'd heard, still not sure she'd heard it right.

She didn't want Emily Rose running away with it even if she had heard right. She could run one of two ways, and Jemma didn't want her to go in either direction. Luckily, Mrs. Braden saved her for the moment, announcing the sweet tea she'd brewed earlier was ready.

CHAPTER 18

That evening, Jemma was still rattled when Davis came to pick her up after his shift. Seeing him made her feel a little better, though. An escape, even if momentary. She got in the car and kissed his cheek. The smell of grease and fried meat overpowered the clean scent of his cologne, but she still enjoyed pressing her face to his neck. "I'm glad to see you."

He rubbed her back. "Likewise. Again, sorry about this morning. I really didn't mean to blow up at you."

"It's okay. Really. I said it's done and it's done." She hugged him close.

She laced her fingers through his, looking down at their hands. Being with him again, she had to back away from what she'd felt at the lake house. She needed that safe distance. She wasn't going to let love—or worse, the illusion of it—destroy her life ever again. She wasn't going to give up her entire future for an unrealistic dream.

Still, she had that odd feeling of wanting to protect him after seeing that peek of vulnerability. First, when she'd asked him about his marriage to Tara in the parking lot of the apartment complex. Then, that morning at the lake house. She didn't want to have those thoughts, but they wouldn't leave her alone. She wanted everything to be simple—to be the way she'd planned. But life didn't seem to like to work according to her plans.

Leaving his right hand in hers, Davis used his left to pull away from the curb.

"Thursday night, I'm going to a jazz club with Em Rose." Her head rested against his shoulder as she spoke. "You wanna come?"

"You probably want some time alone with her, huh? I know she leaves soon for New York. I'll tell you what. Rosa's been asking around for people to take her shift that evening. I'll do it and then she can take my day shift Wednesday and I can have a whole day *and* night with you for a change. How about that?"

Jemma grinned, snuggling closer to him. "Sounds perfect. And I'll come over Thursday night when you get off work?"

"Also sounds perfect." He squeezed her hand.

When she and Davis got to his house, a black haired girl was standing in the next yard, grinning at them.

"Hi, Davis. Hi, Jemma," the girl said.

"Hi," Jemma murmured, wondering how the girl knew her name.

"Jemma, this is my neighbor, Ayn."

"Yeah, I noticed you guys driving up and I wanted to say hi. Are you two back together? I've seen you over here a few times."

"Back together?" Jemma looked from Davis to Ayn and back again, having no idea what was going on. Davis shrugged and mouthed *who knows?* to Jemma.

"Yeah, Davis said you were the one who got away." Ayn's green eyes lit up. She turned her eager gaze on Jemma.

"Ayn, we have to go inside now. We'll catch you later." Davis grabbed Jemma's hand and started for his front door.

"I hope you are 'cause he's been a lot less mopey since you showed up." Ayn's voice followed them across the yard.

"Bye, Ayn," Jemma said. "Nice meeting you."

"Bye!" Ayn waved and jogged back to her house.

"Your neighbor, huh?" Jemma asked as Davis unlocked the front door.

Davis nodded. "And the nosiest person in the entire universe."

Jemma laughed. "The entire universe, Davis? I haven't seen her once in all the times I've been over here."

"Doesn't mean she hasn't seen you," he said in a singsong voice, closing the front door after them.

He hopped in the shower and she went to his room to wait for him. After sitting at his desk, she flipped through channels on his television until he came back into the room wearing only sweat pants, his wet black hair plastered to his head. He hadn't been huge before—not bulky, but solidly muscled. Now, he was skinny. Still, he was perfect to her.

She stood and stretched, watching him walk over to her.

"You know what I was thinking about in the shower?" he asked, taking her hands in his and pressing them to his cheeks.

"No clue." She smiled, pushing her hands up through his damp, black hair.

"I was thinking about how great it would be if we could erase our memories. Erase all the bad that's happened."

"Haven't you seen *Eternal Sunshine of the Spotless Mind*? That's dangerous stuff."

"Yeah. But still."

"You know what I was thinking about while you were in the shower?"

"What?"

She gave him a wicked grin. "You in the shower."

He chuckled. "Were you?"

She kissed his throat at his Adam's apple. "And about you getting out of the shower."

"And what else?"

She kissed his chest, then moved her lips to his collar bone. "This. Kissing you."

"I wish it was last night again," Davis said. "There was something I wanted to say to you. But I made myself not say it."

"There's too much talking going on right now." She reached up to kiss his chin.

"Oh, and what should be going on right now?"

She put her arms around him and hugged him close. "I'll show you."

She wasn't going to let him say something that could have changed her entire world. She'd made up her mind about the way the future had to be. Leaving was the only way. She was afraid of what she'd become if she stayed.

The next morning, Jemma woke up early. She stretched at an angle, careful not to disturb Davis, who was still asleep. She hadn't been able to sleep well and so she slipped out of bed a little after dawn. She grabbed her running shoes and her bag and tip-toed out of the room. She changed into her running gear in the bathroom because she didn't want to disturb him.

Most of the night, she'd watched Davis sleep while trying to turn off her thoughts. It was hard, though. She kept thinking about the fact that maybe the new person she'd thought she'd become was just an illusion. And Derring was shattering that illusion. Maybe after all of her hard work and trying to beat it, she'd ended up being like Lynette after all. Selfish. Bitter. Willing to push everyone and anyone aside to do what she wanted. Putting herself first, not caring who got hurt in the process.

After her run, she checked her email on Davis's computer, took a shower, and got dressed. Davis slept through all of that so she started cleaning his room. Cleaning was her thing. Some people shopped to clear their minds, some baked. She cleaned or ran, and running hadn't done the trick that morning.

While she worked, she started to think about her family and her old life in Derring. Maybe she'd been running too long. She guessed part of her realized that. And perhaps that was the real reason she'd come back. Not to prove something that was impossible to prove, but to begin to actually be okay with what had happened instead of only pretending she'd put the past behind her. To reconnect with her old friends and to stop running. That way, moving to Florida really would be a new start and not just her running further, trying to put even more distance between her and the real problem.

When she got bored with piling up his dirty laundry and dishes, she thought about cooking breakfast. She had to go downstairs to start his laundry and throw dishes in the sink anyway.

She was headed for the door when Davis stirred. Yawning, he asked in a croaky voice, "Where you going?"

She held a bundle of dirty clothes to her hip. "To start some laundry. And breakfast. Your room is disgusting, by the way."

"I know, by the way." He waved to her, gesturing that she should come back to bed. She sighed and dropped the laundry. Kicking off her sandals, she walked across the room to him.

She sank down onto the bed and Davis curled up behind her and settled his head into the crook of her neck. He placed his hand over her arm and she relaxed against him.

"You okay?" he said into her ear while stroking her arm.

It would have been too easy to get used to that. She closed her eyes and answered, "Yes." She didn't want to think about how nice it would have been to wake up that way every morning. She really didn't.

"I can tell something's been bothering you. You can tell me anything. You used to know that." He kissed her neck.

What they were doing didn't feel all the way right, but it didn't feel wrong, either. "I've been thinking. A lot. Would you do something for me? Well, help me with something?" There was something she needed to do that she'd been avoiding for way too long. She hoped it would help her genuinely move on instead of just pretending she had. But she didn't think she could do it alone.

"Anything." Davis lay his cheek against hers.

She turned to face him and pressed her forehead to his. "I want to put it behind me. And I think I need some help with that. All of it. I want you to come with me to where the apartment was. And to—and to their graves."

"Of course. Tell me when."

She closed her eyes. "Soon. Today. I want to get it over with. I've gone too long already without moving on."

"Okay." He trailed his fingers up and down her arms in a slow, hypnotic way.

"I can't let her—she can't keep ruining my life, and I need to let her know that. I need to let myself know it." Jemma didn't realize she was crying until Davis wiped the tears away with the sides of his thumbs.

"Shh. She can't hurt you now." He whispered the words so close to her face that she felt the warmth of his breath on her cheek.

"And Bill can't hurt you now, either." She looked up at him, putting her hand to his cheek. "Have you made peace with him? And what about your brothers?"

A look of pain flickered across his face before he could smooth it over with a smile. "Don't you worry about Bill. And don't worry about them, either. We have an understanding."

"You need to talk about it."

"No. I want you to let it all out. Let me be here for you. This won't be like before. I feel like all I ever did back then was dump my problems on you. It's your turn."

"Okay." Not letting go was only hurting Jemma. And there was no reason not to let go. It was best for herself, for everyone. "I have to let it go. Please help me let it go. All of it."

"Of course I will." Davis stroked her cheek with the back of his hand.

At that moment, she saw herself giggling with her little brother. Lynette came into the room where Jemma sat with the book she'd been reading to Demonte in her lap. Lynette slapped the book away, screeching at Jemma that she was worthless. She found out later that what set the woman off was the fact that Jemma hadn't paid the electric bill that Lynette hadn't left her enough money to pay. "I couldn't save him." She swiped at her tears.

"It's okay," Davis said quietly, gathering her close to him.

She buried her head in his chest until she could stop the sobs. Before either of them could say anything else, she lifted her face toward his and he kissed her bottom lip softly. She wanted the distraction and she needed him. She pressed her hands to the sides of his face and then let one slide over his shoulder and down his side.

Her hands reached his navel and he chuckled. "That tickles."

"Does this?"

"Oh, no. That does something else. And if you don't stop causing that to happen, we're going to both be in trouble."

She grinned. "What kind of trouble?"

She shrieked with laughter as he grabbed her by the thighs and pulled her under him.

"This kind of trouble." He trailed kisses across her collar bone.

"Well then. Maybe I like being in trouble." Jemma stopped him in the middle of a kiss. "Am I bad person, Davis?"

"Nothing's bad about you." He wrapped his arms around her in a soothing hug.

"I feel that sometimes, I haven't been—I'm not—all I should be to Emily Rose, to you—to everybody I care about."

"Don't worry about any of that. We all know you love us."

Jemma lay there, feeling the pressure of his body against hers, the warmth of his breath in her ear. Just feeling because that was safer than thinking.

"I wish you could see all the good about you. Because there is so much good about you. What about all you did to save Emily Rose's wedding day?"

"You saved her wedding day."

"Not by myself I didn't. But not only that. You were by her side on the day you knew meant the most to her. You give all you can. Don't beat yourself up for the things you can't change. Think about the wonderful things." He kissed her temple, barely brushing his lips against her skin. "And there is a lot of wonderful."

Jemma held Davis's face in her hands and looked up at him with a lazy smile. What if she decided she couldn't leave him again? Would that be wonderful? She couldn't say those kinds of things out loud. They meant big trouble and could have hurt more than they helped. Because realistically, she couldn't see herself being able to stay in Derring without falling apart. She couldn't see the two of them ever working out as a couple. The two of them together would have been too much brokenness in one place.

Davis smiled and kissed her on the nose. "I don't wanna let you go again."

She pressed her lips to his and kissed him hard. Her hungry, needy, greedy kisses didn't scare him off. His need matched hers, kiss for kiss and touch for touch. Her hands pushed against him, her fingers kneaded into his skin. Her mind flashed back to the lake, to the reception, to the sofa before the wedding.

Her kisses became softer but still insistent as she thought about his sad marriage to Tara and the child he'd lost. Bill and Davis having to be in that house alone together again. His lost scholarship. The Vicodin bottle—Jemma always heard the pills jangling around in the bottle in his pocket, even though he was right. He hardly ever took the bottle out of his pocket. All his hurts. She tried to put how much she cared for him and wanted him to heal into every touch of her lips to his. Because she couldn't bear to say those things out loud.

He linked his fingers through hers and she smiled against his lips before going back to kissing him. She lost herself in the world of their kiss so she wouldn't have to think of the complicated things happening and changing in the world outside of it.

CHAPTER 19

Later that afternoon, Jemma decided they had to go before she could lose her nerve. So Davis ate a quick lunch—Jemma insisted that he at least have a sandwich, but she was too nervous to eat—and then they headed for the place she used to live.

The modest apartment complex consisted of several squat, beige buildings clustered together against a forest backdrop. Most of the residents were Section Eight voucher holders, as Lynette had been. All of them had to be below a certain income level to live there, whether they were Section Eight or not. Jemma drew in a sharp breath as Davis pulled up in front of the unit where Jemma had lived. She stared at the letter on the door. Apartment E.

"They rebuilt it," Jemma said, breaking the heavy silence. What had she expected? That they would leave the unit a charred hole in the ground, some sort of morbid monument to all she'd lost?

She stepped out of the car and closed the door. She heard Davis doing the same behind her. She hugged herself and leaned against him when his arm went around her.

"She was worthless as a mother, but she was all we had." She laughed, but there was no humor in it.

"Demonte loved her so much. He didn't know any better. She might not have had an easy life, but . . ." She shook her head. "I've tried so hard to put myself in her shoes. Pregnant at sixteen. Running away from home. To live with some old man who should have been arrested for statutory rape? He ran out on her anyway. He left right after my sister was born." She took a deep breath and pressed her fingers into her sides. "What I can never wrap my mind around is, why did she have to take it out on us?"

Davis kissed the top of her head and drew her closer, but didn't say anything.

"I didn't think she had it in her to care for us until Patrice ran away. Right after that happened, she spent most of her time on the couch, drinking. Then, she met Smooth and things got worse. She always had that crack pipe on the coffee table. Right where Demonte could see. Once I caught him playing with the thing and I lost it. I wanted to kill her. And then she did the deed for me. Only she took Demonte with her."

Jemma sank down to the sidewalk and rested her chin on her knees. Tears slipped down her cheeks, but she didn't make a sound. Davis lowered himself next to her. She heard his knees pop as he did. He put his arms around her.

"He died alone. Under his bed. Police said what probably happened was Lynette passed out, knocked the bottle of bourbon over. Lit cigarette fell from her hand. Demonte was probably so scared. What if he was trying to wake her up and nothing he did worked? Can you imagine how that must have been for him? He was only four. I hadn't taught him to dial 9-1-1 yet. I should have done that. He probably thought he was safest crawling under his bed, waiting for it to all be over." Jemma broke down into sobs and Davis held her tighter.

She looked up at the sound of the front door opening and a woman with her light brown hair in curlers asking, "Who's out here? You okay?"

"I—I used to live here," Jemma said shakily. Davis pushed himself to his feet with some effort and then helped her to hers.

"Oh, my—are you—Jemma?" The woman stepped out onto the front stoop. She wore blue slippers and a pink house coat.

Jemma nodded.

"I'm Valencia. My daughter and I moved in right after they rebuilt this. I heard about what happened to your family. So sad."

"I'm Davis, a friend of Jemma's. She's in town for a few days and she wanted to stop by. I hope that's okay. Being here is very important to her," Davis said, rubbing Jemma's shoulder and back as he spoke.

"Of course it is. Would you two like to come inside?" Valencia said, gesturing toward the inside of the apartment.

"No, thanks," Jemma said. Seeing the outside was enough.

"You sure?"

"Yeah."

"Well, you two stay out here as long as you like. And let me know if you change your mind."

"Thanks. Very much," Jemma said. Valencia nodded and went back inside.

A few moments later, Valencia came back out with two large paper cups filled with sweet tea and handed them to Jemma and Davis. They took them with smiles and thanked her.

"No problem at all. Y'all hungry?"

"No, ma'am," Davis said.

"Okay, you know where to find me." Valencia patted Jemma's cheek and smiled at her. "I'll just be in there. And I want you to know you're welcome back any time."

"Thanks," Jemma said, taking a gulp of her tea. Just enough sugar.

Once Valencia was back inside, Jemma leaned her head against Davis's shoulder. "What if Lynette had been like that?"

"Baby, you can't torture yourself with 'what if.' Trust me. It gets you nowhere."

Jemma grinned up at him. "What did you call me?"

"Huh?"

"It's just that you've never called me anything but Jemma."

Davis's face reddened. He bought some time with a sip of tea. Then, he grinned. "What, you don't want me to do that? Is that against the rules of our non-committal time-sharing arrangement?"

"It's different. I wasn't expecting it. That's all," Jemma said, hugging him close with one arm. She bit her lip, looking back toward apartment E. "He would have been ten now. Going on eleven."

"I know," Davis said, kissing her forehead.

"You're going to tell me not to dwell on it, huh?"

"I'm not going to tell you that. I'm here for you. That's all. Here for you whatever you need, whenever. I will tell you that I don't think you've taken time to grieve. Sometimes, we have to think about the things it hurts to think about. To get it out of our systems. And we have to remember to think about the good, too, and not just dwell on the bad."

"When did you become so insightful?"

Davis kissed the top of her head. "Not me. Codie. That girl has been my rock more than once in life. Now if I could go full time on taking her advice, I'd probably fail at life less."

Jemma smiled up at him. "I don't think you're failing at life."

Davis raised an eyebrow.

She laughed. "Well, not completely."

He joined her laughing. "No, I guess not. After all, I have you back in my life. At least for a little while. I must be doing something right."

She kissed him quickly on the lips.

They stood there for a while longer, silently sipping their tea, each lost in their own thoughts.

Eventually, Jemma said, "Let's go."

"Where to?"

She gave apartment E one more glance. "The cemetery."

Davis nodded, gave her shoulders another squeeze, and then they got back into the Acura. She stared out of the passenger side window as he drove, wondering what it would be like stepping into that place.

She hadn't been back since the funeral. The day she had broken down in front of Emily Rose and Wendell. That'd been the last day she'd allowed herself to lose it over what had happened. At least out loud. Then, after spending a few months at Mary's house as a near-catatonic mess, she'd followed in Lynette's footsteps and run away. Even though she'd always thought—and still did—that Lynette's first and biggest mistake had been running away from home and her problems with her family. And, in some form, Lynette had spent the rest of her life running. Twenty years of running until she ran herself right into the ground. Jemma didn't want to be anything like her, but she was scared there was no way of avoiding it.

They walked into the cemetery. The grass was short, as if recently mown, and flowers lay against some of the headstones. The flowers added smatterings of color here and there to the green of the grass and the gray of the stones. They were the only two there and silence hung in the air just as heavily as the humidity did.

Jemma found the graves without a problem—their location had become etched in her mind on that horrible day six years ago. A double funeral for baby and mother. Demonte and Lynette.

She ran her fingers lightly over the craggy sides of the headstones Mary had helped her order with the money Smooth had given her for the funeral. That was one of the few decent things he'd ever done.

"I love you so much. And I'm so sorry," Jemma said to Demonte's headstone. Tears leaked out of her eyes. She then turned to Lynette's. "I hated everything you ever did to us. I worked forty-hour weeks and still went to school just to hold our family together. You were never a mother to us. I never complained because I thought things would get better someday. And then you took it all from me. You destroyed everything."

Davis put a hand on her shoulder.

"I got him ready for Head Start every morning he had to go."

His hand slid down between her shoulder blades.

"If only I had taught him to dial those three stupid numbers."

"It's not your fault." He rubbed his thumb over the fabric of her shirt.

"I keep thinking, what if I had just emancipated myself? What if I could have made social services and the court let me take him away from there? I looked into it. Researched everything I would have needed to do. I didn't have the guts to do it, though."

He put his fingers on her cheek and turned her face to his. He looked into her eyes and said, "It's not your fault." He said it with more conviction that time.

"I want to believe that. I do."

He moved closer so that his face was inches from hers. "I want you to believe it, too."

Davis wrapped his arms around her. She leaned against him and put her hands over his arms. She closed her eyes and the tears slipped down her cheeks.

It was a while before Jemma could pull herself together. Then, she took a deep breath and opened her eyes.

"But I'm not gonna hate you anymore. And I'm going to stop pretending I don't hate you. I'm done with all of that. I'm not going to let you control the rest of my life." Jemma looked up at Davis. "I want to let go. I really do."

She turned to Demonte's grave. "I'm sorry I couldn't save you. And I love you. I know you have a better life up there than you ever had down here. The life you always deserved."

Davis kissed her hand before pressing it to his chest. "He knows. He loves you, too. He's smiling down on you right now."

Jemma nodded. They stood there for a while and Jemma let her mind go back to all the times she'd played video games with Demonte. Or let him "read" to her, which usually meant Demonte holding a picture book upside down and making up a story to go along with the pictures. His stories were often more entertaining than what was written on the page. The kind of stuff that only a three- and then four-year-old could come up with. Tucking him in at night. Just generally filling the spaces that Lynette hadn't or wasn't able to fill. Some of the best times in her life now that she looked back on them. Davis had been right back at apartment E.

He pressed his chin to the top of her head.

"Do you hate Tara?" Jemma took his hands in hers, looked down at them and then back into his face.

Davis shook his head. "She has some ugly ways. So did Bill. But I like to think it's not their fault. People have things happen to 'em that make 'em the way they are. I love Amanda to death, but I think she and Tara didn't have the greatest relationship. I dunno. Tara didn't talk about it too much. I think Tara felt like her mom wanted her to be something Tara felt like she could never measure up to. And Bill—that's a whole package of things gone wrong."

Jemma grinned. "A package of things gone wrong. I think that could describe me, too."

Davis kissed her cheek. "No. It doesn't."

Jemma turned back to the headstones. She couldn't face the tender and open look in his eyes. It made her want to throw everything away—forget the world—and stay with him forever. "I should have brought some flowers. Or something."

"We could go get some right now."

"Let's go." Jemma took his hand and they walked back to the car. They went to a nearby grocery store and came back with two arrangements. One was full of vibrant yellows, pinks, and reds. And the other arrangement was solid blue—Demonte's favorite color. Jemma left the flowers, Davis said a prayer with her, and then they left.

CHAPTER 20

Once they were back in the car, Jemma put her hand over Davis's and looked up at him. "I'm worried I'll be her, Davis. I wouldn't be able to stand that."

"Jemma." He put his arms around her.

"I think I'm more afraid of that than I am of what I feel for you or anything else. That I'll become just like her. It's hard, dealing all of the things that have been running through my head since I got back here. I'm worried that if I stay, I'll turn into her. Be mean and awful and . . . just. Like. Her. Maybe I already am her. But if I don't leave Derring, there'll be no way to avoid it or change it if it's already happened."

"You'll never be like her, okay? You can't be like her. Is that why you've been avoiding everything all this time? Why you ran away from us?" He kissed her forehead. "She's a completely different person from you. In every way. Just because she's your mother doesn't mean it's your fate to be her. And you're not. You're successful, smart, wonderful. You're Jemma, not Lynette."

Jemma let her head rest against his shoulder, thinking about his words, but not quite sure she believed them. She looked up at him. "You know what's funny? Except it's not? That I sort of fully realized today?"

"What?"

"We used to tell each other everything. Now it's like we're afraid to tell each other anything."

"Not true. I told you about my brothers and the house."

"Yeah, but you don't talk about what happened in Pennsylvania. Or about what moving back in with Bill was like."

"Nothing really to tell," he said flatly, staring out of the driver's side window.

That proved her right, but she knew that pushing him would get her nowhere. Instead, she sank deeper into his side. "I think I want to go back to Mary's tonight." She looked up.

He looked down at her. His face crumpled, but he nodded.

"Just for tonight."

"I understand."

"Hey, we'll spend the whole day together tomorrow. It's just that Mary has the night off tonight, and I really need to talk to her."

"Yeah. I really do understand." He kissed her hand. She reached up and kissed him long and slow.

Once Davis pulled onto the road, Jemma looked straight ahead, watching as he passed the low brick buildings housing offices and the few stores in town. They then passed a row of houses on their way out of town. Still looking out of the windshield, she said, "Smooth wants me to go see him in prison."

"Whoa, really?"

"He has a parole hearing coming up. I have an interview with a parole board representative. He wants to talk to me before the interview."

"You're not going to go see him, are you?"

"I dunno. I thought I didn't want to see him again, but maybe I need to. The way I needed to go to the apartment and the cemetery today. I can't decide how I feel, if that makes any sense."

He grabbed her hand and squeezed it. "You let me know if you need me. I mean it."

"Okay."

"I love you, Jemma. If it's in my power, I'll do it for you. I won't let anything bad happen to you. Not as far as I can help it."

He'd said it again. She leaned over the seat and rested her head against his shoulder. For a brief and crazy moment, she thought that maybe she should stay. So what about the job? She could find another job. She'd never find another Davis. Maybe Davis really could be all she needed. Then she came to her senses as he drove up Mary's driveway and stopped in front of the house. She knew all the reasons that trusting love was a bad idea.

He hugged her before she slid back to her side of the car and opened the door.

"I'll see you tomorrow, okay?" Jemma started regretting her decision not to spend the night with him.

"I'll call you before I come to get you in the morning. Around eight?"

Jemma raised her eyebrows. "You're going to get up that early?"

He grinned. "Ha ha. So I'm not a morning person. I'm thinking of something I want us to do tomorrow. So yes. I'm going to get up that early."

She shut the car door and leaned in through the open window. "See you tomorrow."

"Bright and early." He winked at her.

She watched him drive off, thinking of how much she needed time away from him. She was growing too attached. She'd thought about staying way too much over the past few days. And after he'd been there for her that afternoon, not letting her come unglued, it was especially hard to turn away from her feelings for him. But she had to. She couldn't risk everything for something so uncertain as the possibility that love could fix everything.

Davis thought about Jemma's words long after he was at work and forgetting to bring people water. He also got plenty of dirty looks from the other servers because he hid in the back most of the time so the people from his tables couldn't ask him for things. That way, his co-workers got stuck bringing his cranky customers new salt shakers and ketchup bottles.

Davis was more distracted than usual that night, and it didn't take much to distract him from the job he didn't want to do anyway. Ever since Jemma had brought up Bill, he couldn't get the man off his mind. Some father. There was a long list of things Davis blamed him for, but one of the biggest was helping Davis ruin his chances with Jemma. On top of Davis's own stupidity, there had been good old Bill.

He thought back to one of the last times he'd gone to pick up Bill from the hospital before the car accident. Bill had chronic bronchitis, but still thought it was a good idea to smoke cigarettes. That time Bill had had an episode at work, hadn't been able to breathe or find his inhaler, and he'd passed out. He ended up in the hospital again. The doctor had pleaded with him yet again to stop smoking. Told him he'd done more damage to his lungs. Bill said he would stop. Bill and those broken promises.

Davis remembered sitting across from him, staring into those watery, red-rimmed eyes, hating him.

His dad cleared his throat, but his voice still came out gravelly. "You ain't have to come down here. I have friends. I coulda gotten somebody to pick me up."

Davis nodded, picking at his thumbnail. That was his dad, all right.

"I know you can't stand taking care of me and you wish I wasn't around. I probably won't be much longer. This old body is falling apart on me."

"And whose fault is that?" Davis glared at him.

"I don't need no lecture from you."

"Yeah. You don't need anything from anybody. And nobody better need anything from you, either, huh?"

"What are you talking about, Davis?"

"You always screwed everything up for me. And then you sit here and try to make me feel bad about something I don't even have control over. You're the one who smokes. You're the one who drinks. I do all I can for you and you don't appreciate it. You never apologize for anything you do wrong."

"What is going on with you today?"

"I'm real sick of you ruining my life."

"So now I'm to blame for all the stupid mistakes you make?"

"You know, why wouldn't I blame you, Dad? I lost the woman I loved and got in a shit marriage. You taught me that it's wrong to be attracted to someone outside of your race. You taught me that women are all evil and not to be trusted. You tried to teach me not to respect women at all."

"I told you never to get married. You did that one to yourself, son. She's sure fun to look at, but them ones are the most trouble most of the time."

"You really screwed me up, you know. And what about the fact that I had to literally fight for my life when I was younger whenever you got drunk? Which was more often than not."

His dad looked down at the water pitcher on the tray in front of him. "I was wrong, son. I know that now. What can I do about it? If you hate me, I don't blame you. I reckon it don't make sense to get mad. If you don't want to take me to dialysis anymore, I can find someone else. I understand if you want to leave. Move out."

Things weren't going as Davis had expected them to. He didn't even get to be royally pissed off. His dad looked so sad and defeated and small lying there in the center of his hospital bed.

His dad smacked his dry lips before saying, "Jemma is perfect for you, son. I'm man enough to admit when I've screwed up. I could say it was this or that or the other that made me do the things I did. I could blame a lot of really messed up stuff I've done on others, but I won't. I take full responsibility for ruining the relationships I could have had with you and your brothers. Heck, even with your mother.

"I can't say I didn't deserve it. I was hell to live with. But you stayed by me, Davis. Even if it nearly killed ya. And I love you more than I think you'll ever understand for that."

Davis poured water from the plastic pitcher into a paper cup. He handed the cup to his father both to try to improve the papery quality of his father's voice and to give himself time to think.

Davis sighed and shook himself out of the memory when the cook yelled at him that his order was up. The cook looked angry, as if he'd been trying to get Davis's attention for a while. Davis put the plates on his tray and walked toward the table.

His mind slipped back to Bill as he made his way toward the booth at the back of the restaurant where the plates needed to go. Was his father more of a man than him? Hadn't he tried to own up to all the wrong he'd done? Wasn't he showing his strength by not telling Jemma that all he wanted was for her to stay? He knew the best thing for her would be to go to Florida. She deserved every opportunity life had to offer her—and ten times more. He was determined not to ask her to stay.

Davis was glad it was a table of college age girls he was serving. Maybe he could flirt his way to a tip because he certainly wouldn't get one based on the service.

Jemma and Mary went into the living room after eating the dinner Jemma had cooked for them.

"You are some cook. Since you've been here, I've eaten some of the best meals that I didn't have to cook in a long time," Mary said as they settled into the couch with their mugs of cinnamon spice herbal tea. Jemma had made baked chicken, green beans, and fresh rolls from scratch. There was peach cobbler for later, but both of them were too full for it at the moment. Mary had asked how Jemma could be full when she'd barely eaten anything. Jemma's mind had been so full that her stomach seemed to think it was as well.

"Thank you." Jemma breathed in the warm, spicy aroma of her tea.

"Something's been bothering you." Mary turned toward Jemma. "You can't fool me. I know you didn't give up a night with that boy to sit here with me."

"Mary, I haven't spent enough time with you since I got back. This isn't—"

"You know that's not it." Mary smiled and set her tea on a coaster on the coffee table. "Now, what is it? What's been worrying you so bad, girl? You can't even hardly follow a conversation."

"I went to their graves today."

"Oh, Jemma." Mary put a hand on her back.

"I want it to be over, Mary. I went there. I made my peace. I felt fine when I left the cemetery, but now I'm not so sure anymore. What will it take?"

"Honey, this isn't something you can fix with a Band-Aid or magic words. You will always remember. Both the good and bad. It's a part of who you are and you will be stronger for it."

"I don't feel very strong right now."

"You're a smart and wonderful person inside. You were always happy to swap shifts with people at the store. Work the hours nobody wanted to work. And you never complained. You took time out to get to know all of us and the customers. You treated everyone the same and everybody loved that about you. I loved that about you." Mary moved closer. "You need to find a way to get back to that girl. Stop being afraid to open up and be of all those good things again." She patted Jemma's shoulder. "I think a good start would be to stop lying to yourself."

"Huh?"

"It hurts you what happened. It tears you up, but you never talk about it. You never screamed that I saw. Never threw a fit. Except for that one time on the day of the funeral you told me about when it seemed more about punishing your friends than letting go of the things that hurt you.

"Today, what you did was a good start. But learn to lean on people, Jemma. Take help from a friend. Until you learn to do those things, and learn to really let go and live your life free, you're never going to get where you're trying to go in life. You'll always be bitter and shriveled up inside. And I know that's not you. You're trapping that girl I know you still have somewhere deep down in there. Let her out. For my sake. For your friends' sake. For your own."

Jemma looked down at her hands. "That's what I'm trying to do, Mary. I really am."

"I hope you are, Jemma. I really do. But I have to ask you this question. Why are you really going to Florida?"

"Because everything that's important to me is there. My future—my job—is there."

"Everything important, huh?"

"Mary, I love you. I didn't mean that you're not important. And Derring will always hold some things that are close to my heart, and of course people, too." She tried to shut the image of Davis out of her mind as she said that. "But there's no future for me here."

Mary shrugged. "All I'm saying is everything happens for a reason. Maybe you being back in Derring is about more than a wedding and that man being up for parole."

Mary knew about the interview, but not about Smooth asking Jemma to visit him. She hadn't told Mary about Smooth wanting to see her because she didn't want to upset the woman.

Jemma sat back against the couch, contemplating Mary's words. Maybe this was her chance to put a face and a name to her demons and repulse them once and for all. Jemma didn't think she was meant to stay in Derring, but she did think Mary had a point.

She had a few more days before the interview and she was going to spend them with Davis. They would have the real goodbye she had imagined when she first went back to the restaurant for him that past Friday. She would think only of him. Without the fear of and anger with her past. Then she would deal with Smooth and all that entailed.

Mary and Jemma talked about lighter things for the rest of the evening, but Mary's earlier words stuck in Jemma's head. Maybe Jemma wasn't being honest with herself about a lot of things and maybe that needed to change.

Her talk with Mary did a lot to lighten the burden on her heart. She fell asleep without all the tossing and turning she'd done ever since she'd come back to Derring. In fact, she fell asleep with her head against Mary's shoulder while an old movie played on the television on low volume.

CHAPTER 21

Davis showed up at eight the next morning, as promised. He wore a crisp white shirt with blue stripes and dark jeans. It appeared he'd pressed both shirt and jeans. He'd even gotten a haircut. His black hair no longer fell over his ears and it tapered down in the back to the nape of his neck. He wore sunglasses so Jemma couldn't see the blue eyes she loved so much.

He stood just inside the front door, smiling at her as she gathered her overnight bag and purse from the spot where she'd left them in the hallway. "You look great," he said as he took the bag from her.

"Thanks," she said. She wore a white strapless sundress and matching sandals. He kept glancing at her as they walked toward the car. "What?"

"Nothing. I'm just really excited about today."

She grinned. "Where are you taking me?"

"Somewhere you're dressed perfectly for. It's almost like you can read my mind. Creepy a little bit." Davis shut the trunk and opened the passenger side door for her. He put his index finger under her chin as she started to get in the car. She stopped and looked up at him. "Somewhere I think you'll really like. Hope I'm not wrong."

Jemma was curious as Davis drove off, but he wouldn't tell her a thing. Her curiosity grew when he got onto the interstate. Then, when he went from 295 to 64 West, she was really perplexed.

"Where are we going, Davis? Charlottesville?"

He shrugged, obviously enjoying the game. "Maybe."

"Further?"

"Maybe I'm just gonna run away with you." Davis reached across the console for her hand, and she slipped it into his.

She brought his hand to her lips and kissed it before placing it back in her lap. She pushed the thought away of how nice it would be if this was a normal outing for a normal couple.

The weather was beautiful. Not a cloud in the sky. Not oppressively humid. And the temperature was in the high seventies. It was hard to ask for a nicer day during a Virginia summer.

"What? This is where we're going?" Jemma asked as Davis turned onto a gravel road, passing a sign that said "Bayberry Vineyards." They'd just passed Gordonsville and were outside of Charlottesville. The vineyard was in a little town that couldn't have been a dot on the map nestled between the two larger towns.

"Yeah. You like wine, right? You told me you took that wine class or whatever as an elective in college," Davis said, squeezing her hand.

"This is perfect." Jemma's entire face lit up as she looked out of the window at the rolling hills filled with rows of vines. They pulled up near a white Tudor-style house. Davis parked in the small parking lot where there were only a few other cars.

They walked up to the building hand-in-hand and greeted the petite blonde behind the desk in the office. The building looked like a house converted into an office. The reception area could have been a living room at one time.

Davis introduced himself and recognition filled the girl's brown eyes. She didn't look much older than seventeen and she had that smitten, I've-been-charmed look on her face that Davis could bring to a girl with very little effort. Jemma knew that well.

"Oh, yeah. Mister Hill. Private tasting tour, right? Hold on a minute and I'll get Josh. He'll be the one giving you the tour." The girl stood, smoothed out the wrinkles in her khaki cropped pants, and jogged to the back. They heard a door slam. Jemma figured the girl must have gone outside to get Josh.

"Private, huh? Is that expensive?" Jemma asked, feeling badly at the thought of having set Davis back.

"Nah. Besides, whatever it cost, I wanted to spend it. Otherwise it would have probably gone to rotgut liquor and cigarettes," Davis said before kissing the tip of her nose.

"Good point," she said, wrapping her arm around his waist. "Hey. I thought you said you quit smoking."

"Yeah. Working on it. Kind of," Davis said with a wink.

He was a sneaky one. Then again, his breath was extra minty sometimes.

Josh, a middle-aged, well-built man with dark, weathered skin and kind, brown eyes came inside, grinning a grin full of perfectly straight white teeth.

"Josh Burgundy. Davis? Jemma? Pleasure to meet y'all." Josh held out his hand for them to shake, which they did.

"Well, you two, how about we get started? We'll start out back where the grapes grow and work our way inside to where all the magic happens and we stomp the grapes." Josh laughed at his own joke before continuing. "Just jokin' with y'all. We don't stomp 'em anymore. Let's get a move on so y'all can get to the good part." He ran a hand over his thinning black hair. "Tasting the best grapes around after they've been all doctored up by the finest winemaker and vintner in the whole state of Virginia. Heck, probably in all this fine country of ours."

They followed Josh outside, arms wrapped around each other. Jemma slipped on her sunglasses, unable to stop smiling. She was barely able to concentrate on what Josh was telling them about soil, European grapes, blending grapes, or anything else. Once they moved into the barrel room, she stared at the oak barrels, but was glad there was no test later on the differences between using them for the reds and the steel tanks he showed them in the next room for the whites. Although Josh was nice and his words ordinarily would have been very interesting to her, she was lost in thoughts of Davis.

Davis held her close during the entire tour. Regardless of where he stood, he had at least one arm around her waist. When he pressed his cheek to hers, or when his lips were near her ear, she lost track completely of what Josh was saying. Every touch was familiar and intimate—as if they were doing things they did all the time. She tried hard not to think of it that way, but she couldn't stop herself.

Later, they went into the tasting room. It was a vast cavern of a room dominated by a large stone fireplace, but it still managed to have a cozy feel. They chatted with a few couples, all of them telling Jemma and Davis what an adorable couple they made. Jemma thanked them, not bothering to correct them. When they were done in the tasting room, they wandered into the retail area nearby.

After buying a couple of bottles of a chardonnay Jemma liked, they sat down in the winery's small dining area to a lunch Davis had packed for them. The lunch was simple, but the best thing Jemma had ever eaten, knowing Davis was thinking of her when he made it. Plus, the sandwiches and potato salad really were tasty.

"You have a good time today?" Davis asked before taking a sip of water from a paper cup. He'd brought a large bottle of water for them to share.

"Oh yeah. This is—I never dreamed you planned anything like this." Jemma couldn't keep herself from gushing, showing her true surprise at the thought Davis had put into their day together.

He chuckled. "You were probably expecting something really bad, huh? A total cop-out? Like me taking you to a baseball game or something else you would have hated?"

"Hey. I like sports."

"Not baseball. You say it's too long and boring and you don't understand why they have to have all the innings."

She laughed. "How do you know so much about me?"

"I told you. I listen. A lot more than you think I do, apparently. A whole lot more." He grinned, kissing the corner of her mouth. He started to pull back. She pulled him close again, kissing him softly on the lips.

"I wish I hadn't said I'd go to the show tomorrow night. I don't want to leave you."

"Well, we have tonight, the day tomorrow, and you're still coming over after the show, right?"

"Right after." Jemma kissed his cheek. The look he gave her sent chills all over her body and warmth to all the right and dangerous spots.

"I'll be counting the minutes. I'll probably screw up more orders than usual."

They laughed.

A couple stopped near them, smiling. A tall, olive-skinned man and his shorter companion greeted them.

"Is anyone sitting here?" The woman pointed to the empty bench across from them.

Jemma shook her head. "No. Have a seat." She gestured toward the bench.

They sat. "We are from Spain. This is our honeymoon. We wanted to try this famous Virginia wine." The woman had a heavy Spanish accent and she put a short "e" sound in front of "Spain" so that it sounded like the word started with an "e" instead of an "s". "This is my husband, Guillermo, and I am Maria." Maria flipped her shiny black hair out of her eyes and smiled at them.

"Nice to meet you. I'm Jemma and this is Davis." Jemma put her hand over Davis's, which rested on the table, when she said his name. He squeezed it and she grinned at him.

"You two are so beautiful together. I was saying that to Guillermo before we came over." Maria smiled at them before murmuring something to Guillermo in Spanish. He nodded.

"Maria was saying to me that you two have so much love for each other in your eyes." Guillermo translated with a smile.

Jemma blushed and slid her hand from Davis's. "Are you two enjoying your trip so far?"

"We are. This is our first trip to the United States together. We both came when we were younger at different times. That was before we knew each other." Maria smiled and murmured something else in Spanish to Guillermo. Even though Jemma's Spanish was limited, she figured out that Maria was asking how to say something in English. Guillermo answered her in a murmur.

Maria said, "*Vale, vale,*" and then turned to Jemma and Davis. "We are taking the train to Washington, D.C. tomorrow. We will spend a few days there before flying back to Madrid."

"I've always wanted to go to Madrid," Jemma said with a dream-filled smile.

Davis said, "Could be fun."

She glanced sideways at him without turning her head and felt badly for moving away from him, realizing it'd been stupid to do so just because of what Maria had said. She certainly hadn't wanted to move. She'd be gone in a few days and nothing too disastrous could happen in a few days. She told herself for the thousandth time to just relax. To live in the moment for once.

"You should come. Spain is a very beautiful country, and especially Madrid." Maria smiled broadly. "Maybe you two will come to Spain for your honeymoon?"

Jemma winked at Davis, wanting to play along. "Maybe."

Davis grinned and put his arm around her waist. "We could do that."

"Have you been together for very long?" Maria asked.

"We've known each other for ages, but our relationship's pretty new." Jemma was enjoying her little game. She moved down the bench so that she was closer to Davis, their legs touching.

"Ah, well, you make the beautiful couple and you will have the beautiful babies."

"Maria." Guillermo gave his wife a look.

"Oh, these young American kids. They can take a good joke, right?" Maria laughed again—a rich, throaty sound.

Davis wasn't laughing. He looked directly into Jemma's eyes until she looked away. The game had been a dangerous one. She could tell he was actually thinking about it—he was considering Maria's words.

Maria clasped her hands together. "And now we celebrate. We toast our new friendship with some Virginia wine. This wine, it's okay, but it's no rioja. Then again, what is?" She gave them a broad smile and then started singing the praises of Spanish wine.

They chatted with Maria and Guillermo until the winery closed. The two were so much fun to talk to that Jemma didn't want to leave. Before they left, all four exchanged email addresses and Maria made them promise to look her and Guillermo up if they ever made it to Spain. However, Maria insisted it was a question of "when" and not "if."

Jemma walked back to the car with her arm linked through Davis's. She glanced at him several times, noticing the way the sun shone on his black hair, the hollow in his cheek where there were acne scars left over from high school, how quiet he was.

When she asked him later why he was so quiet, he said he was thinking. She didn't press him after that. She was scared he'd answer her honestly and that her response to him would confuse her even more. As it was, thoughts about how she could make a life in Derring work for herself refused to leave her mind.

CHAPTER 22

Davis didn't drop Jemma off at Mary's until he was already ten minutes late for work. They'd spent the whole day together Thursday, and they didn't do much of anything. It was the nicest doing nothing had ever felt. From Wednesday morning until Thursday afternoon was just like heaven. Even as she walked into the house, she wished she was still sitting on Davis's couch, running her hand through his hair while they watched movies on TCM.

Jemma showered and changed into jeans and a tank top right before Emily Rose pulled into the driveway that night. Emily Rose insisted on driving to the club, which was fine since Mary needed her car to get to work that night.

"So you all psyched for your big move to New York? New apartment. Newly wed." Jemma stretched and leaned back in the passenger seat as they flew down I-95 South, on their way to Richmond. Em Rose had always had a little bit of a lead foot.

She shrugged. "Yeah, I guess."

"Why do you say it like that?"

"Sure, there are more teaching positions available. And of course, there's Michael. I would only move there for him. I mean, I miss him already, and he just left Monday. But I'm not as excited to leave Derring behind as you are, Jemma."

"You actually like being in this place, huh?"

"Yeah. It's where I grew up. Met the best friends I've ever had. Where I learned so much. And high school was fun for me. Even though it was just the three of us—you guys were the center of my world and that was all I needed."

Jemma smiled, realizing that it really hadn't been all bad. She sighed, thinking of making cookies with Em Rose and of walks home from school with Wendell.

"You really hate Derring, Jemma? There was good in being here, too, right?"

"I guess you're right about that." Jemma changed the subject. "So you're going to let a guy tell you what to do?"

"It's about compromise and doing what you can to make each other happy. I can teach anywhere, but Michael needs to be in New York. A good job in finance is hard enough to find these days. Why should he put himself at a needless disadvantage?"

"I guess." Jemma shrugged. "Just seems like you're doing most of the compromising."

"I think I know why you're being so hostile."

"Huh? I'm being hostile? 'Bout what?"

"There's a certain guy you'd love to be with, but you won't let yourself."

"Hey. You used to be completely against Davis and me, remember? What about what you said when I first got back?"

"Yeah, but Davis has proved to me over the past few days that people really can change. Especially after what happened on my wedding day. I think you're what he needed to try." She reached over and put a hand on Jemma's shoulder. "I don't know why he married Tara or did half the things he did, but I see him trying to be a good guy for you and I believe he wants a relationship with you enough to work harder for it than he ever has for anything."

"What, a person can change in a week or so?" Jemma snorted. She wouldn't admit to Emily Rose that she'd had similar thoughts, but had chalked her feelings up to wishful thinking.

Emily Rose put a hand on the back of Jemma's seat. "I don't understand why you two are torturing yourselves when you so clearly want to be together."

"Because we could never make each other happy. Not in a real relationship."

"Really?" Her voice was dry with disbelief.

"Yes. Bad things happen when we're together." Why were all those bad things paling in comparison to the last few days? She needed to remember why staying with Davis would be a mistake. Love, even if it was real and true, had never been enough in her experience. She didn't have time for naïve fantasies. Being realistic always led to the best results. Like she always told herself, happy wasn't necessary. Content was worth the sacrifice.

"It didn't seem that way at the reception."

"Anything can seem perfect for a few hours. That's not how it would be long term."

"You two seemed so crazy about each other that night. And you've barely been apart since. Maybe you should give him a chance to prove things can be different from how they were . . . before. That's all I'm saying."

"We've hurt each other and been hurt by others too much for us to be good for each other."

"Yeah, but do you love him? Love has a healing power like nothing else."

She felt as if she'd been punched by Emily Rose's words. "Where has loving Davis ever gotten me? When has it ever not destroyed me?" Love. Huh. That was easy for Em Rose to say.

"When has anyone else ever made you feel like you have this week?"

Emily Rose had a point, but Jemma refused to admit it. After all, Jemma had turned down a marriage proposal. And if she really thought about it, part of the reason had been she still wasn't over Davis. Maybe she did still love him. But love could end up being more trouble than it was worth. "Sometimes life demands sacrifice. All trade-offs considered, forgetting Davis is the better choice. For both of us."

"There's a thin line between sacrifice and stupidity sometimes."

Jemma glared at her, but didn't say anything.

Once they got to the club, their conversation was light again. They had a couple of beers and talked about New York and Florida and visiting each other until the first act came on stage.

Jemma had very little interest in the first act musically and so spent most of the time watching and analyzing the band. Especially the bassist. He was really getting into the song. He seemed to enjoy what he was doing, and he did it well. Jemma could appreciate that even though she wasn't drawn to the band's overall style.

Watching the bassist with that look of freedom on his face led to her thinking about what she really wanted. And when she thought of that, Davis's face was the first thing that popped into her mind. Davis, who'd once treated her like dirt when she'd worshipped him. Davis, who now gave her looks that made her soul shiver. She didn't know what to do about the fact that she didn't want to let go. Did she have to? Did she really have to? Her earlier conversation with Emily Rose had her wondering about that.

Davis had held her so tightly that awful day when she'd forced herself to face Lynette one last time. Davis who'd whispered to her and talked with her about anything, everything, and nothing at the reception. Who held her so tightly at night. Even if he hadn't told her how much he loved her, his look and his touch would have done it for him.

Maybe she didn't want to get on a train and turn her back on that forever. Waking up with him in the mornings felt so right and natural—like something she should be doing every morning for the rest of her life. And he hadn't brought up sex. Every time made herself stop— because she was afraid of what would happen if they went too far—he backed off and didn't even look pissed about it. At least he never let her see if he was.

And that night in the lake—and after. That night, her heart almost split in two it ached so much for him. She felt as if she'd been living somewhere outside of reality since Emily Rose's wedding. It was too good to be real life. She wasn't sure she wanted to come back to real life if that meant she had to leave Davis. She wanted to keep him, but she couldn't let herself think of the possibility too much. He was a part of the past she'd come back to Derring to let go of. He would be the hardest goodbye, but he had to be a goodbye, too. Otherwise, what if she wasn't able to move forward with her life? What if she wasn't able to avoid becoming the one thing she couldn't bear to be—Lynette Jenkins?

Jemma hadn't realized how lost she'd been in her thoughts until the crowd started cheering for the second group who'd just taken the stage.

Jemma said, "I'm glad we're here."

"Me, too." Emily Rose smiled.

Jemma sat back in her chair and listened to the opening bars of one of her favorite jazz songs. That was the band they'd come to hear. It felt nice, having her good friend back and listening to some good music.

That night on the drive home, Jemma couldn't stop thinking about all the things Em Rose had said earlier. She had to go to Florida, she knew that, but some nagging part of her felt like she was making the wrong decision. Asking Davis to come with her wouldn't have been a good idea at all. No, that could only cause more problems. The problems weren't only in the location, they were in certain people, too. Jemma tried reminding herself of all the reasons she was right and Em Rose was wrong, but she wasn't doing a great job of it.

CHAPTER 23

Emily Rose dropped Jemma off at Davis's house. For the first time since Jemma had gone back to the restaurant for Davis on the day of the rehearsal dinner, she was nervous. She wiped her sweaty palms on her jeans before knocking on the door. She'd decided that she wasn't leaving Derring without making love to Davis. There were complications, sure, but she wasn't allowing herself to think of them. Regardless of whatever else might be true, she needed all of him.

The moment he opened the door, she said, "Davis, at the winery—and the way you held me at my old apartment—and the wedding—thank you. Thank you for everything."

He looked up at her, obviously puzzled by her flustered nature and sudden lack of verbal skills. He nodded. "No prob. I'll always be here for you. You know that."

"Tonight? I just want you to be with me." Jemma came inside and closed the door behind her. She backed him into a nearby wall and pressed her cheek to his before whispering to him. "Just be with me." She pressed her face into his T-shirt, holding him with all the love in her heart. Saying it out loud would wreck everything.

Wordlessly, Davis told her he would give her what she asked for. He lifted her face to his by hooking his fingers under her chin. Bringing her lips up to his, he kissed her softly. She climbed onto his hips and deepened the kiss.

"You've been so good for me, Jemma. Having you here has made me feel a lot better than I have in a while. And now I want to take care of you. In every way you'll let me. In every way I can." He whispered the words into her hair before kissing her ear.

She wanted to take care of him, too, but she didn't know how to say it without being too honest. So she said nothing at all.

Davis carried her up to his room and lay her down on the bed. He sat next to her and pushed his hand beneath her shirt, letting it roam over her stomach. A pleasant warmth spread over her. Goose bumps rose all over her skin. His thumb moved over the undersides of her breasts through her bra. No one else's touches had come close to doing the things to her that his did. Davis was home for her.

"I want to give you everything I can tonight. I'm sorry that it's probably not enough." She trailed her fingers up and down his arms as his fingers traced her collar bone and moved down to the rise of her breasts.

"I want to give you everything, Jemma. How can I do that in only one night?" He kissed her cheeks, moved his lips down to her throat.

She kissed his fingers before placing his hands low on her hips. "All this has to be? Is perfect."

He laughed softly before crouching over her. "My words coming back to haunt me, huh?" He slid his fingers under the strap of her bra and caressed her skin.

"All I want is you," Jemma said. Too honest. She couldn't take it back, but she wouldn't say anything more damaging. She tucked her fingers inside the waist band of his jeans. He crouched lower, resting his forearms on either side of her head.

"You know how important this is to me? Us making love?" Davis whispered the words over her lips before kissing them. "You're Jemma. My Jemma." He moved the strap of her tank top aside and kissed her shoulder.

She threw her tank top to the floor and did the same with his shirt. Skin pressed to skin, her breath coming in gasps, she hugged him close.

"You've always been the only one for me." Davis murmured the words into her stomach. She reached for him and he brought his lips back to hers.

"Shh." She kissed his shoulder. She dropped his jeans onto the floor and then slipped out of hers.

How did he know all the right places to touch her? She melted into Davis's touches as his lips and hands played over her skin. Each kiss was unhurried and soft. Each touch was a pleasant, slow burn. She'd never been on fire for anyone before, but with Davis on top of her, putting his tongue in all the right places, she was that night.

Davis removed her bra and trailed kisses down her body until he reached her belly. He pulled her bikini briefs away from her hips. He urged her thighs further apart with his shoulders and she spread them wide for him. His fingers pressed inside of her, touching skin that had long been slick with desire for him. She gasped, her mind completely numb. While his fingers were at their very important work, he trailed kisses and almost gentle pulls of his teeth along her inner thighs.

Once he was again on top of her with his forehead pressed to hers, he kissed her long and slow. She heard the package rip open, but she was so distracted by his kisses and touches that she never realized when he slipped the condom on. One moment it wasn't there and the next, it was.

He pulled her to his body, and the moment for which she'd been aching for for over six years finally happened. He filled her and at the same time consumed her. She gave into her need for him.

He moved very slowly against her, hips kneading hips. Those gorgeous blue eyes never left hers. He ran his fingertips over her lips before kissing her, and she could still feel both fingers and lips after he pulled back. Even when his hand moved down to her breasts, his eyes remained on hers. She put her hand on the bicep of the arm that rested by her head, his elbow anchored into the pillow.

It was while his thumb moved in maddeningly slow circles over the dark circle of skin at the apex of her breast that she gave in. Biting her lower lip, she gave a deep, rich moan as she felt herself tightening around him, throbbing against him. He covered her with kisses, whispering his love for her into her skin, as they finished together.

Jemma never said it out loud that night, but she had the feeling that wasn't necessary. She was pretty sure he knew from the way she touched and kissed him. And her responses to his confessions of love. The way he'd held her eyes with his, refusing to allow hers to lie to him.

"I know you don't want me to say this, but right now I can't imagine you leaving me." Davis kissed her cheek.

Jemma pulled the sheet closer, not knowing how to deal with that or the fact that she'd just fully realized how big the difference between sex and making love actually was. She'd only had sex with two other guys, and it had never been anything like that with either of them. But she had to stop. At that moment, any thinking at all would drive her crazy. She'd been working on instinct since knocking on Davis's door that night and shutting off the complicated stuff. She had to keep that going.

He was a part of her. No matter what else happened, she couldn't deny that. She was losing a part of herself. Again.

Davis pulled her against him and she lay her head on his chest. Hugging his waist, she closed her eyes. His fingers were still tracing patterns on her shoulder when she drifted off to sleep.

Jemma slipped out of bed early the next morning, not having been able to sleep well. She smiled down at Davis, touching the backs of her fingers to his cheek. He moaned, shifted slightly in the bed, but his eyes never opened.

She was falling hard for him again and she knew that was bad. But was he really the same? Either way, she had to go to Florida. Her train ticket waited on her desk back at Mary's place. Her job was in Jacksonville. So was her life now. Being with Davis might have felt right—especially after the night they had spent learning the secrets of each other's bodies—but it was so very wrong. They'd only end up hurting each other in the end, even if it seemed like a good idea on the surface.

She forced herself to turn away from him. She threw her hair into a haphazard ponytail with a rubber band she found on the top of the dresser, pulled on a pair of sweats she found in the corner of his room across from his bed. She shrugged on a t-shirt of Davis's and headed out of the room.

She went into to the kitchen to make a pot of life-giving coffee. She spied a head of black hair peering through the kitchen window in the next house. It had to be Ayn. As soon as Ayn saw she was spotted, she flitted away from the window and made a big show of moving pots and pans around as she zipped around the kitchen.

Jemma laughed softly, shaking her head, before she turned away from the window. Then she heaved a heavy sigh as she thought of Davis upstairs. After last night, without either of them saying a word about it, she knew Davis knew the truth. He had to know that she wanted to stay more than she'd ever admit.

She heard him walk in the moment she started brewing the coffee. He wrapped his arms around her and captured her with a kiss. He didn't let go until they were back upstairs in the bathroom with the door shut behind them.

"The coffee," she managed to say between kisses.

"It'll be there when we're done. You really care about coffee right now?" He murmured the words into her ear before teasing it with his tongue.

"No." She moaned the word long and slow against his lips.

"Why did you let those people think we were a couple? At the vineyard?" He whispered against her throat.

"Because I wanted it," Jemma answered without thinking. His kisses had her defenses down.

"I want it, too." He lifted her onto the sink. After moving between her legs, he pressed his body to hers for a long moment, his face buried in her shoulder.

After a very long, hot shower, they stood in front of the mirror that was above the sink, wearing only beige towels.

Davis grinned and pressed his cheek to hers. They stared at their reflections staring back at them.

"Tell me what you see." He kissed her shoulder while watching her reflection in the mirror.

She laughed. "What?"

"Just tell me. Play along."

"Okay. I see this really hot guy I had a crush on in high school, only his eyes are different now. He's seen a lot in the six years since I left him here."

"And what about the girl?" He put his hands on her shoulders. She put hers on top of his.

"She's smiling with her lips, but her eyes are uncertain. She wants to be happy but she's afraid."

"Why's she afraid?"

"Because she knows . . . that nothing good can stay," Jemma said, quoting her favorite Frost poem, her voice barely above a whisper. Neither reflection smiled now. Davis spun her to face him and sat her on the sink.

"I hate that I hurt you." His arms went around her waist.

She looked away from those burning blue eyes. "I know. We don't live in a perfect world. People get hurt. Wounds make us wary—perhaps too cautious for our own good. Anyway, that's life."

"What would your perfect world be like, Jemma?"

The words were out of her mouth before she could stop them. "You would have always loved me. We'd have gone to Penn together. You would have taken the lacrosse team to the national championship every year and you'd say you couldn't do it without me. We'd have gotten married right after graduation. I would have had a huge, poofy, ridiculous dress and a million bridesmaids—my sorority sisters. We'd be pregnant by now. And—it would just be normal and not complicated to love you with all of my heart."

He kissed her temple. "You've thought about this a lot."

Embarrassed, Jemma nodded. "I used to think about it all the time."

"Me, too."

"And what do you see?"

He pressed his forehead to hers. "You. Just you. In fact, this could be my perfect world right here, right now."

"My heart's always been filled with you. For what it's worth." She couldn't stop betraying herself for some reason.

His forehead moved to her cheek. "I'm filled with so much love for you that sometimes I think it's gonna kill me not to be with you. You know. For what it's worth."

Jemma swallowed hard against all the things rushing up inside her. She thought back to those last few horrible days in Derring before she'd run away. She'd promised herself. Never again. She'd promised to not so much as take a chance.

"I never gave up on hoping you'd come back to me," he said.

"Don't do this. Please."

"I know I don't deserve you, but you're all I want."

"I'm going to Florida. I can't stay here." She pushed against his chest so that he'd back up and give her the space she needed.

"You're all that's best about me. You've always been." He reached for her hand.

She hopped off of the sink and turned away from him. "We can't work together. We're too screwed up for that. We'd never be able to give each other what we need."

"I can't think of anything I could ever need that doesn't include you." Davis started toward her and she walked out of the bathroom. He followed, calling after her. "I think two broken halves can still make a whole. I need you to believe that, too."

Turning to face him, she avoided his eyes. "We're bad for anybody, but we're especially bad for each other.

There's nothing you can say or do to change my mind about that."

All of the color and life drained out of Davis's face. "This is too much like before."

"Well, that's because as much as we don't want it to be, 'before' will always be there. Davis, we both need to move on from that. And we can't do it together."

"You still hate me for what I did, don't you? I'll never be able to fix that, will I?" Something changed in Davis's face. It seemed to shut down somehow.

"I don't hate you, Davis. And it was no one's fault." She crossed her arms over her chest and concentrated on the dark colored carpet in the hallway.

"You know what? Go ahead, Jemma. Run away. Again. It's what you're good at. I don't give a damn."

"Same old jerk, huh? See? You see what I mean? This is what I was just talking about." She looked up, almost relieved to see the Davis standing there who would allow her to walk away. Good, he was proving her right by not trying to be reasonable. He refused to see that she was trying to do what was best for both of them.

Davis didn't say another word to her. He stormed off to his room. He yanked off his towel and threw clothes out of the dresser until he found what he wanted. She stood in the hallway with her arms still crossed over her chest, fighting tears, forcing herself to stay put, and not go running after him when he stormed down the stairs.

CHAPTER 24

Davis walked out of his room after grabbing his wallet and keys. He refused to look at her even though she stood in the hall and he felt her stare as he walked past. He jogged down the stairs and slammed the front door behind him. He knew it was his fault. He'd caused that morning to happen by being an idiot six years earlier when she needed him more than anything. That hurt the most. There was nothing left. Nothing left to do. Nothing left at all.

He hadn't packed anything. He didn't know where he was going anyway. The only thing he cared about was getting away from there.

He didn't look back to see if she'd followed him outside. Didn't want to know. He got into the car and jammed the key into the ignition. The engine roared to life and he tore out of the driveway.

Driving with his head slumped against the driver's side window, he tried to start thinking rationally again.

"How did I screw things up so bad?" He had to laugh at himself. "I have the worst timing in the world or I'm an idiot. Or both."

He sat up straight. He slammed his fist into the dashboard so hard that he thought for a moment that he'd broken his hand. He pulled his hand back, shaking it gingerly. He was losing her again and there wasn't a thing he could do about it.

Davis didn't realize where he was headed until he saw the signs for 95 North. Then it was clear. He was going to the only person who would understand and help him put the pieces in order again. The only person who ever had. Maybe he should marry her. If Jemma could choose pragmatism over passion, he could, too. Maybe she was on to something.

He grabbed his phone from the passenger seat.

Codie answered on the first ring. "Hey, Davis."

"I'm headed up there."

Stunned silence. And then, "Why?"

"Because she's going to Florida. I can't stop her. She won't stay for me, Codie. And it's all my fault."

"Oh, Davis. What time do you think you'll be here?"

Davis floored it and passed a long line of cars before flipping back over to the middle lane. "At this rate, hopefully by seven."

"I'll see you soon, then."

Jemma concentrated on packing her things so she could get out. She'd left more and more of her stuff at his house during the time she'd spent there since the wedding. No more of that. Oh well. She knew she'd made the right choice. Davis was too much of a danger. Too much of an uncertainty. So why did she feel so horrible?

She stuffed dirty clothes along with clean ones into her bag. She threw a pair of sneakers in. And then she grabbed a threadbare t-shirt. The same t-shirt that she had pressed her face into days ago lying in the same bed at which she stared. She threw the t-shirt across the room, knocking over his lamp.

Emily Rose raised her eyebrows. "Good arm, Jemma."

Jemma sank to the floor and stared at her unzipped bag with clothes spilling over the top of it. She'd called Emily Rose to come pick her up since Davis had stranded her there by taking off in his car.

Emily Rose put her hand on Jemma's shoulder. "Maybe I was wrong last night. I don't know. Seeing you like this . . . I'm sorry if I said something that led to this disaster."

"No, Em Rose. This is my very own disaster of my very own making." For so many reasons, that was true. Jemma zipped her bag and stood up.

"Ready to get outta here?"

Jemma nodded.

"Florida, huh?" Emily Rose asked as she headed for the door.

Jemma shrugged, kicking at the carpet with her big toe.

"You don't seem as excited about it as you've been since you got here."

Jemma stared at Emily Rose for a moment before she realized that there was no point in not being completely honest. She wasn't about to start building that wall between herself and Emily Rose again. "Sometimes I don't think I'm cut out for this life I've chosen for myself."

"What makes you say that?"

"The more I try to make things right, the more everything just falls apart. Nothing makes sense anymore. What's the point? Of anything? At all?"

"Wow. Debbie Downer to the thousandth degree."

Jemma let out a choked sound. She wasn't sure if it was sob or laugh. Maybe it was a little bit of both. "It's true."

"You have to do what you think is best. And maybe you're right. Maybe you can't start over by staying here. So go to Florida if that's what you have to do to be happy. You'll make the right decision. I know you will because you're strong, Jemma."

"It doesn't take much strength to run away." Jemma remembered Davis's words to her before he'd stormed out of the house that morning.

"But it takes a whole lot of strength to come back. Even more to admit you were wrong. And this time, when you leave, you're not running if you're going for the right reasons."

Jemma smiled. "I'm so glad I got you back."

"Me, too." Emily Rose laughed and walked over to hug her. Jemma slumped against her friend, trying to ignore the pang of emptiness she felt full force.

Davis sank into Codie's overstuffed couch and pulled his knees into his chest. The right one screamed in protest, but he barely noticed. The screaming in his heart was much louder.

"I can't love her this much. How can I still be alive and hurt this much?" He shook his head.

"Love is cruel that way," Codie said, sitting next to him on the couch. She pushed her brown hair away from her face. Codie was pretty enough with her shoulder-length hair newly layered and her large brown eyes. She was such a small thing, too. Adorable. But she was no Jemma. Nobody ever would be.

"That's all? No words of wisdom? No scolding? That's all you're going to say about it?"

Codie spread her hands wide and smiled. "That's all I got for you."

Davis looked down at the carpet. "Codie, you ever think about you and me?"

"You and me what?" Codie sounded confused, but Davis didn't look up to see the expression that went with that tone.

"Well, you know, as more than friends?"

She laughed and put a hand on his back. "You're talking crazy talk. I know you're hurting right now, so I won't hold it against you."

"I could use a drink." He sighed and let his feet drop back to the floor. He forced away the grimace he felt coming on and managed to keep his face smooth.

"You drinking a lot these days?" Codie asked. Davis noted the sadness in her voice.

"Just sometimes," he said, sparing her. "No, not a lot." She didn't need to know the truth. He'd done this to himself. It was his job to bear the burden of his mistakes. Besides, it was kind of true. He hadn't been drinking all that much for the past few weeks.

"Oh. Well. I really feel this is going to work out for the best."

"I think it already has. I shouldn't be getting into other people's lives and ruining them, anyway."

"You know what we're gonna do?" Codie stood and placed her hands on her narrow hips.

"What?"

"We're going to watch one of those awful, gross comedies you like, talk about stupid stuff, and order disgustingly greasy pizza because I'm a really, really good friend."

Davis finally smiled. "Yes. You are."

"Don't you forget it."

"Not even if you'd let me."

Codie went to find her phone and order the pizza. Meanwhile, Davis called the restaurant to let them know he wouldn't be in for the next few nights because he was sick. It wasn't so far from the truth. His manager wasn't happy.

"What do you mean, sick?" he said.

"I mean sick. As in I'm not coming in tonight. Probably not tomorrow night, either."

"Don't bother coming in Monday night then. I thought we were past this crap. Didn't I tell you the last time I re-hired you that you were getting one more chance? Guess what? Chance blown."

"Fine." He pressed his fingertips to his forehead. He'd been fired too many times to be fazed by it. And it had been the "last time" many times before as well. The guy just needed a week or two to cool off.

"You can pick up your last check when you drop off your aprons. You won't be getting it direct deposit."

"I know the drill."

His manager grumbled a few choice words before slamming down the phone. Davis shrugged and tossed his cell phone onto the coffee table.

He lay down on her couch and tried unsuccessfully to shut out pictures of the night before that he'd spent with Jemma.

Friday night, Jemma sat at a small table in a bar with Emily Rose and Meg. It was Emily Rose's last night with them. The next morning, she would be leaving for New York. All night, Jemma kept telling herself she didn't miss Davis. That she barely thought about him. So they'd spent a few fun days together. Fun was over. And it was almost time for her to leave anyway. She thought maybe if she repeated it to herself enough, she'd start to believe it.

Not far into the night, the conversation turned to the wedding and marriage in general, which turned into talk about Meg's recent engagement to her boyfriend. Meg and her boyfriend had gone away for a few days after the wedding, and he'd popped the question at their favorite restaurant. He was being shipped off to Afghanistan soon and he'd wanted to ask before he went. They were getting married the first opportunity he had to come home—as soon as he got his first leave from duty over there. Nothing fancy. Just a trip to city hall.

"That's so romantic," Jemma said with a smile, stirring the ice in her drink with the cocktail straw, resting her chin in her hand.

Emily Rose turned to her and raised her eyebrows. "Says Miz Anti-Romantic? You must be drunk."

"No, really, it's sweet. He wants to be with you so much. And you're getting married as soon as he comes back?"

"Yeah, pretty much. As long as he comes back in one piece," Meg said with a worried laugh.

Emily Rose put a hand on Meg's arm. "Oh, Meg. That's so scary. I'll be praying for him."

Meg nodded, and shook her black hair over her shoulders. "Yeah, well, don't let me kill the party. Em Rose, your wedding was gorgeous. I want Ed and me to have a reception like that one day. We've talked about it for after his tour is over."

"Yeah." Jemma pushed away thoughts of dancing with Davis at that very reception. "Everything was perfect."

"I can't take all the credit." Emily Rose rolled her eyes. "You'll have to thank Ms. Fletcher for taking over my wedding."

"Aw. I'm sure things'll get better now that she realizes you're not going anywhere."

"I hope so," Emily Rose said with a sigh.

Emily Rose and Meg started talking about mother-in-laws and wedding decorations and Jemma sat back with a sigh. She realized at that moment just how much she'd screwed up. She wanted what Meg and Emily Rose had with their men. None of the excuses she'd given Davis that morning were good enough. She hadn't given one good reason for her to leave him behind.

She wanted that one who made her heart jump. The one she'd run off. She didn't even know where he'd gone. He refused to return any of her calls.

"What's wrong?" Emily Rose asked. "You look so sad all of a sudden."

Jemma was about to reply when a man put a hand on the back of her chair and leaned over to talk to her. "I'm about to leave, but I had to come over here to tell you that I cannot leave this bar tonight without at least saying hi to you."

"Do I know you?" Jemma looked up into the man's tan, handsome face. He had dark eyes and a wide, charming smile. She didn't think so, but there was something familiar about him.

"I know I want you to." He straightened and extended his hand. "I'm Alex."

"Alex . . ." She bit her lower lip, thinking. She did know him from somewhere. Suddenly, it hit her. Davis, that clown Parker, and Alex had been co-captains of the lacrosse team. "Alex? From Derring High? The lacrosse team?"

Alex looked a little thrown off, but he nodded. "Yeah. You are?"

"Jemma Jenkins."

"Jemma?" Alex took a step back and gave her a scrutinizing look. "Jemma Jenkins? Really?" He scratched the back of his head, still looking unsure of what he was seeing.

"Yeah." She knew she looked different, but she hadn't realized she looked that different.

A grin slowly replaced the look of confusion. "Well, you sure changed a lot, huh?" Alex moved closer. His friends waved to him and he held up his hand and mouthed something to them. "I guess they're ready to go, but wow. You are smoking. If only Davis knew what he was missin' out on now." Alex walked back to his friends who were waiting for him by the door. Little did he know; Davis wasn't missing it all that much, apparently.

Jemma pushed her braids away from her face where they'd fallen. "Alex Ford," she murmured.

"How about that?" Emily Rose said, and Meg agreed.

Jemma had to laugh. "Yeah, how about it?"

Later that night, Jemma lay with the side of her head pressed to Emily Rose's, their bodies in opposite directions. They were lying on Emily Rose's floor. The room was eerily empty as Emily Rose had packed up most of her things and sent them either to New York or put them in her parents' attic. The Bradens were going to convert Emily Rose's room into a room for Branson as part of their effort to get Tara to bring him to visit more often.

"I'm sorry," Emily Rose said.

Jemma put her hands up in front of her face, staring at her polish, wondering how much longer she could go before her next manicure. Otherwise, her mind would go where she least wanted it to. "For? You didn't do anything."

"I took you to that bar. Alex brought back bad memories. I could tell."

"Like you knew he was going to be there." Jemma laughed. "You're a horrible person, Em Rose. I'm never speaking to you again."

"Yeah, yeah. Still, I'm sorry you had to be reminded of, um, him tonight."

Jemma dropped her hands onto her stomach and looked up at the ceiling. "So how's Michael doing with the job stuff?"

"He's still interviewing, but he has a couple coming up next week he has really good feelings about. It's always iffy, though. And money is going to be really tight until he finds something. I'm probably going to substitute teach until next year. I didn't jump on the job search right away because I wasn't sure if I'd go to work this year. We'd talked about starting a family right away. But with Michael having such a hard time finding a job and his shrew of a mother threatening to cut him off financially, we need all the money we can get. It's kind of late in the summer now, but I'm going to see what's available. Maybe I can still find a full-time teaching position."

"She's worse than I thought. You two will make it, though. But in New York? Shouldn't there pretty much always be open positions?"

"Yeah, but I'm not sure I want to teach in public schools."

"That's the problem. They need more good teachers like you."

"Yeah, well. We'll see," Emily Rose said.

Jemma sat up and fanned herself with a folded piece of paper she'd taken from Emily's box of miscellaneous things and packing supplies. "You really don't want to, huh?"

"I have this conversation with Michael almost every night. I'm tired of having it. Can we please talk about something else?"

"Okay. For now." Jemma lay back down.

Emily Rose nudged the side of Jemma's head with hers. "So you thought any more about this Smooth thing?"

When wasn't she thinking about her impending visit to the prison? Oh, right, when she was thinking about Davis. "Yeah." Jemma heaved a heavy sigh and rested her arm across her face.

"And?"

"I'm going to call down to the prison soon. See when visiting hours are."

She'd put off scheduling the visit ever since she decided to go see him. It was time to stop doing that, though. She had to talk to him and she might as well get it over with as soon as possible. Dealing with Smooth was the next step she had to take in confronting her past. Whatever came of it, she knew what she had to do. She couldn't run anymore. Running had always caused more trouble.

CHAPTER 25

Jemma woke up Saturday morning, still on the floor. She looked toward the rain spattered window across from where she lay. She'd been awakened by the sound of thunder, but the brief thunderstorm was already passing by the time she opened her eyes. She'd lain there for a while before admitting to herself she was awake.

She felt disgusting. She'd fallen asleep the night before without meaning to and was still in the same clothes she'd worn to the bar. Ugh, the bar. Her head hurt when she remembered seeing Alex. Because that, of course, led to thinking of Davis.

Despite her unsettled stomach and her cantankerous mood, she was going to see Emily Rose off with a smile on her face. She was going to miss Em Rose, but she reminded herself that it wasn't going to be like their last goodbye. It wouldn't be six years again before they next saw each other.

Jemma made her way downstairs and found Emily Rose in the kitchen with her parents. After chatting a bit with the Bradens and grabbing a piece of toast, Jemma wandered outside with Emily Rose.

"You okay? And by that I mean tell me what's up with you. Because something obviously is," Emily Rose said.

Jemma sagged onto the swing and pressed her chin into the chain that suspended it from the roof of the porch. "I blew my only chance at what I really want."

"Are you finally admitting your real feelings?" Emily Rose sat next to her.

Jemma shrugged. "What does it matter if I am? He's done with me now."

Em Rose put an arm around her. "Don't be so sure."

She rested her head on Em Rose's shoulder. "I haven't heard from him since he left me at his house. He just—disappeared."

"Maybe he's waiting for you to call."

"He wouldn't answer when I called."

"When was the last time you tried?"

"Yesterday. Afternoon."

"Well, maybe after sleeping on it, he feels just as rotten as you do and he feels too stupid to call you first."

Jemma chewed her lower lip thoughtfully. She wondered how much hope she should put into Emily Rose's words. Hope had never gotten her very far in the past. Still, she couldn't stop thinking about Davis and how if she already missed him so much, maybe going really would be worse than staying. Or at least going alone would be.

"You love him, Jemma."

She looked down at her hands.

"You know he loves you, too, right? Anybody and everybody can see that."

"So what do I do now?" Jemma asked, not really expecting an answer.

Emily Rose squeezed her shoulders. "This time, you stay."

"Huh?"

"That's it. That's my advice. You stay."

"That's some crappy advice."

Emily Rose laughed. "Maybe. Maybe not."

They sat in silence for a while, enjoying the cool breeze that followed the morning's quick summer thundershower. There were good reasons to leave Derring, weren't there? But if she had to keep reminding herself of those reasons, were they really good ones?

"So you all were talking about Tara when I came in the kitchen this morning. Something about her calling last night?"

"Yeah. She only calls when she wants something." After a brief pause, Emily Rose said, "I guess I do feel kind of sorry for her. I think I'm getting over any envy I ever felt for her. Thanks to—well, it's not important who."

"It's okay. You can say his name."

"Davis really did help me a lot on my wedding day."

"What does she want?"

"It really does sound like she's in trouble, so maybe it was mean of me to say it like that. There's a lot going on with her. She's fighting with Thom, her husband, again. They fight a lot whenever he comes back from being on his ship. He lets people fill his head with rumors of things she was doing while he was gone and then he jumps all over her. Last night, Mom said Tara was so out of it. Like she was strung out on something. And now Thom's threatening to leave her and fight her for custody of Branson."

"That's messed up," Jemma said, thinking back to the conversation she'd had with Tara on Em Rose's wedding day. There was always more to a person's story than what was on the surface. It was always too easy to judge without taking a closer look. "But I'm glad to hear you say that about how you feel about her. You should have stopped giving her power over you a long time ago."

Emily Rose squeezed her hands. "Yeah."

She pushed away thoughts again of wanting to know more about Davis and Tara and their marriage. It seemed to be such a sad and painful story. People didn't always want to share, though. She should have known that better than anybody. She put her hands on Emily Rose's shoulders. "Thanks for putting up with me. Through, you know, everything."

Em Rose hugged her. Resting her head on Jemma's shoulder, she said, "I'm sorry for yelling at you the other day. You really have been a good friend. There probably wouldn't have been a wedding without you."

"I probably needed you to yell at me. But you know what? No more apologies between us. We're going to start fresh. Right now. There's nothing to apologize for because we're going to let all old wounds heal. No more festering."

Emily Rose grinned. "Sounds good to me."

"Me, too." Jemma hugged her closer.

Later, after Emily Rose said goodbye to her parents, she and Jemma headed out to the car with the last of her things. Em Rose was still trying to convince Jemma not to give up on Davis when she opened the car door. Jemma put a blue tote bag in the back seat and shut the door.

"Jemma." Em Rose gave her the I'm-trying-very-hard-not-to-cry look.

"Hmm?" Jemma said.

She threw her arms around Jemma and squeezed. "You know, I still believe that even in the worst of circumstances, we can be the very best of ourselves."

"I want to believe that, too." Jemma hugged back. She really did, but she didn't know how to quite get her mind around it. She didn't know how to see past the idea of being forever broken—emotionally mangled—by her past. She wasn't sure it would ever be possible for her to trust things like love, forever, and all the other things people promised. She let go of Em Rose and sadness gripped her. The gloomy morning sky seemed to darken a little more.

"I told you, Jemma. Everything's going to work out." Emily Rose threw her a last reassuring smile. "I'll call you later. See how everything's going."

"Have a safe trip back," Jemma said, hugging herself as Em Rose slipped into the car. She waved one last time before pulling away from the curb.

Sunday morning, Jemma's bare feet slapped against the linoleum as she paced the floor in Mary's kitchen. She'd awakened at four in the morning and hadn't been able to go back to sleep. Forcing herself not to think about Davis almost drained as much energy as thinking about him.

She'd finally gotten out of the bed after a few hours of tossing and turning and gone into the living room to channel surf. She'd still been in her pajamas, lounging on the couch, when Mary came home from work a little while after the sun came up.

It was time to stop stalling. She went to her room to get her laptop. She looked up the visiting hours at Smooth's prison. She had to tell him to his face. To look into the face of the man who'd stolen everything from her and make sure he knew from her own lips that she wouldn't let him steal anything else.

After that, she went back into her room to set down her laptop. She thought about her scrapbook, which she'd stuck in the bottom dresser drawer. She liked to keep it close, but didn't like to keep it where she could see it—she didn't like to be constantly reminded of what it contained. But maybe looking at it was just what she needed that day.

Retrieving it from beneath her nightshirts and hose, she walked over to the bed and sat down cross-legged with it. She opened it to the section labeled "The Davis Years" and flipped past the track listings for that CD she'd made for Davis before she could read the names of the songs. She scanned over some cringe-worthy poems she'd written about him while trying to remember what she'd put in the letter she'd written and given to him along with the CD.

All she could remember was how much she'd loved him. How much she always had. The one line she remembered from the letter was admitting to him the words that often ran through her mind: *Your kisses are like home.*

Davis woke up sore and wincing on Codie's couch Sunday morning after sleeping most of Saturday away. He'd spent most of his time at Codie's so far in a semi-comatose state. He stood up slowly, listening to his knees crack and pop. Just one sound effect away from Rice Krispies, he thought with a sour smile. He then limped to the kitchen. His knee was being a real asshole that morning. He poured a glass of water and pulled out the Vicodin bottle. He shook a few pills into his hand. Then he sighed and threw them down the sink. After a pause, he emptied the rest of the bottle into the drain and then switched on the garbage disposal. The last thing he needed was another vice.

He went to Codie's pantry, where he knew she kept her over-the-counter meds, and found some aspirin. He gulped down a few of them with his glass of water. He rested his forehead against the side of the refrigerator.

"Davis?" Codie yawned. She was near the kitchen's entryway. She stood there in flannel pajamas and an over-sized yellow T-shirt. Possibly the ugliest T-shirt he'd ever seen.

"Hey there, canary lady," Davis said, limping over to her and leaning against the counter next to where she stood, taking most of his weight off his right knee. On the days his knee chose to really be a pain in the ass, mornings were the worst.

"You're so funny." Codie rolled her eyes.

"Yeah, well, you know. I do what I can."

She wrapped her arms around him. He half-heartedly hugged back. "You okay, Davis Hill?"

He shrugged. "Yeah."

"You sure about that?"

"Codie, I—yeah." He didn't want to talk about it. He knew what she would say to that.

She gave him a little frown. "I don't feel like things are the way they used to be between us."

Davis smiled weakly. Nothing was the same. How could half a person give all he used to give to anyone? That was the main reason he had to leave Jemma alone. Even though he was angry and it hurt, he understood that what she'd done was for the best. She deserved more than half a person. She deserved everything in the world she wanted. He was not one of those things. And with good reason. He had to come to terms with that. To respect it.

He said, "Don't go all Hallmark on me. We're good. Hey, you're obviously the first person I run to when things fall apart."

"Yeah, if only you'd let me help put them back together." She gave him a sad, tired smile. "You know, you should try to call her."

"No. She was right. My head was clouded by what I wanted and I forgot all about what was right." He wasn't about to drag Jemma down with him.

Codie sighed and shook her head.

"I still think you should marry me and make me a kept man," he said. They laughed although he was only half-joking and even then mostly about the latter part.

"Quit before I decide to take you up on that. The dating pool's shallow these days after all."

"I love you, Codie my friend. You're the best."

"Things are going to work out, Davis my friend. You two are gonna make it." She grasped his elbows, shaking them for emphasis. "I can tell no one's ever meant to you what she does. I've always been able to tell that. She brings out all the things that are great about you like no one else can."

Davis rolled his eyes. "Yeah, yeah. Whatever."

She slapped his shoulder. "Wait. You'll see that I'm right."

He gave her his best attempt at a smile. "I'm going to go take a nap."

"Didn't you just wake up?"

"Yeah." He didn't see anything all that great about being conscious at the moment, though. Plus, maybe the aspirin would kick in if he lay down for a little while. He noticed the wounded look in her eyes and said, "When I wake up, we'll go for a walk or something?"

She nodded. "Yeah. Sure. I have some work I should be doing, so I'll just go—do that."

He settled into the couch and pulled her afghan over him. Why had he come up here and just dumped on her? She wanted to help and he was hurting her by making it impossible. Why did she put up with him? He closed his eyes, trying to think of ways to be a better friend to Codie and of ways to forget about Jemma.

Davis woke up early that afternoon to the sound of his cell phone vibrating against the coffee table. He squinted at it, head pounding, before making a swipe at the thing.

He almost fell off the couch in the process of reaching for it. Groaning at the sight of Cole's number on the caller ID, he put the phone to his ear. He hadn't thought about Cole since that day he'd run into Seth at the post office. Seth had told him his brothers would call, but Davis forgot about it up until that moment. "What?"

"Nice to finally talk to you, bro," Cole said.

"What?" Davis repeated.

"We need to talk about the house."

"You can't kick me out. The house is mine, too."

"We have a proposition for you. That's all I'll say over the phone. We're staying at the Red Roof near the interstate. We went by your house, but nobody was home. Your car's missing. Neighbor said you hadn't been home in a couple days. I think her name's Ayn? Where are you anyway?"

"Out of town," Davis said flatly.

"Well, when can you be back in town? This is urgent."

"Just tell me what you want."

There was a short pause before Cole said, "This isn't the sort of thing that can be discussed over the phone. But I will tell you this. If you can't get your butt back here by tomorrow, you won't be happy. We have an appointment with Seth."

"You can't talk to my lawyer without me."

"All three of us, dummy. And we'll get our lawyers involved if you don't play nice. Don't make me drag you into court for something this stupid, Davis. I'll do it if I have to."

Davis winced. Maybe he should have listened to those voice mails from Seth before deleting them. "All right. I'll be there by tonight. What room are you staying in?"

"Three thirty-six."

Davis hung up and slipped his phone into his pocket.

"Your brother?" Codie asked. She must have walked into the room some time while he was on the phone. She wore jeans and a cream colored blouse. It looked cleaner in there, too. She'd been productive while he was conked out. Always the considerate type, she'd probably tip-toed around him while he slept.

Davis nodded. "Both of them. In Derring. I guess it's time for the final showdown."

"Do you want me to come with you?"

"You have to work."

She put a hand on his shoulder, sinking down next to him on the couch. "You're more important than work."

"No. This is between me and them. Thanks for being a good friend, though. Always."

Codie wrapped her arms around him. "I'm always gonna be here for you when you need me."

"Thanks," Davis said. He didn't deserve anyone being so good to him, but it was sure nice to have Codie in his life.

He limped to the front door and she followed.

"I'll call you when I get back," he said.

"Okay." She nodded. She stood in the doorway and he walked into the hallway.

He turned at the end of the hall to wave to her and caught her swiping her sleeve across her eyes. His heart broke a little more. Being friends with him couldn't be an easy thing. All he could ever seem to do was hurt people. Maybe he just needed to stay away from everybody.

CHAPTER 26

Davis grabbed a cup of coffee and drove back to Virginia with only two bathroom breaks. Traffic wasn't too bad, and he got back earlier than he'd expected to. He went to Room 336 at the Red Roof and knocked on the door. When it opened, he started to say something, but then closed his mouth. The shock of seeing an unexpected face had made him forget what he wanted to say. He stared back into his own eyes on a slender brunette who appeared to be in her mid-forties.

Davis stumbled back a few steps. It couldn't be.

"Oh, Davis." She let out a choked sob and reached for him. "You've grown into such a handsome young man. You've grown so much."

Davis guessed she would be shocked. After all, the last time she'd seen him, he'd been four. Of course he would have grown a little in twenty-one years.

Davis looked up to see Cole and Ashby standing further back in the room.

"Your brothers brought me to you," she said, flipping her hair over her shoulders.

So his brothers still talked to his mother. She really had abandoned Davis. Just him. Really had thrown him away.

"This is what we couldn't tell you about on the phone," Cole said from somewhere inside the room. "Mom."

"Oh, Davis. We can finally be a family." She clasped her hands together. Tears shone in her eyes.

"Looks like you already have one of those," Davis said, spying the wedding ring on her finger as she stretched her arms out to him again.

She pulled back and twisted the ring around her finger a couple of times. "There's so much you don't understand."

"I'm sure. Right now, though, I need to talk to my brothers," Davis said. He walked into the hotel room. His mother followed him.

Davis stood in the center of the room, facing Ashby and Cole. Lydia cowered in the corner, watching all three of them.

"So what is this? Why did you bring her here?" Davis repeatedly clenched and unclenched his fists. He trembled with rage he fought to control. It was a losing battle.

"Like I said, we need to talk about the house," Cole said, giving Ashby a nervous glance. Ashby gave him a slight nod.

Davis glared at his brothers. "What about my house?"

"We want you to let her stay there." Cole looked at Ashby, but spoke to Davis. "It belongs to all three of us. You know that."

"What? No, no, no. First, you dump Dad on me and now this? Hell no." They should have known they had no right to ask something like that.

Cole sighed and pushed his hands through his hair. "She has nowhere else to go. When she came to Ashby and me, she was living on the street."

"Why can't one of you take her in? You're the ones with the fancy jobs and all the money." Davis shook his head, still trying to wrap his mind around what Cole was suggesting.

"You know we have families. We have kids. There's not really room. You have that whole empty house."

"Kids I never see. You cut me out of my nieces' and nephews' lives."

"You never ask to see them, Davis. You never even call." Cole looked down at his tanned hands. He'd always tanned easily, unlike Davis.

"What's the point? I know you don't want me in their lives. Uncle Davis, the loser black sheep of the family. And you're not done screwing me over yet, huh? You're going to rub it in that you all have real lives? The kind you stole from me?" Davis moved over to the table near the windows at the front of the room, leaning against it for support. Cole looked so smug and stupid, standing there in his standard sports coat and khakis.

"Stole from you? What?" Cole's eyes flashed as he turned to Davis.

"You took my lacrosse scholarship from me. You threw me back in that house with Dad and let me rot there."

"So you still blame me for you messing up your knee, huh? You jumped out of a moving car to try and impress some girl and it's my fault?"

"You let me drink way too much that night. You were egging me on to do it. 'C'mon Davis, have one more shot,' you said."

"I didn't know you'd jump out of that car like a damned fool. It's always someone else's fault. Why don't you ever take responsibility for anything in life? That's your damn problem." Cole slammed his fist against his thigh.

"It's not about me taking responsibility. You should have never let me get in that car after you let me drink like that."

"Oh. So it's my responsibility to tell you when you've had enough to drink?"

"Then you threw me out of your house while I was still recovering."

"I wanted you to stay, but you spent all your time fighting with my wife, cussing in front of my baby, and you stayed drunk and glued to my couch."

"You never tried to help me find a job or get back in school or anything. You wanted me to fail. You wanted me back here so you wouldn't have to worry about *him* anymore."

"Such a screw-up, Davis. Always have been. Always will be. You threw away the kind of life people dream about."

"Yeah, well, I had such great role models to learn from, huh? Brothers who told me it was better if I didn't tell anybody Dad beat the shit out of me 'cause they'd split our family up if I told. Well, you two left me as soon as you could anyway." Davis threw an ugly look into the corner where Lydia still cowered. "A mom who didn't want me to the extreme that she legally severed herself from me. Yeah, so I screwed up. Is that really a surprise?"

Lydia stood. "I never wanted to leave you."

Davis ignored her, turning his attention back to Cole. "She is not coming to live in that house with me. She made her decision over twenty years ago. She doesn't get to come back now."

Cole turned to Ashby. "I can't talk to him. I'm gonna punch him in the face if I say one more word. I'm going out for a smoke." He walked out of the room.

Ashby turned to Davis with a sigh. "We've come to a decision. You either let Lydia move in, or we're going to force you to buy us out."

"You know I can't afford that." And his credit was trashed—no way he could get a loan to do it.

"Take it or leave it. Those are the only two alternatives you have."

"You'd really force me out of the house if I don't let this traitor move in with me? You two really hate me that much?"

"She just needs a place to stay for a few months. This is best for everybody." Ashby wouldn't look at Davis as he spoke.

"Wrong. All you care about is money. You two have wanted to sell that house out from under me since the funeral. And then she dropped the perfect excuse into your laps. You knew I wouldn't agree to this. You're trying to force me out of there."

"It's not like that."

Lydia said, "Please. Let me explain."

Davis turned to her. "I don't have to let you stay. You gave up your rights to everything, remember? Including me."

Lydia's face seemed to cave in. "I know, Davis. And I'm sorry."

"So you couldn't come back for the funeral, but you can come back for a free place to live, huh?"

"I didn't know what else to do. I wasn't ready for kids. Taking care of the three of you . . . putting up with his neanderthal ideas of what a wife should be . . . I was twenty-three. He was twice my age. But I didn't have any other choice. I was broke. I thought he loved me. I thought I could learn to love him. I was wrong." She walked toward him and he backed away. "I'm not expecting forgiveness. Not right away."

She shouldn't have been expecting it at all. He took a step toward the door.

She wrung her hands. "I hated my life with him. I thought that if I left you and your brothers behind, he'd let me go without a fight. He always seemed to love you kids more than me. I'll never be able to tell you how sorry I am."

"That doesn't change anything," Davis said, but he didn't stop her when she came up and threw her arms around him.

"If I'd known, Davis. If I'd had any idea. I tried to call, but he changed the number. He wouldn't let me have anything to do with you all. The last time I called before he changed the number, he told me you all hated me."

"I learned to hate you. Every time he laid his fist into me, I learned to hate you a little more."

She sobbed into his chest. "I screwed up. I admit that. I want us to be able to start over now. Please."

Davis pulled away from her. "I can't do this today."

"Davis," Ashby said in a warning tone.

"Come to the house tomorrow morning. I need some time to think."

"Would you really rather be homeless than live with her?" Ashby called to him as he crossed the room.

"Maybe," Davis said as he exited the room.

Davis spotted Cole out in the parking lot, shoulders hunched over, sucking on a cigarette. He walked up to his brother and stood there, not knowing what to say.

His brothers would never be sorry for anything. Especially Cole. Not for Davis getting in that car. Not for his wasted life. They would never be sorry because they would never care.

"I wonder how we ended up like this." Davis wasn't expecting a reply and he was surprised when he got one.

"Ended up like what?" Cole took a long drag, and Davis fought the urge to bum a cigarette. That was the one bad habit he hadn't started back up in the past few days.

"A family of traitors who hate each other."

Cole exhaled, nostrils flaring. He looked down at his cigarette. "Him. He caused all of this."

Davis stared at his brother a long time. Cole didn't back down from the stare. "I don't think that's true."

"Oh?" Cole dropped his cigarette butt to the asphalt and crushed it out with an expensive-looking brown leather shoe.

"He didn't ruin everything all by himself."

Cole stared across the parking lot. "You woulda done the same thing if you'd been the oldest. Gotten yourself the hell out of there."

"Oh? So you and Ashby get away and I get forgotten."

"We tried to get you out. You sent yourself right back to him after the accident."

"I could tell you didn't want me at your house. So I left."

"What? I never said—or thought—anything like that. You're my brother. Of course I wanted you there." Cole took a deep breath. "But I also wanted you to treat my family with respect. Did I want you lying on the couch all day, destroying your liver, and generally turning into Dad? No. But when I tried to talk to you about it, you wouldn't hear it. All you wanted to do was shout and throw things. Act unreasonable. Just like him."

"I'm nothing like him." Davis's jaw clenched.

"Really? You're not a belligerent drunk who alienates everyone who tries to love him?" Cole lifted his eyebrows in mock surprise.

Davis drew back his fist. Cole didn't flinch.

"Go ahead. Prove my point." He didn't back off from Davis one inch.

Davis muttered that he wasn't worth the effort and walked off.

"That's the other thing he was good at. Running away from his problems," Cole called after him. Davis didn't break his pace, but the irony wasn't lost on him as his mind went back to his last words to Jemma.

Jemma sat forward in the hard plastic chair and kept her face set in an emotionless mask. Seeing Smooth again wasn't as hard as she'd expected it to be. She was ready to tell him everything she'd always meant to.

She said, "I don't know why you wanted to see me today, but I would never do anything to help you get out of here. You were wrong for what you did. If you rot in here, you deserve it."

"You're probably right," Smooth said.

Jemma was shocked into silence because when she'd pictured this meeting in her head, she'd told him off without him saying so much as a word. She certainly hadn't expected him to agree with her.

"Yes, I deserve what I got. You were right when you screamed it at me that day outside of the courthouse at the end of the trial. I always remembered how you looked when they dragged you away that day."

She narrowed her eyes at him. "Really?"

He nodded. "I think I started growing a conscience right then and there." He smiled. "Don't you know I never tried to appeal my conviction? Lawyer said we had a good chance of winning on some kind of evidence technicality. If I had any sense, I would have taken a plea bargain from the start. I made life harder than it had to be for so many people. I'm done with doing that."

Jemma realized that he was different. His demeanor, his tone of voice, his eyes. Nothing seemed the same about him. "Smooth . . ."

"My name is Larry, Jemma. I'm not that person anymore. I go to chapel here every Sunday. I really want to change. Whether you believe it or not, what I did to your family was the most horrible thing I've ever done and being in here . . . has made me want to be different. Now, there are a lot of knuckleheads here who can't see the light, and I don't know if they ever will. Not that I blame them. I don't think there are any really bad people. Just people, some of them in worse situations than others. And some of those people make bad decisions, but no. No bad people."

Jemma sat back in her seat, still eyeing him warily. No bad people, huh?

He spread his hands on the table in front of him and continued. "I blame the system more than anything. Broken system, broken people. It's hard for a man to really be a man when everything's set up against him. But the point is I was a part of the problem for too long." He gave her a small smile. His eyes were full of sincerity. "Now, I'm trying to be part of the solution." He chuckled. "I lead a book discussion group. Me, Jemma. I bet you thought I didn't know how to read."

She knew it was supposed to be a joke, but she was too busy trying to wrap her head around all he was saying to force a laugh.

"We've read a lot of Harris, but now we're starting *The Autobiography of Malcolm X.* Way better than the movie. But what am I saying? You've probably already read it. Probably read way more books than I ever will before I met you. You've always been so smart."

"That's great, Larry. The book club and . . . all of it." Jemma wanted to say something that really captured how she felt inside, but her vocabulary eluded her.

He leaned forward and clasped his hands together. "One thing I learned in here is the past is for learning. It's not for punishing others or yourself. It's not for dwelling on and getting angry about things you can't change. It's for learning how to do better in the rest of your life. And being grateful you get another chance to try and do better." He held up a hand and shook his head the moment she tried to say something. Then, he said, "I'm not expecting instant forgiveness or for you to run down to the parole board and sing my praises. And maybe you can never forgive what I did. I just wanted you to hear those things. From me. There are just some things that can't be expressed the right way in letters."

"Right." Nothing he'd ever said to her before had made so much sense.

Larry smiled. "You go on and do well for yourself. That's all I want for you. After all I done wrong and all I took from you, I pray every night for you to have that. I know I can never fully apologize for all I've done, and I can't change the past, but I can at least offer you my heartfelt well wishes."

"I'll tell them the truth." Jemma's heart instantly felt lighter. "Nothing more or less than that. Including the fact that you're more than what I thought you were. That you've changed."

His voice cracked. "I'm glad to hear you say that."

They talked for a while longer about Larry getting his GED and his trying to be a mentor for some of the guys he'd met. Later, when she left, his words about learning from the past rang through her head. Their echoes stuck there hours later, bouncing around along with what Mary had said.

CHAPTER 27

Monday morning, Davis's brothers showed up bright and early as promised. In fact, he was awakened by a phone call and Cole's angry voice telling him they'd been knocking on the door for five minutes. Davis rolled out of bed, pulled on the first pair of sweats that caught his eye and limped down the stairs, grimacing at the morning stiffness in his knee.

He threw open the door for the three of them, grunted a greeting, and then retreated into the family room. They followed.

"Well?" Cole raised his eyebrows.

Davis sneered at him. He looked like he thought he was entitled to the answer he obviously expected Davis to give. Davis watched Lydia go around the room with her hand pressed to her mouth, looking at pictures of the three brothers—her sons—growing up in soccer, football, and baseball uniforms and shirts and ties for school pictures. Ashby paced around the room, fidgeting with his wedding ring and tapping his foot against the floor whenever he attempted to stand still.

"Davis, our appointment with Seth is in less than an hour. I suggest you tell us what you have to tell us or else go get showered. 'Cause you could really use one of those."

Davis's stare went back to Cole. Not only was he going to take what little Davis had left, he was going to be a jerk about it. Then again, what else could he expect from Cole?

"We don't have time for this." Cole glanced at his watch. He was probably calculating in his head the quickest he could get back to Pennsylvania and get on with his life. Dump Lydia off and go. That was their M.O., Cole and Ashby. Dump the family problems on Davis and go. Davis, the skeleton keeper.

He'd made his decision almost as soon as he left the hotel the night before. He was sick of them. They kept thinking they could boss him around and they were wrong. He nodded. "She can stay here."

Lydia rushed over, beaming up at him as she was a full head shorter. "Thank you. I knew you had it in your heart, son. I knew it."

Cole nodded. "You made the right decision."

Davis locked his cold stare first on one brother and then the other. "But I won't. You two are going to buy me out of the house."

"Davis, no," Lydia said.

"Don't be stupid. Where will you go?" Cole said.

"Don't worry about it. You've never worried about me before. Your little plan backfired on you, huh? I can't afford to buy you two out, but you can certainly afford to buy me out." He laughed bitterly. "Besides, isn't this what you wanted anyway? You have your friggin' house. Now you can re-sell it, burn it, do whatever you want with it. But I'm leaving."

"Don't be an idiot," Cole said, running a hand through his short, thick hair. He looked like he'd rather use that hand, along with the other one, to strangle Davis.

Davis ignored his comment. Before he turned to leave the room, he said, "I guess I better grab that shower. We'll need to keep that appointment with Seth to talk all of this over."

Davis headed for the stairs, leaving his stunned brothers and hysterical mother behind him. He had no idea where he would go or what he would do. But it was too bad Florida wasn't an option. Not that he should allow himself to think that way, but he couldn't stop little thoughts like that from popping into his mind, and he'd given up on trying.

On her way home Monday afternoon from running errands and long after visiting Smooth, Jemma decided to take a route home which took her by Davis's place. She slammed on the brakes, stopping just past the driveway, shocked to see his car there. She pulled over to the curb and parked. She didn't know what she was going to say, but she knew she had to see him. Her last memory of Davis wouldn't be of him speeding away while she watched from his bedroom window.

She wasn't going to tell him how much she wanted to be with him and that she was thinking of not leaving. He couldn't know those things. First things first. She had to see if he would answer the door and take it from there. After all, the last time she'd tried to call, which had admittedly been Friday, he hadn't answered.

She stood at the front door, just staring at it for a moment. She raised her hand to knock several times before she got up the nerve to actually do it.

He answered the door with a drunken grin. "Jemma." He stumbled backward so she could come in.

"How much have you had, Davis?" Jemma followed him into the family room. She pushed a pile of takeout cartons out of the way so that she could sit on the sofa.

"Psht. Just a sip," he slurred, sitting, or more like falling, across the chair facing her.

He was sloppy drunk. She hadn't seen him like that the whole time she'd been home. He'd had a glass of wine or two with her, but he hadn't gotten anything close to what he was like at that moment. He'd told her one night that he drank a lot and was afraid of becoming his father. She hadn't thought he'd been in any danger of that until he'd opened the door for her moments earlier.

Davis upended a rectangular bottle filled with dark liquor and Jemma sighed, shaking her head. He looked at her. "What?"

"You've probably had enough."

Davis smirked before taking another large gulp from the bottle. "You don't know what's enough for me. You're not around enough to know. I developed a high tolerance over these last six years, Jemster."

She went up to him and grabbed the bottle. He gave it to her without much resistance. She set it on the end table furthest away from him and walked back over. She let him pull her onto his lap. Putting her head on his shoulder, she combed her fingers through his hair in a slow rhythm.

"I'm losing my house," Davis said. "Well, his house, I guess."

Jemma stopped running her fingers through his hair and looked up at him. "What happened?"

"My mom is back. My idiot brothers want me to let her live here. We went to the lawyer today. Worked it so that they're going to buy me out. She can have this house. I've been trapped in here with a bunch of bad memories. And it's the last thing tying me to them. Good. Riddance. At least I get some money out of it."

"Oh, Davis." She wanted to know more about his mom being back, but the look on his face told her asking wouldn't have been a good idea.

"Don't 'oh Davis' me. I don't care." He pushed at her and she stood. "I shouldn't anyway," he muttered. "I earned this damned house, though." He pulled himself to his feet, wincing a little.

"Is it your knee?" Jemma asked, worried.

"What knees? I'm golden. I got whiskey." He grabbed the bottle she'd taken from him earlier. It fell through his drunk-slow fingers and hit the floor. "It's like I don't have any knees. I don't really. Well, I got one maybe."

"Davis, please tell me you haven't been drinking all day."

"What do you care?"

"Please."

He heaved a huge sigh. "No. I have not." He lumbered toward the stairs.

Jemma went to the kitchen, retrieved an ice pack from the freezer and hunted down a clean dish towel after searching through several drawers and cabinets. She went up to his room and lay next to him. Without saying a word, she wrapped the ice pack in the towel and gingerly placed it over his right knee. She then patted his shoulder before lying her head on it.

"You're staying?"

She nodded, and her cheek rubbed against the fabric of his t-shirt. "Yeah."

"What about the car? Doesn't Mary need it?"

"She's not working tonight."

"I'm fine. I don't need you to do this. You can go home if you came here just to take care of me. And feel sorry for me," Davis said.

"I know," Jemma said, rubbing her hand over his chest. "I know."

He put his arm around her, hugging her to him. A few minutes later, he was out. She lay wide awake in his arms, wondering what in the world she would or could do about him.

The next morning, the moment Davis stirred, she looked up at him. He rubbed a hand over his bloodshot eyes and mumbled something about whiskey.

She sat up on the edge of the bed. She couldn't just leave him there. The pain she felt radiating from him almost broke her heart.

"How you feeling?" she asked.

"I don't need looking after." He glanced at her before rolling over to the edge of the bed and pulling himself to first a sitting and then a standing position while leaning heavily to the left.

"I didn't say you did."

Davis grunted in response.

"You want to talk about it?"

"What?"

"The house? Your mom? Any of it?"

He grunted again.

Jemma looked down at her hands, knowing she was crazy for suggesting what she was about to. She didn't expect a positive answer. But she took a deep breath and did it anyway. "You could come to Florida."

"Oh, that'd be a great idea. That's exactly what I want to do. We should invite Wendell, too. And Stephanie."

"Davis—"

"Yes, it'd be great. We could get a place together and be like *Three's Company*, millennium edition, only there'd be four of us."

"It was just an idea," Jemma said, feeling defensive after getting the burst of attitude from him. She no longer felt like apologizing for how she'd acted the week before.

"A bad one." He glowered at her from across the room.

She stood and straightened her jeans and shirt out the best she could before pushing her braids away from her face.

"I don't need you to rescue me. You're only asking me to come 'cause you pity me," he said.

"I wasn't trying to 'rescue' you. I was trying to be a friend."

"Well, I'm sorry, but it's kind of hard for me to be friends with someone I'm in love with. I'm not going to pretend everything's fine and wonderful when it's not. You can leave me, but I'm not going to play the confused loser game with you."

She'd been right. He'd just proved how little a word like love really meant. "Yeah, confused, I dunno. But the loser part sure fits you." Jemma slammed the door behind her. Wiping angry tears from the corners of her eyes, she hurried down the stairs and out of the front door.

She didn't know what she'd been thinking by coming there and especially by asking him to come to Florida, but at least Davis had proven her point. Shown her that she'd been right all along. In a way, it was a good thing that she'd gone to see him. Up until that morning, she'd actually been enough of a fool to start second-guessing her decision about him.

Tuesday afternoon, Lydia brought over the few suit-cases she had. He overheard her, Ashby and Cole talking about how light her load was. Apparently she had a few things in storage back in Denver, but still she didn't own much. Davis heard her and his brothers going in and out of Bill's old room, but he didn't so much as open the door to his. He sat on his bed, playing a video game with the television on mute. He was barely paying attention to it, though. He kept dying and having to start the game over. His mind was on Jemma and what a jerk he'd been to her that morning. And on his new housemate until he found somewhere to go.

That was the other thing. He didn't know where he'd go. Especially now that he was fired again. The money he got once they closed on the sale of the house would last for a little while, but he still needed a job. One of the cooks at the restaurant was looking for someone to share his new apartment in Richmond, but Davis wasn't sure he wanted to have a roommate or live in Richmond.

Once Lydia got settled in Bill's room and Ashby and Cole left, she came to his. He called out for her to come in after hearing her knock.

She walked in, putting one foot in front of the other at a snail's pace. "This place is going to be a great investment for your brothers. And they are going to make a killing on it once the market turns around. You've kept it in great shape." Cole and Ashby were going to use the house as a rental property once Lydia moved out and then sell it after its value increased enough.

He glanced at her. Was she trying to pour salt in the wound, or did she have no tact at all?

She sat on the edge of his bed, near his feet. "I just want things to be okay between us. Would it help if I told you what happened?"

"To tell you the truth, I dunno." Davis paused the game and looked in her direction.

"Let's at least give it a try. I really don't want you to leave your home. This place is yours more than it will ever be mine."

He kept his face emotionless and stared at her sitting at the foot of his bed. He swung his legs over the side of the bed so that he sat close to the headboard. He stared down at a faded cola stain on his tan carpet, waiting for her to tell her story.

"I was young. When I married Bill. As you know. I was twenty-three and broke and I believed everything he said to me. As I'm sure you know, that man was full of lies."

He turned his head toward her, but other than that made no move at all.

"Bill and I—I don't know if I ever loved him. If I did, it wasn't the type of love you marry for. And I think when he realized that, that's what set him off. Made him a bitter, ugly man. When he found out about my boyfriend, that's when the drinking started."

"You cheated on him." Davis's voice was a perfect monotone.

"Yeah. And still being young, stupid, and selfish, I chose myself over you kids until it was too late. I gave up my parental rights and . . . well, I told you the rest earlier. Bill was pretty convincing. I figured there was no point in coming back."

"How'd you find Cole and Ashby?"

"I hired a P.I. I needed to know what happened to my kids. By the time I got in touch with them, you'd already had your accident. They told me it was best to stay away from you. That you had turned into another version of him and didn't want anything to do with your family. It took me weeks and finding out about Bill to realize that I needed to stop listening to other people."

"Really. You know, it's suspicious to me that you show up a few months after Bill died. Now that there's a house to be had. My accident was four years ago."

"I was still mixed up inside. I've done a lot of things I'm not proud of. I didn't know if I was worthy of being back in any of your lives. Your brothers made me feel like I wasn't for a long time. I still don't know if I am. All I know is I want you in my life."

"What about your other family? Don't I have brothers and sisters I don't know about?"

"Sean—Sean never wanted any kids. And my third marriage didn't last long enough for us to talk about kids. I still wear the ring, but that's been over for a while now. And after what I did to you all . . . I didn't figure I deserved any more kids anyway."

"Well, you made one good decision. I guess that's better than none."

"I understand that you're angry. I only hope you can forgive me one day. I need you, son. I need all three of you."

"So you've been married twice since Bill?"

"Yeah. Like I said, I've made a lot of mistakes. But now I want to repair whatever I can."

"Wow. It only took you twenty-one years to choose me? Not bad at all."

"Davis, please."

"Or did you really choose me? You know what I think? I think you just want a free place to live. Well, you can have it. I don't need anything from him anyway. Or you, for that matter."

"I've been out of work for a while. I'll be out of here as soon as I can get myself together. Please. I don't want to run you out of your own house."

"What's a while?"

"What?"

"You say you've been out of work for a while."

"Well, there were a couple of lawsuit settlements. The divorce settlement from Sean. A car accident. A slip and fall in a grocery store . . . Money ran out and it's been so long since I worked, it's hard for me to find something now since my work history is kind of sparse."

Davis scoffed. "Whoa. Really? So all your other free-loading got cut off and you hunted down your sons to see what they had, huh? Too bad the ones with all the money pawned you off on the have-not, huh? But at least you got a house out of the deal."

She shook her head. "I had other options. I could've gone to live with my sister. I just wanted to be near you. To be back in your life."

Davis doubted it, but he couldn't talk to her anymore right then. "Could you just get out? Please?" Davis pressed his fingertips to his temples. He felt his stomach coiling around itself.

Lydia stood, but continued to hover by his bed. "Davis, are you okay?"

He cast an ice-glazed gaze at her, and she finally understood. "Okay. I'll be in my—in the room if you need me." Placing her hands to her mouth, she hurried to the door.

She turned to face him, leaning against the doorframe. "I'm going to go get settled in. Take all the time you need. But please, come talk to me when you're ready. Don't you think this family's been through enough heartbreak?"

"Whose fault is that?" He turned his back to the door until he heard it close.

CHAPTER 28

Tuesday night, Jemma and Mary sat at the kitchen table with mugs of tea. Now that it was all over, she was able to tell everything without being concerned that Mary would needlessly worry about her. Jemma went over what had happened when she visited Larry at the prison. She also told Mary about the interview she'd had with the parole board representative earlier that day.

"You were right. I really do feel better now that I've dealt with everything." Jemma sat back in her chair and took a sip of her peppermint tea.

"You don't look like you feel much better." Mary spoke the first words she had since Jemma had told her all that had happened.

Her smile faltered as her mind went back to that morning at Davis's, but she refused to admit defeat.

"It's okay to admit you want to stay. You know I'd love to have you here."

"I know. But I want to go."

"Lynette may be dead and gone, but you're still letting her run you off, I see. That woman sure has some kind of power over you."

"Lynette doesn't have anything to do with this. This decision is for me." Jemma tensed. She was tired of people accusing her of running away.

Mary looked unfazed by Jemma's reaction. She looked at her mug and then up at Jemma. "If you say so. But no matter what you say or do, I'm going to be right here. Whether you go to Florida or Timbuktu, there will always be a place for you in my heart and in my house."

"I appreciate that, Mary. I really do. But I have this opportunity. To go to Florida and start over. I can start fresh now that I've dealt with everything that happened before."

Mary sipped her tea. "Whatever's in your heart is what you should do."

"Florida's in my heart."

Mary smiled and patted Jemma's hand.

Maybe Davis was also in her heart, but that couldn't be helped. She had those memories of him from the past couple of weeks, and no one could take them from her. She had much better memories of him than she had the first time she'd left. And wasn't that all she'd expected out of the deal? A few happy moments and some good memories? They'd ended a little earlier than she'd expected. So what?

Wednesday afternoon, Davis went to his room as soon as he got home. Lydia followed him in. He needed to talk to her, so that was convenient.

"I spent the whole day cleaning. What do you think?" Lydia beamed sunshine at him with her huge smile.

"House looks nice," Davis said before rubbing his hand across his face.

"Thanks." The smile slowly fell from her face.

"I just came from Seth's office. Cole and Ashby are talking to the bank they want to use. Things look good for the loan. Seth says the papers should be drawn up soon. Probably in less than a week from now." Davis toyed with his keys, glanced up at her occasionally.

"You're still thinking of moving out? It's such a silly idea, Davis. There's plenty of room for both of us here."

"That's what I was out doing. Seeing Seth and running other errands. Getting packing supplies and asking around at apartment complexes and places. There are a few trailers for rent, too. Saw some adds on the bulletin board at the laundromat when I was walking around town."

"So you haven't found a place yet?" Lydia looked a little too hopeful about that.

Davis gave a small frown. "I have some leads."

"You don't even have a place to go."

"I'm moving out next week and that's all there is to it."

"I'm only trying to make you see that it makes sense for you to stay, Davis."

He tightened his grip on his keys. "I don't want anything to do with you. I can hate you if I want and you can't blame me for that. I'm entitled to that after all you did to me."

She looked at him as if he'd stabbed her in the gut. Her shoulders sagged forward and she walked to the door. She paused for a second without turning around. Then she walked out, quietly closing the door behind her.

Davis sat on the corner of his bed after she left the room. He had his fist pressed to his mouth and a bad taste inside of it. He couldn't believe he felt like he'd been out of line. But he also couldn't shake the feeling that he'd just said something incredibly stupid.

He got up and paced the room, the feeling gnawing, eating away at him. Finally, he groaned and walked next door to Bill's room. He still had trouble thinking of the room as belonging to her.

Her words had somehow gotten to him. He began to see her from a new angle. A more human one. As a victim of circumstance creating three new victims of circumstance. He still had a lot of things to work out when it came to his feelings for her, but maybe moving out wasn't the best option. He wouldn't work much out by avoiding her.

Besides, he really had earned a right to stay. After taking care of Bill for years, he had a right to every square inch of that house. And if Bill hadn't run him out of the house, why move out because of Lydia? She couldn't be any worse to live with than him. Definitely not.

He stood in the open doorway. She slouched next to the window that faced the front lawn, staring out of it. He knocked on the open door. She turned and gave him a weak smile, waving him into the room.

Stalling for time, he looked around Bill's room. He hadn't been in there since the funeral except to get Bill's important papers for Seth. The room was nearly unrecognizable, and that was a good thing. For one thing, he could see the floor, and it was vacuumed. He was surprised she'd been able to find the vacuum; he certainly didn't know where it was. She'd taken down the green sun-faded curtains and had draped light blue fabric over the windows.

"I'm going to make curtains out of that. Eventually," she said, breaking the silence, when she noticed him staring at the windows.

He nodded, his gaze traveling over the mint green sheets on the bed and the dusted surfaces of the desk and wardrobe. The only things that seemed out of place now were her suitcases lined up against the wall at the back of the room.

"Looks good in here," Davis said, sitting on the corner of the dresser.

"Thanks." She stood with her back to the window, looking across the room at him.

"I guess I came in here to apologize. So maybe I should get to it." Davis stared down at his fingernails, wondering if they'd always been that dirty and he'd just never taken the time to notice.

Lydia nodded and crossed her arms over her chest.

"It's hard. I want to be angry at you, but what's the point? I mean, it's not like I have much family. I guess I should try to save what little there is."

"I would have been willing to do anything to hear you say that." She wiped at the corners of her eyes with her jacket sleeve. Davis kept the A/C up pretty high, and he guessed she wasn't as hot natured as him.

"I don't wanna go through all this bull anymore." Davis ran his hands through his hair and then raked them over his face before letting his head rest in them.

Lydia walked over and hugged him to her. "I know, Davis. I know."

"I need to talk to Cole and Ashby, I guess."

"We could call them together."

"Nah. I need to go see them." He pulled back from the hug. They were leaving in a few hours. He needed to say what he had to say before they did. Face to face.

When Cole first opened the door, Davis thought he would slam it right back from the look on his face.

"What do you want, Davis? Seth called, everything's set for the closing. We're moving as fast as we can," Cole said. "We'll be out of your way soon."

"I just want to talk," Davis said. "Can I come in?"

Cole heaved an exaggerated sigh. "I guess."

Davis walked in and saw open suitcases on both beds. "You guys heading out?"

"Tomorrow. We have to get back to work." Cole put extra emphasis on the word *work*.

Davis forced himself to remember that he hadn't come over to fight and that Cole was naturally a jerk. That was just a fact of life. He sat in a chair near the window and drummed his fingertips against the table in front of him. "Where's Ashby?"

"He ran out to pick up dinner. I sent him to that rib place in Ashland. Man, being close to that place is one of the few things I miss about this dump town." Cole scratched the back of his neck and took a seat on the edge of the bed closest to Davis. "What do you want to talk about?"

"I'm staying in the house." Davis gulped in a breath and exhaled slowly through his nose. "I'm gonna work on things with Mom."

"You've finally come to your senses."

"But I want all of us to work on things." He turned toward his brother. "With each other, Cole. You, me, Ashby, and Mom. We should try to save what we have left of a family."

"What is this? You still thinking we're trying to dump Lydia off on you and this is your insurance against it?"

"No, Cole. You're such an asshole." Davis focused on his mission—the reason he'd come there. "But you're also my brother. And if you meant what you said the other night about trying to reach out, well, I'm not pushing you away anymore. Either prove me wrong or prove me right about wanting all of us to be able to put this behind us. Step up or step out."

"She's a bum and a leech. I'm not asking you to keep her there any longer than it takes her to get herself together. My conscience wouldn't let me throw her out on the street. Why should I want anything to do with her? Why should any of us?"

"That's what I thought about Bill when I first moved home. I wanted to be in and out of that house as fast as I could. Stay a month at most, I told myself. But the day I came home from PT and saw him passed out on the living room floor, all that changed. That was right around the time his kidneys started failing. I realized that there are things more important than being angry and proving a point. I almost forgot that when Mom came here. All those feelings about her I'd buried came to the surface, and it was ugly. You know what? I'm going to try not to forget that anymore."

Cole was quiet for a long moment. When he looked at Davis again, his brown eyes were tired and unfocused. "You really believe she deserves another chance?"

"I have to believe she can change. How else can I hold out hope for me?"

"You're nothing like her."

"I'm no saint, either."

"Point taken."

They laughed.

"Besides, it's almost like therapy. I think trying to understand her will help me understand myself better. I hope so anyway." Maybe if he ever got another chance at love, he wouldn't screw it the hell up the way he had with Jemma. Maybe it was possible for him to become a better person. He had plenty of time to work on it because he wouldn't be getting over Jemma any time soon—if he ever did.

"I'm not so sure."

"Cole, something kept you from kicking her out on her ass. I'd be willing to bet that same something wants to get to know her and see what she has to say for herself."

"This, uh, all this family bonding you want to do, that mean things are cool between us?"

"I think they're on their way to being. Really well on their way."

"Good. Davis, I gotta tell you, despite all I said the other day, I've felt horrible. I just didn't know what to say to you. I had no idea how to get things back on track between us. I mean after the funeral . . ."

Davis nodded. The funeral hadn't been one of his better moments. What kind of son showed up drunk to his father's funeral and had to be ushered out before the eulogy? The kind of son who had Bill for a father. Still, thinking of that day made Davis feel terrible.

"Well, I think we can do it, Cole. Pull things back together for all of us," he said quietly.

"I hope we can, Davis. I really do."

Davis stayed and talked with his brother a little longer before telling him he had to leave. Davis wanted to catch Seth in the office and tell him the news about the house. He knew Seth stayed around the office until at least seven most nights.

Cole walked him to the door.

He put a hand on Davis's shoulder. "So what's this about a girl, huh? Your neighbor, Ayn, says Jemma was over your house the night before we brought Mom there. Now, would this be the same Jemma you used to talk about all the time when you were in Philly with us?"

Davis tried to smile, but couldn't quite manage it. "Yeah."

"What's going on with that?"

"Nothing."

"Nothing?"

"Absolutely nothing." Davis stepped out of the room. It took a lot of effort for him to not let the lie show on his face. He wanted to go to Jemma that minute, but they needed to stay away from each other. She'd been right all along. He wanted her to go to Florida and have a good life—the kind of life he could never give her.

Cole leaned against the door. "You know, the wife still asks about you. Kids, too. Ashby's family would be happy to see you, too. Come up sometime and visit us. See your nieces and nephews."

Davis nodded. "I think I will."

He walked down the breezeway, pulling his cell phone out of his pocket. He stared at it all the way down the stairs and was still staring at it as he headed for his car in the parking lot. Finally, as he got in the car, he put it back in his pocket. He made himself realize that calling Jemma wouldn't bring anything good to either of them.

CHAPTER 29

Jemma spent the night before she left scouring Mary's house from top to bottom. Cleaning helped her think, and she was trying to make sure everything was in order for her move to Jacksonville. The activity gave her structure that she needed—it allowed her to focus so that her mind wouldn't stray into dangerous territory.

The movers had taken everything from storage in South Carolina to her new apartment in Jacksonville. She'd already sent a check to the landlord for her first month's rent and deposit. She'd done that before leaving South Carolina. Everything was in place for her new beginning. She was finally going to complete her transition to her new and better life in just a few hours.

Jemma sang along with the lyrics blaring from the stereo in the living room as she scrubbed at the kitchen sink. One good thing about Mary living far from civilization was that she could turn the music up as loud as she wanted to—when Mary wasn't around.

Jemma couldn't remember the last time someone made her feel as whole and at home as Mary did. But Mary had to be wrong. She had good reasons for not staying, didn't she? She had an amazing job in Florida. And although she'd made her peace with her Derring life, there was nothing in that town to keep her there. Not anything that she could have, anyway.

Thinking like that wasn't going to do her any good. She scrubbed harder at the countertop. Frustrated with the song that started playing next, she hurried over to the stereo. She changed the CD from her favorite singer-songwriter compilation to Mary J. Blige. Then she headed to the bathroom, ready to attack the bathtub under the pretense of giving everything a good scouring as a surprise and a thank you to Mary.

"Not Gon' Cry" started playing on the stereo and Jemma started bawling. She threw her sponge into the bathtub and stripped off her yellow latex gloves. She pressed her rubber-scented hands to her face and sobbed.

Thinking about Emily Rose's words to her before she left for New York and Smooth's words at the prison had filled her with regrets and second guesses. Then, Davis Hill filled her mind. Of all things her mind could have gone to, she thought of the night they'd made love.

Her first time had been awkward and almost impersonal. It'd been with one of her classmates. They'd gone out a few times and she hadn't been able to come up with a reason not to sleep with him. He'd been a nice enough guy. Not the best of reasons, but she didn't have any real regrets about it.

With Davis, she'd felt like a virgin all over again. Just thinking about his kisses heated her blood. He'd let her know without speaking a word that he belonged to her that night. He'd been hers and only hers. No one would ever make her feel like Davis had again. That wasn't possible because there was only one Davis.

Then there was her first and only serious boyfriend. The guy who'd asked her to marry him a few weeks before graduation. He'd been nice enough during the "on" parts of their on-again off-again relationship. But she'd never really felt a click with him. The sex hadn't been great with him, either, although it hadn't been as horrible as it had with the first guy.

Davis was the only one who seemed to want to give more than he wanted to take. Making love with him had been a mistake. The memories of that night were making it almost impossible to stay focused on what was best for her—for both of them, really.

"It's not good to want a self-destructive person who almost destroyed me, too." Jemma said it out loud, as if that would make the words sink in better.

She scrubbed at a spot on the side of the tub long after it was gone. And after her arm ached with the effort. Until her arm lay trembling and uncooperative against the side of the tub. Then she pressed her hot face to the cool ceramic and cried again.

Why did she want what she couldn't have, and shouldn't want in the first place because it was bad for her? She wanted him so badly that forcing herself toward the right choice made her nauseous. Spending all of that time with him hadn't been a good idea. But she wouldn't have changed a moment for anything in the world—well, except maybe for the last, few sad ones.

After she finished cleaning, Jemma went back to her room to finish packing. She checked through the drawers of the dressers and desks to make sure she hadn't left anything behind. That was how she spotted her scrapbook in the bottom dresser drawer.

"Hmm. How'd I miss this?" She took the book over to the bed with her and lay it on the bedspread. She ran her hands over the red and white cover. Without really wanting to, but not being able to stop herself, she turned to the section it most hurt to look at. Her eyes fell on a picture of Davis's Acura, and she slammed the book shut.

She folded her body close to the window and rested her forehead on the windowpane. She sat like that for a long time. And eventually came to the conclusion that as much as she'd tried to deny it to herself, Mary was right. She was running again.

Later, still staring out of that window long after her neck was stiff and sore, she realized that the solution she'd come to was a bad one.

The next morning, Jemma stared at the phone. She knew what she had to do, but that didn't make her any less afraid to do it.

Finally, with a heavy sigh, she picked up the phone and dialed a number.

A tart voice greeted her from the other end. "Dale, Bigby, and Associates."

"Hi, Amerie. This is Jemma," she said to the receptionist she remembered from her summers at Dale Bigby. "Can I speak to Dana?"

She fought not to talk herself out of it while she waited to be connected to Dana.

"Dana Marks." Her crisp, assertive tone came through the line so clearly that Jemma almost looked around the room to see if Dana was in the room with her.

"This is Jemma. I'm really sorry, but . . . I'm not going to be able to take the position."

"You're kidding. You're supposed to start in three days. We were expecting a new assistant director in three days."

"I know, but I've had—well, something's come up. An emergency. And I can't move to Florida now. I'll do whatever I can to help you through telecommuting until you can find a replacement."

"Jemma, this is really disappointing."

"I know." Jemma winced. Dana was the type of person who could make you feel worthless without breaking a sweat.

After a terrifying conversation with Dana, which mostly consisted of Jemma apologizing several different ways, she was exhausted. She went back to bed, not wanting to face the fact that she had thrown away the new life she'd spent so much time and effort building for herself.

Jemma had found the courage to own up to what she wanted and, more than that, to go after it.

She waved to Ayn when she got out of the car, calling out in a cheery voice, "Hi, Ayn."

"Hey." Ayn waved back, looking over Jemma's ensemble. Jemma still wore pink pajama bottoms and a white tank top along with her running shoes. She hadn't taken time to change before heading to Davis's.

Her smile finally faded once she thought no one would answer her knocks on the door. She almost turned away when the front door opened. An attractive, slim woman resembling Davis stood there, peering at her. She had to be Lydia.

"You must be Davis's mom," Jemma said.

"You must be Jemma." A worried smile flitted across the woman's face. She twisted her wedding ring around her finger a few times.

"You know who I am?" She hadn't thought about Davis telling his mom about her. It hadn't crossed her mind. Especially after the way she'd left him the last time she'd come to his house.

Lydia glanced behind her and then turned back to Jemma, something in her face having changed. "Of course. Come in, honey. He's inside." She seemed unsure about every word she spoke, but Jemma didn't understand why until she walked into the house.

CHAPTER 30

Jemma stopped cold at the look Davis gave her. It was the closest thing to a look of pure hatred she'd ever seen on his face, and it hurt to have it directed at her.

"What are you doing here?" he asked, no warmth in his voice at all.

"I'm staying. I want to be here. I want to be with you," she said.

He just stared at her. Her words had no impact on him at all. She hadn't made a mistake. She couldn't afford to think that way.

Lydia startled Jemma. She hadn't realized the woman was still in the room. "I'll be outside. You two should have some time alone."

Jemma nodded. After Lydia walked away, she turned back to Davis and watched his face carefully. Even scruffy and unwashed, he was beautiful to her. But the look on his face wasn't beautiful at all.

"You were right before. It could never work," Davis said.

She reached out to touch his face, but he pulled away. "No. I wasn't. We can't control life, but we should cherish what we have while we have it. I'm sorry for the crazy way I've acted. I have . . . issues. I know. But I want to try to make this work. If you'll try with me."

Her heart pounded in her chest as she watched him. Not so much as one muscle twitched in his face. It couldn't be too late. She'd finally realized that he was all that mattered and she couldn't be too late. Just couldn't be.

Finally, he looked away from her and said, "It's done, Jemma. You should have gotten on that train this morning."

She grabbed his hand. "No. We're so close to all we've ever wanted and I won't let you throw it away. Track ten, Davis. Lenny Kravitz. The CD I burned for you. Remember? I need you."

"Nobody needs me. I'm nothing but a waste." Davis's shoulders slumped and he pulled his hand away.

"Wrong. You're everything. Everything, anything, and the only thing that matters. You have to understand that. That night at the lake house. The nights we spent together here. Us making love. That was all I've ever needed. My heart is filled with you. I am filled with you. Every part of me."

Davis looked away, but not before she saw a misery in his eyes that hurt her. "I can't give you what you need. I'm Bill all over again. I mean, the other day when you came over and I was pickled drunk? That wasn't proof enough for you?"

She took a step forward, but didn't try to touch him again. "You're not. You're worth so much more than that. I—"

"No, Jemma. It's done."

A sharp pain hit her stomach. "It feels like I'm dying."

"I don't want to be with you."

"Why would you say something like that?"

Davis shrugged. "I'm an asshole. An unemployed drunk. Just move on. Go."

"I know the time we spent together meant something to you. We both do. You're lying if you say it didn't."

"I can't put up with this anymore. We were both right, just at different times. We really were broken from the start. And nothing can trump that. We were always a bad idea."

"Romeo and Juliet were a bad idea in the eyes of some."

"Well, they both ended up dead, didn't they?"

"Davis, no. Don't do this."

"Jemma, yes."

He turned his back to her and refused to say another word. After pleading with his retreating form as he went up the stairs, she gave up and made her way to the front door. His mother stood in the front yard. Jemma shuffled past her and toward the sidewalk.

She blocked the driver's side door to Mary's car. "Jemma, honey, can we talk for a moment?" Her kind blue eyes searched Jemma's face in a pleading manner. Davis's eyes.

"I don't know what there could be to talk about." Jemma sniffed back tears. "Davis just said all there is to say."

"Please."

"Ms. Hill, I—"

"Randall, but call me Lydia."

"Lydia, then—"

"What would it hurt for you to hear me out? All you have to do is listen. If you don't like what I say, I'll walk back into that house and you'll never have to hear from me again."

Jemma studied the chipped nail of her index finger as she considered Lydia's words. Something inside of her relented because she still felt too much for Davis. What she felt threatened to overtake her resolve to walk away, but she stayed. Despite everything that'd happened, she wanted to hear what Lydia had to say.

"Okay." She folded her arms over her chest.

Lydia nodded. A smile broke out over her fair features. "He's trying to push you away, isn't he?"

Jemma stared over Lydia's shoulder.

"He didn't mean it. There's no way I can undo whatever my son did in there, but I know he thinks this is for the best. He thinks you won't get hurt anymore if he pushes you away. He's good at that. Pushing people away is his answer for everything." She put a hand on Jemma's arm. "But from what I've seen, and what I'm seeing now, it seems that both of you are hurting more like this."

"He seemed pretty sure he wanted me out of his life a few minutes ago." Jemma nodded toward the house.

"He's miserable. Which he is a lot of the time, I know. But I found him asleep on the couch last night and he was talking to you in his sleep. He was asking you not to go—not to leave him. And you know what else? The look on his face when he first saw you just now. That's the most life I've seen in him since I got here."

"He was probably alive with the hatred he feels for me now."

"No, Jemma. I've been around for a while. I've seen a lot of people give a lot of looks. Plenty of those looks were none too nice. He was alive with something else in that living room. Sure wasn't hate."

"Even if what you say is true, and even if he wanted my help, it's not my job to save him," Jemma said. She purposefully ignored the fact that he'd been a different person during the time they'd spent together. He'd seemed lighter and freer—maybe happier than she'd ever seen him before.

"It's not your job to love him, either. But you do."

"I'm tired of fighting with him." She pressed her palm to her face and wiped tears from the corner of her eye. "One of us is always messing up, so maybe it's not meant to be. If we were meant to be together, it wouldn't be so hard for us to feel the same way at the same time. Our love is destructive." She shook her head. "No one should be in a relationship that makes them this crazy."

"You really believe that, Jemma?"

She shrugged. "Yeah." She had to.

"Then why'd you come here today?" Lydia flipped her hair over her shoulders.

"Apparently, I'm a slow learner."

"I'm afraid for both of you if you really believe that."

"Why?"

"He's disintegrating and you remind me so much of myself. Not the love part—Bill and I—well, that's another story for another day. But the running away part. Take it from an old pro. Running never solves anything. You always end up right back where you started from. And usually worse off than the first time around."

"I'm not going anywhere. I decided not to go to Florida. I'm not running."

"You're not? You can avoid your problems, avoid dealing with them, without leaving town."

"Nope. I'm not." She'd visited Lynette and Demonte's graves. She'd gone back to the apartment complex. She cried. She'd thrown the fit she needed to throw. She'd made her peace. Mary had been there for her just as before. And the one in the house behind Lydia had been there for her, too, but that was done now. "There's nothing here for me to avoid. Nothing at all."

"Davis is here."

"Davis doesn't have anything to do with me. Nor does he want to."

"You know he does. Just look at the way you try not to flinch every time I say his name. You look so sad. Just like him."

"What does it matter if he doesn't want me? Why should I torture myself thinking about him?" Jemma suddenly burst out.

Before Lydia could respond, their attention was drawn to the sound of something heavy clattering against wood. They looked toward the direction of the sound.

Ayn picked something up from the porch and scampered into her house.

Jemma looked up at the window to Davis's room, wondering if he was in there at that moment. Thinking about the nights that she'd spent up there.

"Don't give up on him. Please." Lydia put a hand on Jemma's arm.

"I don't think I have a choice," Jemma said softly.

"He'll come around." Lydia opened the car door for her.

"I doubt it." Jemma got into the car. She rested her head against the steering wheel for a moment before she could pull herself together enough to drive away.

CHAPTER 31

Jemma went back to Mary's house and walked straight to her room. Mary followed her. She threw herself across the bed, ignoring Mary's unasked questions. Even though Jemma's face was pressed to the bedspread, she knew Mary was standing in the doorway.

Mary finally broke the silence. "I knew something was funny when I woke up and my car was gone and your suitcases were still here."

Jemma shrugged, still face-down on the bed.

"I thought you were leaving today."

Jemma turned her head to the side so she could answer Mary. Her tone was wobbly and dead as she talked around the sob that seemed to have taken up permanent residence in her throat. "I'm not. Not Derring, anyway. I'll start looking for an apartment and a job tomorrow, I guess."

"You know that apartment thing is not necessary. It's not even going to happen. You're going to stay right here with me or else hurt my feelings something terrible."

Jemma looked over her shoulder. Mary didn't look smug. She didn't look anything.

Jemma said, "I decided maybe you were right about some things."

"Was I right about Davis?" Mary took a few steps into the room.

"I dunno." She clearly didn't know anything when it came to him.

"I guess things didn't go so well."

"Yeah. That's pretty much done. He needs someone who's not like me. And I need someone who's not . . . like him. I knew it all along. I should have listened to myself."

Mary gave her a pointed look, but didn't say anything. She just walked out of the room and down the hall.

Jemma called Emily Rose Saturday afternoon. That was after she'd spent a good while on the phone fighting with her landlord in Florida to get out of the lease. She'd then lain in bed, staring at the wall and second-guessing every decision she'd made since not getting on the train. Although she knew she'd made the right decision, it was hard for her to see how and why it was the right decision.

Finally she decided to stop feeling sorry for herself and to talk to the person who would understand better than anyone else what'd happened.

Jemma poured the whole story out to Emily Rose. She felt better when she got out the last word about leaving Lydia standing there, staring after her as she drove away.

"That is—I don't even have words. I should be there with you right now."

"That's my life for you. Now Davis doesn't want anything to do with me, I have no job, and I still can't believe I'm staying. I don't know what I'm going to do with myself."

"Do you regret any of what happened?"

Jemma thought about that for a moment. She wondered if Lydia had been right and if it mattered whether she was or not. Regardless, Davis was not going to be in her life any longer. He was probably right about them being bad for each other. Still, she was glad she'd had a few perfect days with him.

She slowly shook her head although she knew Emily Rose couldn't see her doing it. "You know what's weird? I don't. Not one moment. I'm glad I had the time with him that I did. And I'm glad I decided to stay in Derring. I want to be here. I wanted to go to Jacksonville for all the wrong reasons."

"You know what I learned on my wedding day?"

"What?"

"Love is stronger than stubbornness."

"That supposed to make me think Davis and I aren't done? Because we are. He made his decision. He's probably right."

"You say that now."

"Yeah," Jemma said, not wanting to talk about it anymore. "How's New York? You like the apartment?"

"It's fabulous. Huge. Well, for a one-bedroom in Manhattan, anyway. You'll have to come visit soon. We have a futon and you'll have to sleep there, but it'll be fine. We'll have so much fun." Emily Rose went on to gush about the apartment more and more and Jemma was safe from any more talk about Davis.

Losing him for the last time was bittersweet. And no, she didn't regret it. She'd meant that. But still, there was the pain of knowing she could never have again the thing she wanted most in the world. What Michael and Emily Rose had. And Meg and her fiancé. The thing she'd had at the winery. Not having it wouldn't kill her. But losing it wouldn't be easy to survive, either. One step at a time. One moment at a time. Wasn't the first step admitting there was a problem? And she'd done that.

Emily Rose was wrong about one thing. Love was poison—a dangerous drug. She was addicted to something very bad for her that felt so good and she knew she couldn't have that thing anymore. Learning to take seriously that promise she'd made to stay away from love was going to be a painful yet necessary process.

After taking Mary to work Sunday night, Jemma sat in the living room, staring at the dead television screen. There was nothing she wanted to see. To do. She just wanted to sit there and try not to think about all the no's. No money, no job, no life, no desire to have one.

She must not have heard the knocking at first because when it did register, it was quite insistent and impatient. As if the person knocking had been at it a while and would knock the door down if she didn't answer it soon.

With a heavy sigh, she got up, muttering about having no idea who would come there at nearly midnight. She looked through the peephole, saw Davis's face, and collapsed against the door. She was so weak with shock, she couldn't move enough to open it.

"Jemma?"

She opened her mouth, but nothing came out.

He must have taken her silence to mean she was angry or reluctant to see him because he said, "I need you. I've been a huge idiot asshole about all of this."

She pressed her palm against the door.

"I thought you'd be better off without me. But now I see that neither one of us is better off like that. Us being together is the most important thing. You were right about that." He paused for a moment and then said, "Haven't you figured it out yet? I'd do anything for you. I can't even think of what life was before I knew you. Did any time before you came back into my life exist? It certainly didn't matter. I don't wanna think about what it'll be like when you're gone again. Because I don't want you to be gone again. You are me. Without you, I'm just Davis. And that's not enough."

Jemma pressed her trembling fingers to her lips.

"Remember that day? You probably don't remember. I bet you didn't even see me, come to think of it. It was back in high school. You were spending the night with Emily Rose and I was there to pick Tara up for a date. You were so perfect to me. It almost broke my heart to look at you. I loved you so much in that moment. I knew that no matter what came between us, my heart would always be chained to you."

She opened the door.

Davis stood before her, his blue eyes bright with unshed tears. "I wanted you. I wanted to run my fingers across the smooth, brown skin of your arms. To pull you close and bury my face in your hair. To tell you that no one and nothing could ever change how I felt about you. Twirling that lock of hair in your fingers, dancing around in that orange tank top, not knowing you were stealing my heart. Unconscious beauty. That's part of what's always made you so perfect to me."

Finally, Jemma swallowed the lump down in her throat enough to speak. "I'm nowhere close to—"

"I said perfect to me. That's all that matters."

Those words nearly brought Jemma to her knees.

"You are the light inside of me where it's dark and almost dead. Even when I don't want to admit it. This love is oppressive. But in a good way."

"So, you want me to believe that love is magic and that after all of this, we can be together? We can be happy?" Jemma wanted to believe even as she spoke the words. "Just yesterday, you didn't seem to believe that yourself."

"I know I hurt you. I know you're sad. But if you don't come back to me, I might be stuck inside this mean, small person I am forever. I'm asking you to save me this one last time. I'm hoping your heart's big enough to fold me inside of it, flaws and ugliness and all. I can't promise that I'll never be a jerk again. But I can promise that I'll never leave your side again."

"You can really promise me that?"

"I want you to marry me, Jemma. I don't know how I could make a more legit promise to be with you always than that."

"You want me to what?"

He smiled. "Be my wife. Be with me always."

"Like Tara was?"

Davis looked away and his smile faltered. "That was a mistake. I told you that. It's always been you. I don't know how I can make you see that, but I promise to spend the rest of my life finding a way. And making up for all the bad I've done to you."

"I loved you with all of my heart, Davis, and it nearly killed me. Twice."

"And now? Could you love me now?" Davis moved forward and wrapped his arms around her. She didn't fight it, but she didn't hug back, either.

"I never stopped. But giving into it again . . . I need to be sure. Really, really sure."

"I know." He kissed the top of her head. "Let's go get our ring. Set a date. Please, tell me what I have to do to keep you. Don't tell me there's nothing I can do. Like last time. I won't believe that."

She put her arms around him and ran her hands up and down his back. "I don't want a long engagement. We get married Labor Day weekend."

"Done."

"And you tell Mary."

"I already have. I went to see her at the store because I knew I wasn't going to lose you this time without a fight. The fight of my life for the love of my life."

She pulled back a little and studied his face, trying to put words together in her head. His teeth closed over his lower lip and the corners of his mouth turned up in a grin. He took her hand. "Let's go."

She let him pull her along. "Where we going?"

"The jewelry store."

"The jewelry store won't be open for hours."

He shrugged. His eyes shone in a way she hadn't seen in ages. That light was her undoing. "We'll be the first customers of the day."

"You're nuts," she said. "Hold on, I have to get my stuff." She ran into her room, grabbed her purse, and ran out of the house with him. She paused only to lock the front door. Even though Mary's house was surrounded by the woods and her closest neighbor was a few miles away, Jemma felt better with the door locked.

They clambered down the steps, managing to not trip over each other most of the way to the car.

"It's hard to believe yesterday happened right now," she said as they got in the car.

His face grew serious and he took her hands, lacing their fingers together. "I wish it hadn't."

"What happened between then and now?"

"I've done a lot of talking with a lot of people in a short amount of time." He kissed her fingers. "A long talk with Lydia. A little soul-searching. A talk with Mary, too. I called Cole and talked with him, and Codie, too. I realized how right everyone was but me." He looked at her with soulful eyes. "And I thought a lot about how horrible life without you really is."

She kissed his cheek.

He rested his forehead against hers. "You were right. I've been holding back."

She squeezed his hands.

"Bill was never easy to live with, but I think I started to understand him by the end." He told her about Pennsylvania, the party he'd gotten drunk at the night he screwed up his knee, living with Cole and getting kicked out of his house, and moving back in with Bill. He told her everything. About his drunken appearance at Bill's funeral. All that'd happened after. Right up until the moment his brothers and mother had come into town and all that happened as a result of that. He ended by telling her that his brothers had gone back to Pennsylvania after promising to bring their families down for many visits in the future.

When he was done talking, she reached up and kissed him softly, linking her fingers behind his neck. And then they made love in the car because they knew they'd never make it back inside the house. They needed each other too much to allow that to happen.

They drove around for the rest of the night with the windows down, letting the heavy yet cool air into the car. They talked and laughed about everything and nothing, just wanting to hear the sound of each other's voices. Their hands remained locked together over the console the entire time.

They were indeed the first customers at the jewelry store that morning. The owner was holding his morning coffee and yawning when they got out of the car and met him at the door, holding hands. He froze, holding the key in front of the lock to the door. His bulbous nose made the rest of his face look small in comparison.

"Hi, Mr. Ennes," Jemma said. He was one of two jewelers in Derring, and he'd been there all of Jemma's life.

"Morning." He nodded at both of them, his expression remaining bemused and foggy with sleep. He'd never been a morning person.

"Can we come in?"

He unlocked the door and pushed it open. Then he made the wise move of stepping back so that he was not bowled over by the overenthusiastic couple.

"We need a ring," Davis said to Mr. Ennes, but his eyes remained on her.

Mr. Ennes ran a hand over his graying hair. "Um, well, I, uh, I'm not really open yet. Just got here. Store opens at nine . . ." He looked down at his watch.

Jemma looked at her cell phone screen. It was a little past eight thirty.

"I know it's early, but we just got engaged and we have to have a ring." Davis kissed Jemma's bare hand and then held it up for emphasis.

Mr. Ennes gave a slight smile. He locked the door and headed over to the counter. "Congratulations, you two. Let's see what I have here."

Jemma and Davis picked the perfect ring together, thanked Mr. Ennes, and left.

"Let's go show it to Mary. And then your mom," Jemma said, staring down at the ring.

He kissed her cheek. "Whatever you want."

She smiled. They put their arms around each other and walked to the car.

CHAPTER 32

Emily Rose shrieked into her ear for a good five minutes when Jemma called to tell her. She scolded Jemma for not calling her the minute it happened—even though she'd been the first person Jemma called—for all of five seconds before devolving into squeals about wedding plans.

"So have you guys set a date yet?" Emily Rose asked when she calmed down enough to use full sentences again.

"Yeah. We're doing it Labor Day weekend."

"This year?"

"Yeah, in less than two months."

"Jemma, that is not enough time. Do you know nothing about weddings?"

"I know I don't want a big one. I don't want all the fancy stuff. That was never me. I just want Davis."

"Well, you're at least having a reception."

"Who's gonna plan it?"

"Who do you think?"

"You're in New York. Don't you have a job?"

"Not yet. I think I'm going to end up subbing this year after all. Anyway, what's more important than you and Davis getting married? This is huge. I have to tell everyone I know."

Jemma laughed. "With you on the case, I'll save a lot of money on invitations."

"Leave it to me and Mom. You won't be sorry."

"I believe it."

"Great. I gotta go. I gotta tell Michael, I gotta tell Mom. Have you told Mom yet? Even if you have, I still have to call her. We have a reception to plan. You haven't given us much time!"

Jemma held her phone to her chest after she ended the call and smiled.

Jemma and Davis had asked the Bradens if they could have their reception at the lake house, and they'd been overjoyed. Emily Rose said she'd almost died from how romantic it was for them to have it there. Their only request in return was that they have the wedding there, too, instead of at town hall. Eventually, Jemma agreed.

Jemma hadn't wanted a big wedding, and, for the most part, she'd won on that. Lydia had insisted on redesigning her wedding dress and giving it to Jemma as something old. Lydia had her sister send the dress from her storage unit in Colorado to Lydia in Virginia. She'd shortened and updated it so that it was way better than anything Jemma could have gotten from a store. Lydia had done a great job, and Jemma thought she should go into business for herself as a seamstress. Lydia had been too modest to take her seriously.

The dress was simple, silk and form-fitting. It hit just below Jemma's knees. It had spaghetti straps. The top was bodice-like, but not too constricting. Jemma cried the first time she tried it on.

The night before the wedding, Jemma, Emily Rose, and Mrs. Braden set up a few things on the beach so that they'd have less to do the next day. They were putting out the chairs, hanging a few decorations, and preparing some other things that wouldn't get destroyed by being outside overnight.

Emily Rosé said as she handed Jemma a chair, "Things really came together, huh?"

"Yeah." Jemma took the chair, unfolded it, and set it in the sand. "Thanks. I don't know that I'd be here without you. And I don't even want to think about not being here."

"No thanks needed. You're happy and that's all that matters." She hugged Jemma. "After all the years of— well, the important thing is you're really happy. And that means so much to me."

"Ugh. I'm gonna cry again. Why can't I stop?"

They laughed.

Things were so good. She'd decided to freelance for Dale Bigby until she could decide whether she wanted to look for a marketing job or start her own business as a consultant. She'd felt kind of horrible leaving them stranded like she had, and a lot of the things they needed help with could be done via telecommuting. Dana had been thrilled about the idea, and that was a huge relief. With everything falling into place, she finally felt peace.

Happiness. She finally felt like she didn't have to be on the defensive just to survive.

"Here they come," Emily Rose said.

Jemma smiled at the loud group coming toward them, singing a song she didn't recognize. Davis's brothers, Michael, and Seth were stealing him for the night so that bride and groom could keep the tradition of not seeing each other before the wedding. Davis was in the middle of the group, and he was the loudest and most obnoxious singer of the five.

"Yeah." She couldn't believe there'd been a time, and not so long ago, when she hadn't realized he was everything she needed.

He pulled Jemma aside and into a long, wonderfully suffocating kiss.

"I'm gonna miss you so much," he whispered into her hair.

"We're gonna see each other in a few hours." Jemma wrapped her arms around his waist, smiling.

"Yeah, but those are going to be really, really long hours."

"You're right."

"Hours? I can't do this." He bent down and brushed his lips against hers.

She pulled him to her in a deep kiss.

"Okay, if I don't leave right now, I don't know if I'll be able to." He gave her a last quick kiss and then pulled away. "I can't wait until tomorrow."

"Me, either."

"Parting is such sweet sorrow," he said with a wink. They laughed. "But we won't end up dead any time soon."

"Thank you for making me happier than I've ever been, Romeo."

"Thank you for giving me all the chances I needed to get it right, Juliet."

"Okay. Now get going." She blew him air kisses and waved him away.

He caught every single kiss, backing to the spot where his brothers and Seth stood, shouting for him to hurry up.

They went to a bar near the motel where they were going to spend the night. Davis hadn't wanted a bachelor party, but they insisted on "at least one drink." He knew what that meant. For them, anyway. He ordered a Coke.

Seth sat next to Davis at their table. "I guess I'm earning my keep, huh?" He laughed.

"If you say so," Davis said, laughter rippling through his words. Seth was handling the sale of the house. Davis was keeping his house. Better than that, his brothers were signing it over completely to him. By the time he got back from his honeymoon, the papers would be ready and he'd sign, making him the sole owner. Lydia was going to stay there as long as she needed to. That was good since they were still trying to get to know each other. And they still had some rough spots to work through in their relationship.

He didn't care too much where he was or what he was doing, though, as long as Jemma was with him. He'd really lucked out with her. After all he'd put her through, she still hadn't given up on him. Thank goodness for that because she meant the world to him. She always had. He planned to make sure she knew that all day every day for the rest of their days.

"I say so. Now, we just have to get you a job," Seth said.

"Yeah. Know any magic?" Davis had burned just about all his bridges in Derring County when it came to employment.

"No, but I know a guy. Friend of mine who works over at Parks and Rec. They're thinking of starting up a lacrosse division. They could use a good coach."

"Yeah, but that's a part-time thing, right?"

"You didn't let me finish. I think you should go back to school."

"You do?" He'd never really thought about it before.

"Yeah. Why not? Coach high school lacrosse. We've needed a real coach at Derring High ever since your old coach retired. Ever think about that?"

"No," Davis said slowly.

"Maybe you should."

He turned his glass in circles on the table and watched the condensation pool on the table's lacquered black surface. "Yeah. Maybe I should." He sat back in the booth and looked around at the faces of his brothers, Michael, and Seth. "You have a card? For that Parks and Rec guy?"

"Not on me, but come by my office as soon as you get back from your trip."

"Will do," Davis said. He took a sip of his drink and sucked up an ice cube to chew on. "Definitely."

"Good."

"And thanks again. For the loan," Davis said. He'd borrowed money from Seth to pay for his honeymoon trip.

"Yeah, you keep calling it a loan, but it's a gift. A wedding gift. And if you ever try to pay me back, I'm not taking the money."

Davis grinned. "I know you were joking earlier, but you've more than earned your keep."

He shrugged. "I have three daughters. I love 'em to death, but it's nice to have a son sometimes, too."

He laughed, throwing an arm around Seth. "Works for me."

CHAPTER 33

Jemma managed to smile at all the familiar faces smiling back at her. Her stomach churned with nerves, and walking down the aisle on sand was no easy task even in low-heeled sandals. Despite her nerves and the sand, seeing the faces of the people who meant most to her warmed her heart. Emily Rose, Wendell, Lydia, and even Davis's brothers. And of course Mary. Mary was right next to her, as a matter of fact, giving her away.

Jemma looked next to Davis where Codie stood. She was Davis's best man or woman or whatever. She wore a slinky silver dress that worked well on her small form. She smiled at Jemma and mouthed that she was so happy. Jemma smiled back.

After Mary gave her away, Jemma's world became Davis. It was a good thing they were having a DVD made because she missed her entire wedding, lost in Davis's eyes. Still not able to believe it was happening. She had to be prompted to say "I do" and she stumbled all over her vows. Davis thought it was adorable and said so in his vows, which were the only part of the ceremony she was able to concentrate on. Well, besides the kiss, of course.

"I want you to know I've never been happier and my life is perfect now," Davis said as they headed back down the aisle through the clapping, shouting throngs.

Jemma nodded, unable to think of a thing to say. She smiled and waved and laughed and enjoyed her moment.

The reception was mostly on the deck of the lake house and in the sand below, but people milled in and out of the house. Jemma and Davis danced their first dance to "Just Like Heaven" in the living room, even though it wasn't exactly slow enough for a first song at a wedding reception. Nothing about getting them to that point had been conventional, so they didn't see the point in trying to start being conventional with their first dance.

Afterward, Jemma danced until her feet were numb. She was glad she had remembered to bring her flip-flops along. She danced with everyone at the reception, it seemed. Carolina grabbed her after a few songs.

While they danced, Carolina said, "Did Em Rose tell you? The audition went great—I got the callback and things are looking good for me getting picked up for the tour."

"That's fantastic. Congrats," Jemma said, happy that things had worked out well for Carolina, too.

"I'm so happy for us." Carolina stopped dancing and grabbed Jemma's shoulders. "I'm glad we both figured out which dreams were worth fighting for and went after them."

"Me, too." Jemma felt tears coming on yet again. She fanned her face with her hands.

They hugged.

Jemma, Emily Rose, and Carolina danced to several songs. Then the music changed, and they returned her to the groom. Later, surprise of all surprises, Stephanie asked to cut in with Wendell standing right next to her.

Stephanie kissed her cheek. "You're glowing. I'm so happy for you. Really."

"Thank you." Jemma said, tears threatening to spill over for the thousandth time that day. Stephanie took Davis's hands and Wendell took Jemma's.

"I'm happy for you," Wendell said. "I really mean that."

"Thank you."

"He finally got his act together for you, huh?"

"I think we got our acts together for each other," Jemma said.

"Good," he said. "Remember when we were kids and you used to write Mrs. Jemma L. Hill all over your notebooks?"

She laughed. "Shut up."

"Well, you can do it for real now." He grinned. "Congrats."

She looked up at him as the song ended, her arms still around him. "Thanks."

"Of course."

Wendell went back to Stephanie and Davis grabbed Jemma.

"I love you, Mrs. Hill," Davis said, his arm tightening around her waist.

"Love you, too." She grinned, thinking of what Wendell had said earlier. "Hmm. So nice to hear that."

"Nice to say it, too." Davis pressed his chin to the top of her head. "Who would have seen all this six years ago?"

"I'm just happy we've all come as far as we have," Jemma said. She smiled, looking around the room.

Emily Rose and Michael danced. Emily Rose's head rested on Michael's shoulder, and he held her close. Cole and his wife sat with their arms around each other, whispering to each other and smiling. Ashby danced with his daughter, her tiny feet on top of his shoes. His wife watched the two of them with a look of adoration on her face. Codie sat next to her date, the two of them laughing about something. Carolina flirted with Wendell's friend, Brad. He'd come to the wedding with him and Stephanie. Brad and Carolina had been inseparable for most of the evening.

Mary sat at a table with a couple of friends. When Jemma looked at her, Mary gave her a huge grin and two thumbs up. Jemma laughed, nodding at Mary. Her mother.

After the dance, they went back to their table. Jemma dropped onto Davis's lap, careful to put her weight on his left thigh. "I'm completely wiped."

Davis put his arm around her. "That makes two of us. Wanna get outta here?"

"Yeah." She rested her arms on his shoulders. "You still haven't told me where we're going yet."

He winked at her. "I know."

"It better be somewhere great."

"It is. Don't you worry."

"Well, let's get out of here so I can find out for myself."

She stood up and reached out for Davis's hands, which he gave, and together they pulled him to his feet.

Codie ran a hand through her dark hair, grinning up at them. "You two headed out?"

"Yeah. Codie, thanks." His face grew solemn, and he gave her a meaningful look. "For everything. Always."

"You know I wouldn't have it any other way," Codie said, standing and patting his arm. She looked at Jemma. "You got a good one. He's a handful, but a good one."

Jemma smiled. "I know. Thanks for being such a good friend to him."

"Yeah, well, you know you're stuck with me now, too, right? I don't see myself as losing a Davis. I'm gaining a Jemma."

"Good." Jemma laughed.

"Well, I guess I should let you two crazy kids in love go."

"We'll call you when we get there," Davis said. He was good at keeping their destination a secret. Jemma had been listening closely, hoping he'd slip and give it away while talking to Codie, but no such luck.

"Okay. Now get outta here." Codie waved them off.

They started walking toward the kitchen to find Mrs. Braden.

Lydia rushed up to them. "Where are you two going?"

"Getting out of here," Davis said, running a hand over his hair and looking around at the laughing, carousing guests. "You guys are having plenty of fun without us, and we have a long day ahead of us before our flight tomorrow evening."

"Flight?" Jemma turned to him, wondering what he was up to.

He grinned and squeezed her shoulders.

"Oh, yes. That's right," Lydia said. A knowing look passed between mother and son. "We have to finish up here then." Lydia grabbed Jemma and whisked her away from Davis, stuffing her bouquet into her hands. Jemma looked back at Davis helplessly and he shrugged, his hands up in the air.

After the bouquet tossing, garter belt throwing, well-wishing, and car vandalizing, Jemma and Davis were finally on their way out of there.

"So where are we going?" Jemma asked, curling against his side. His arm went around her.

"Right now? To a hotel in D.C."

"What? I don't have anything packed."

"Sure you do. Mary slipped a bag in the trunk for you earlier."

Jemma squeezed his waist. "I don't even get a clue about tomorrow?"

Davis kissed the top of her head. "Not one."

"This could be dangerous. For you, I mean. If I don't like it."

He laughed. "You'll like it. Really."

Jemma held her left hand in front of her face and admired the two rings there. The man they linked her to was worth more than both of them put together.

The next evening, on the shuttle from the airport hotel parking lot, Davis handed her a ticket, along with

ABOUT THE AUTHOR

Nicole Green is a graduate of the University of Virginia. She is also a graduate of the College of William and Mary's Law School. She currently resides in Arlington, Virginia. She is a member of SCBWI and the Virginia Romance Writers Chapter of RWA. You can visit her online at her blog: http://lisezvous.blogspot.com or her website: http.www.nicolegreenauthor.com. She would love to hear from you.

2011 Mass Market Titles

January

From This Moment
Sean Young
ISBN-13: 978-1-58571-383-7
ISBN-10: 1-58571-383-X
$6.99

Nihon Nights
Trisha/Monica Haddad
ISBN-13: 978-1-58571-382-0
ISBN-10: 1-58571-382-1
$6.99

February

The Davis Years
Nicole Green
ISBN-13: 978-1-58571-390-5
ISBN-10: 1-58571-390-2
$6.99

Allegro
Adora Bennett
ISBN-13: 978-158571-391-2
ISBN-10: 1-58571-391-0
$6.99

March

Lies in Disguise
Bernice Layton
ISBN-13: 978-1-58571-392-9
ISBN-10: 1-58571-392-9
$6.99

Steady
Ruthie Robinson
ISBN-13: 978-1-58571-393-6
ISBN-10: 1-58571-393-7
$6.99

April

The Right Maneuver
LaShell Stratton-Childers
ISBN-13: 978-1-58571-394-3
ISBN-10: 1-58571-394-5
$6.99

Riding the Corporate Ladder
Keith Walker
ISBN-13: 978-1-58571-395-0
ISBN-10: 1-58571-395-3
$6.99

May

Separate Dreams
Joan Early
ISBN-13: 978-1-58571-434-6
ISBN-10: 1-58571-434-8
$6.99

I Take This Woman
Chamein Canton
ISBN-13: 978-1-58571-435-3
ISBN-10: 1-58571-435-6
$6.99

June

Doesn't Really Matter
Keisha Mennefee
ISBN-13: 978-1-58571-434-0
ISBN-10: 1-58571-436-4
$6.99

Inside Out
Grayson Cole
ISBN-13: 978-1-58571-437-7
ISBN-10: 1-58571-437-2
$6.99

2011 Mass Market Titles (continued)
July

Rehoboth Road
Anita Ballard-Jones
ISBN-13: 978-1-58571-438-4
ISBN-10: 1-58571-438-0
$12.95

Holding Her Breath
Nicole Green
ISBN-13: 978-1-58571-439-1
ISBN-10: 1-58571-439-9
$6.99

August

The Sea of Aaron
Kymberly Hunt
ISBN-13: 978-1-58571-440-7
ISBN-10: 1-58571-440-2
$6.99

The Finley Sisters' Oath of
    Romance
Keith Thomas Walker
ISBN-13: 978-1-58571-441-4
ISBN-10: 1-58571-441-0
$6.99

September

Except on Sunday
Regena Bryant
ISBN-13: 978-1-58571-443-8
ISBN-10: 1-58571-443-7
$6.99

Light's Out
Ruthie Robinson
ISBN-13: 978-1-58571-445-2
ISBN-10: 1-58571-445-3
$6.99

October

The Heart Knows
Renee Wynn
ISBN-13: 978-1-58571-444-5
ISBN-10: 1-58571-444-5
$6.99

Giving It Up
Dyanne Davis
ISBN-13: 978-1-58571-446-9
ISBN-10: 1-58571-446-1
$6.99

November

All I Do
Keisha Mennefee
ISBN-13: 978-1-58571-447-6
ISBN-10: 1-58571-447-X
$6.99

A Love Built to Last
L. S. Childers
ISBN-13: 978-1-58571-448-3
ISBN-10: 1-58571-448-8
$6.99

December

Fractured
Wendy Byrne
ISBN-13: 978-1-58571-449-0
ISBN-10: 1-58571-449-6
$6.99

Everything in Between
Crystal Hubbard
ISBN-13: 978-1-58571-396-7
ISBN-10: 1-58571-396-1
$6.99

Other Genesis Press, Inc. Titles

Other Genesis Press, Inc. Titles (continued)

Other Genesis Press, Inc. Titles (continued)

Do Over	Celya Bowers	$9.95
Dream Keeper	Gail McFarland	$6.99
Dream Runner	Gail McFarland	$6.99
Dreamtective	Liz Swados	$5.95
Ebony Angel	Deatri King-Bey	$9.95
Ebony Butterfly II	Delilah Dawson	$14.95
Echoes of Yesterday	Beverly Clark	$9.95
Eden's Garden	Elizabeth Rose	$8.95
Eve's Prescription	Edwina Martin Arnold	$8.95
Everlastin' Love	Gay G. Gunn	$8.95
Everlasting Moments	Dorothy Elizabeth Love	$8.95
Everything and More	Sinclair Lebeau	$8.95
Everything but Love	Natalie Dunbar	$8.95
Falling	Natalie Dunbar	$9.95
Fate	Pamela Leigh Starr	$8.95
Finding Isabella	A.J. Garrotto	$8.95
Fireflies	Joan Early	$6.99
Fixin' Tyrone	Keith Walker	$6.99
Forbidden Quest	Dar Tomlinson	$10.95
Forever Love	Wanda Y. Thomas	$8.95
Friends in Need	Joan Early	$6.99
From the Ashes	Kathleen Suzanne Jeanne Sumerix	$8.95
Frost on My Window	Angela Weaver	$6.99
Gentle Yearning	Rochelle Alers	$10.95
Glory of Love	Sinclair LeBeau	$10.95
Go Gentle Into That Good Night	Malcom Boyd	$12.95
Goldengroove	Mary Beth Craft	$16.95
Groove, Bang, and Jive	Steve Cannon	$8.99
Hand in Glove	Andrea Jackson	$9.95
Hard to Love	Kimberley White	$9.95
Hart & Soul	Angie Daniels	$8.95
Heart of the Phoenix	A.C. Arthur	$9.95
Heartbeat	Stephanie Bedwell-Grime	$8.95
Hearts Remember	M. Loui Quezada	$8.95
Hidden Memories	Robin Allen	$10.95
Higher Ground	Leah Latimer	$19.95
Hitler, the War, and the Pope	Ronald Rychiak	$26.95
How to Kill Your Husband	Keith Walker	$6.99

Other Genesis Press, Inc. Titles (continued)

How to Write a Romance	Kathryn Falk	$18.95
I Married a Reclining Chair	Lisa M. Fuhs	$8.95
I'll Be Your Shelter	Giselle Carmichael	$8.95
I'll Paint a Sun	A.J. Garrotto	$9.95
Icie	Pamela Leigh Starr	$8.95
If I Were Your Woman	LaConnie Taylor-Jones	$6.99
Illusions	Pamela Leigh Starr	$8.95
Indigo After Dark Vol. I	Nia Dixon/Angelique	$10.95
Indigo After Dark Vol. II	Dolores Bundy/	$10.95
	Cole Riley	
Indigo After Dark Vol. III	Montana Blue/	$10.95
	Coco Morena	
Indigo After Dark Vol. IV	Cassandra Colt/	$14.95
Indigo After Dark Vol. V	Delilah Dawson	$14.95
Indiscretions	Donna Hill	$8.95
Intentional Mistakes	Michele Sudler	$9.95
Interlude	Donna Hill	$8.95
Intimate Intentions	Angie Daniels	$8.95
It's in the Rhythm	Sammie Ward	$6.99
It's Not Over Yet	J.J. Michael	$9.95
Jolie's Surrender	Edwina Martin-Arnold	$8.95
Kiss or Keep	Debra Phillips	$8.95
Lace	Giselle Carmichael	$9.95
Lady Preacher	K.T. Richey	$6.99
Last Train to Memphis	Elsa Cook	$12.95
Lasting Valor	Ken Olsen	$24.95
Let Us Prey	Hunter Lundy	$25.95
Let's Get It On	Dyanne Davis	$6.99
Lies Too Long	Pamela Ridley	$13.95
Life Is Never As It Seems	J.J. Michael	$12.95
Lighter Shade of Brown	Vicki Andrews	$8.95
Look Both Ways	Joan Early	$6.99
Looking for Lily	Africa Fine	$6.99
Love Always	Mildred E. Riley	$10.95
Love Doesn't Come Easy	Charlyne Dickerson	$8.95
Love Out of Order	Nicole Green	$6.99
Love Unveiled	Gloria Greene	$10.95
Love's Deception	Charlene Berry	$10.95
Love's Destiny	M. Loui Quezada	$8.95
Love's Secrets	Yolanda McVey	$6.99

Other Genesis Press, Inc. Titles (continued)

Mae's Promise	Melody Walcott	$8.95
Magnolia Sunset	Gisellé Carmichael	$8.95
Many Shades of Gray	Dyanne Davis	$6.99
Matters of Life and Death	Lesego Malepe, Ph.D.	$15.95
Meant to Be	Jeanne Sumerix	$8.95
Midnight Clear	Leslie Esdaile	$10.95
(Anthology)	Gwynne Forster	
	Carmen Green	
	Monica Jackson	
Midnight Magic	Gwynne Forster	$8.95
Midnight Peril	Vicki Andrews	$10.95
Misconceptions	Pamela Leigh Starr	$9.95
Mixed Reality	Chamein Canton	$6.99
Moments of Clarity	Michele Cameron	$6.99
Montgomery's Children	Richard Perry	$14.95
Mr. Fix-It	Crystal Hubbard	$6.99
My Buffalo Soldier	Barbara B.K. Reeves	$8.95
Naked Soul	Gwynne Forster	$8.95
Never Say Never	Michele Cameron	$6.99
Next to Last Chance	Louisa Dixon	$24.95
No Apologies	Seressia Glass	$8.95
No Commitment Required	Seressia Glass	$8.95
No Regrets	Mildred E. Riley	$8.95
Not His Type	Chamein Canton	$6.99
Not Quite Right	Tammy Williams	$6.99
Nowhere to Run	Gay G. Gunn	$10.95
O Bed! O Breakfast!	Rob Kuehnle	$14.95
Oak Bluffs	Joan Early	$6.99
Object of His Desire	A.C. Arthur	$8.95
Office Policy	A.C. Arthur	$9.95
Once in a Blue Moon	Dorianne Cole	$9.95
One Day at a Time	Bella McFarland	$8.95
One of These Days	Michele Sudler	$9.95
Outside Chance	Louisa Dixon	$24.95
Passion	T.T. Henderson	$10.95
Passion's Blood	Cherif Fortin	$22.95
Passion's Furies	AlTonya Washington	$6.99
Passion's Journey	Wanda Y. Thomas	$8.95
Past Promises	Jahmel West	$8.95
Path of Fire	T.T. Henderson	$8.95

Other Genesis Press, Inc. Titles (continued)

Path of Thorns	Annetta P. Lee	$9.95
Peace Be Still	Colette Haywood	$12.95
Picture Perfect	Reon Carter	$8.95
Playing for Keeps	Stephanie Salinas	$8.95
Pride & Joi	Gay G. Gunn	$8.95
Promises Made	Bernice Layton	$6.99
Promises of Forever	Celya Bowers	$6.99
Promises to Keep	Alicia Wiggins	$8.95
Quiet Storm	Donna Hill	$10.95
Reckless Surrender	Rochelle Alers	$6.95
Red Polka Dot in a World Full of Plaid	Varian Johnson	$12.95
Red Sky	Renee Alexis	$6.99
Reluctant Captive	Joyce Jackson	$8.95
Rendezvous With Fate	Jeanne Sumerix	$8.95
Revelations	Cheris F. Hodges	$8.95
Reye's Gold	Ruthie Robinson	$6.99
Rivers of the Soul	Leslie Esdaile	$8.95
Rocky Mountain Romance	Kathleen Suzanne	$8.95
Rooms of the Heart	Donna Hill	$8.95
Rough on Rats and Tough on Cats	Chris Parker	$12.95
Save Me	Africa Fine	$6.99
Secret Library Vol. 1	Nina Sheridan	$18.95
Secret Library Vol. 2	Cassandra Colt	$8.95
Secret Thunder	Annetta P. Lee	$9.95
Shades of Brown	Denise Becker	$8.95
Shades of Desire	Monica White	$8.95
Shadows in the Moonlight	Jeanne Sumerix	$8.95
Show Me the Sun	Miriam Shumba	$6.99
Sin	Crystal Rhodes	$8.95
Singing a Song…	Crystal Rhodes	$6.99
Six O'Clock	Katrina Spencer	$6.99
Small Sensations	Crystal V. Rhodes	$6.99
Small Whispers	Annetta P. Lee	$6.99
So Amazing	Sinclair LeBeau	$8.95
Somebody's Someone	Sinclair LeBeau	$8.95
Someone to Love	Alicia Wiggins	$8.95
Song in the Park	Martin Brant	$15.95
Soul Eyes	Wayne L. Wilson	$12.95

Other Genesis Press, Inc. Titles (continued)

Soul to Soul	Donna Hill	$8.95
Southern Comfort	J.M. Jeffries	$8.95
Southern Fried Standards	S.R. Maddox	$6.99
Still the Storm	Sharon Robinson	$8.95
Still Waters Run Deep	Leslie Esdaile	$8.95
Still Waters...	Crystal V. Rhodes	$6.99
Stolen Jewels	Michele Sudler	$6.99
Stolen Memories	Michele Sudler	$6.99
Stories to Excite You	Anna Forrest/Divine	$14.95
Storm	Pamela Leigh Starr	$6.99
Subtle Secrets	Wanda Y. Thomas	$8.95
Suddenly You	Crystal Hubbard	$9.95
Swan	Africa Fine	$6.99
Sweet Repercussions	Kimberley White	$9.95
Sweet Sensations	Gwyneth Bolton	$9.95
Sweet Tomorrows	Kimberly White	$8.95
Taken by You	Dorothy Elizabeth Love	$9.95
Tattooed Tears	T. T. Henderson	$8.95
Tempting Faith	Crystal Hubbard	$6.99
That Which Has Horns	Miriam Shumba	$6.99
The Business of Love	Cheris F. Hodges	$6.99
The Color Line	Lizzette Grayson Carter	$9.95
The Color of Trouble	Dyanne Davis	$8.95
The Disappearance of Allison Jones	Kayla Perrin	$5.95
The Doctor's Wife	Mildred Riley	$6.99
The Fires Within	Beverly Clark	$9.95
The Foursome	Celya Bowers	$6.99
The Honey Dipper's Legacy	Myra Pannell-Allen	$14.95
The Joker's Love Tune	Sidney Rickman	$15.95
The Little Pretender	Barbara Cartland	$10.95
The Love We Had	Natalie Dunbar	$8.95
The Man Who Could Fly	Bob & Milana Beamon	$18.95
The Missing Link	Charlyne Dickerson	$8.95
The Mission	Pamela Leigh Starr	$6.99
The More Things Change	Chamein Canton	$6.99
The Perfect Frame	Beverly Clark	$9.95
The Price of Love	Sinclair LeBeau	$8.95
The Smoking Life	Ilene Barth	$29.95
The Words of the Pitcher	Kei Swanson	$8.95

Other Genesis Press, Inc. Titles (continued)

Things Forbidden	Maryam Diaab	$6.99
This Life Isn't Perfect Holla	Sandra Foy	$6.99
Three Doors Down	Michele Sudler	$6.99
Three Wishes	Seressia Glass	$8.95
Ties That Bind	Kathleen Suzanne	$8.95
Tiger Woods	Libby Hughes	$5.95
Time Is of the Essence	Angie Daniels	$9.95
Timeless Devotion	Bella McFarland	$9.95
Tomorrow's Promise	Leslie Esdaile	$8.95
Truly Inseparable	Wanda Y. Thomas	$8.95
Two Sides to Every Story	Dyanne Davis	$9.95
Unbeweavable	Katrina Spencer	$6.99
Unbreak My Heart	Dar Tomlinson	$8.95
Unclear and Present Danger	Michele Cameron	$6.99
Uncommon Prayer	Kenneth Swanson	$9.95
Unconditional	A.C. Arthur	$9.95
Unconditional Love	Alicia Wiggins	$8.95
Undying Love	Renee Alexis	$6.99
Until Death Do Us Part	Susan Paul	$8.95
Vows of Passion	Bella McFarland	$9.95
Waiting for Mr. Darcy	Chamein Canton	$6.99
Waiting in the Shadows	Michele Sudler	$6.99
Wayward Dreams	Gail McFarland	$6.99
Wedding Gown	Dyanne Davis	$8.95
What's Under Benjamin's Bed	Sandra Schaffer	$8.95
When a Man Loves a Woman	LaConnie Taylor-Jones	$6.99
When Dreams Float	Dorothy Elizabeth Love	$8.95
When I'm With You	LaConnie Taylor-Jones	$6.99
When Lightning Strikes	Michele Cameron	$6.99
Where I Want to Be	Maryam Diaab	$6.99
Whispers in the Night	Dorothy Elizabeth Love	$8.95
Whispers in the Sand	LaFlorya Gauthier	$10.95
Who's That Lady?	Andrea Jackson	$9.95
Wild Ravens	AlTonya Washington	$9.95
Yesterday Is Gone	Beverly Clark	$10.95
Yesterday's Dreams, Tomorrow's Promises	Reon Laudat	$8.95
Your Precious Love	Sinclair LeBeau	$8.95

Order Form

Mail to: Genesis Press, Inc.
P.O. Box 101
Columbus, MS 39703

Name _____
Address _____
City/State _____ Zip _____
Telephone _____

Ship to (if different from above)
Name _____
Address _____
City/State _____ Zip _____
Telephone _____

Credit Card Information
Credit Card # _____ ☐ Visa   ☐ Mastercard
Expiration Date (mm/yy) _____ ☐ AmEx   ☐ Discover

Qty.	Author	Title	Price	Total

Use this order form, or call **1-888-INDIGO-1**	Total for books	_____
	Shipping and handling: $5 first two books, $1 each additional book	
	Total S & H	_____
	Total amount enclosed	_____
	Mississippi residents add 7% sales tax	